Love is in bloom . . .

Straightforward Kay Bing has never been one for subterfuge, although she did embellish her resume just a bit to land a design job at Free Leaf Concepts, a cutting edge botanicals firm. Determined to make a good first impression, she's exploring the highly secure company greenhouse when her assistant—the much too attractive Oliver Pierce—confides that he's actually working undercover to investigate whether Free Leaf has created a potent new street drug. Kay doesn't believe it for a minute—until someone plants designer mushrooms in her salad. Suddenly she and her sexy colleague are teaming up to unearth the roots of a dangerous operation . . .

Oliver not only has a personal stake in the investigation, his entire career in law enforcement is on the line. Stubborn, sensible Kay is a distraction he can't afford, but as they dig deeper into the case, they discover a chemistry that's too heated to deny. When even one wrong move could be deadly, Oliver may have to risk it all to keep Kay from harm—and convince her they should be partners for good.

Books by Roxanne Smith

Long Shot Romance
Men Like This
Relapse In Paradise
Running the Numbers

Bound By Design
To the Studs
Love On the Vine

Published by Kensington Publishing Corporation

Love On the Vine

Bound By Design

Roxanne Smith

LYRICAL PRESS
Kensington Publishing Corp.
www.kensingtonbooks.com

First Electronic Edition: July 2017
eISBN-13: 978-1-5161-0083-5
eISBN-10: 1-5161-0083-2 =

First Print Edition: July 2017
ISBN-13: 978-1-5161-0086-6
ISBN-10: 1-5161-0086-7

Printed in the United States of America

Best friend and partner in everything just this side of crime since 1999

Acknowledgements

Dawn Dowdle, always.

Marci Clark, my one and only (and favorite!) editor.

For this particular book, I owe special thanks to my kids, Brandon and Cheyenne, for letting me ruin their summer, as I spent it writing instead of doing cooler, funner, swimmier things.

Chapter 1

Kay Bing sat on the pristine white leather monstrosity deemed a sofa, her arms and legs crossed defensively. "You invited me over to fire me. That's fantastic, Neve. That's just great. For once, you could've at least been your usual bitchy self about it so I'd have your smart mouth to aim for when I socked you. Duke can quit training you to behave like a normal human being any day now. Really, only one of you is supposed to be the thoughtful, considerate type. Otherwise, it's cloying. Nobody likes cloying."

Neve smiled sweetly. "I can still dismember you with a few words, sweetie. I simply choose not to. Besides, I'm firing you to help you, so maiming you would be counterproductive. And Duke and I could never be *cloying*," she added with a disgusted grimace. "I'm emotionally distant, and he's endearingly frustrated."

Kay would never understand the strange dynamic at work between Neve and Duke. She rubbed her forehead and fought off a brewing headache. She was Kay Bing! She was happy and zesty, feisty, fun, and upbeat. Since when did she get headaches and moan? "So move in with him. Close the distance. End the frustration. And quit putting off the wedding. You're killing the guy."

"You look terrible, by the way." Neve swiftly changed the subject. "Just terrible."

"I thought a spray tan would lift my spirits."

"Well, it's dampening mine. Embrace the pale." She sat forward suddenly and grabbed Kay's knee, earnestness replacing her faux haughtiness. "I know you think you hate me but that's because I've yet to tell you the reason why you're about do the exact opposite. In fact, you're going to declare your undying love for me and challenge Duke to a duel for my affections.

Because I, your great mentor and friend, have secured for you a position at one of the most prestigious outfits in the city."

"Neve." Kay dropped her head into her hands so her palms gently cradled her poor forehead. She kept trying to rub away headaches, and now she had a pimple. "If I can't dredge up any zest as Neve freakin' Harper's assistant, what makes you think—"

"Common sense. Quit crying for three seconds, and get your hands off that zit. It's like you're worshipping it."

Kay glanced through her fingers at Neve. The woman was her personal hero. The biggest hotshot interior designer in the greater Little Rock area. She was everything Kay aspired to be one day. But sometimes, like now in particular, Kay wanted to stab her in her gorgeous amber eyeballs with a dinner fork. She settled back, crossed her arms, and invited her mentor to continue with an arched brow. Kay wasn't all that intimidating on the surface, she knew it. But a few close to her, Neve included, had seen what she could do in a tight spot. That had earned her enough respect to arch her brow daringly and not be met with a chorus of scoffs.

Neve's smile dazzled. "See how nice it is when your mouth is closed? You should try it more often. Now, what makes *me* think is difficult to explain, given how most everyone around me suffers from some measure of mental encumbrance." She gave Kay's knee a final squeeze and snuggled back into her spot, tucking her feet beneath her bottom. "I called your parents. I found out that once upon a time, before you realized your dream of interior design, you were quite the little gardener. You had an aunt who ran a florist shop, may she rest in peace, and you spent many of your formative years helping her with professional arrangements. Then I learned you actually designed the courtyard of her shop when she had it remodeled, and you did it at the vastly impressive age of sixteen. From what I gather, it was remarkably well done. Your first experience with design hailed from plumerias and peonies. Whether it's wood or beavertail cactus, the basics are the same. Think about it. It's all contrast and symmetry. Each flower has a certain shape, their leaves likewise, and each a different shade of green on a massive spectrum. You had to coordinate with not only the flowers and their foliage, but whatever grew alongside it. It's the same thing you love, just a different medium. You're an artist, switching from oils to acrylic."

Kay knew her mouth was slightly open, but who'd have thought—she stopped herself there. Neve. Neve would've thought, because Neve's mind functioned on a different plane of reality than ordinary folks. It was almost a lucky thing she was also cocky, abrasive, rude, and potty-mouthed, because she'd be otherwise perfect. As it was, she was just acerbic enough to be likeable, given one had the right sense of humor,

"Finn and I split, so you called my parents." Kay nodded. "Of course you did. I'm almost scared of what you're going to say next."

"You should be." Neve reached for her coffee mug and took a sip. She licked her lips. "Because I had to pad your résumé a bit. I'm not tooting my own horn or anything, but my recommendation goes a long way. What it can't do, however, is give you work experience you don't have. So, my lying fingers did that. I typed you up a fancy résumé—by the way, you worked with Duke on Vale House, the geraniums were a bitch—and now, my dear friend, you have an inspiring job far above your current station as a mere assistant, and something new and fascinating, yet old and dear, to sink your teeth into. Not to mention my prominent word resting on your teeny-tiny shoulders. I'd say no pressure, but it'd be a horrible lie. Don't make me look like an idiot."

Forget open, Kay's mouth went full guppy. Open and shut. Open and shut. She had nothing and everything to say, starting with what meds Neve might be on. "You faked my résumé—"

"Lightly padded." Neve grinned. "And now, you're the new head designer at the most prestigious high-end landscaping service in the city. The NASA of all things green, responsible for creating some of the most unique, award-winning hybrid plants in the country."

Kay covered her mouth. She couldn't stand looking like a guppy. "You don't mean..." she mumbled through her fingers.

"Free Leaf Concepts? Of course I do. Who else? That's who I call when I get leafy ideas for my jobs. I don't really do leafy stuff. But you, you've got all kinds of leafy experience."

Kay chewed her lip and let the idea swim around in her head. Yeah, okay. She did have some leafy experience, didn't she? In fact, landscaping had been her first bug, the one that bit early. Only later had she decided her interests were more inside than out. But she still had a green thumb hanging around somewhere. It hadn't been lopped off completely.

Free Leaf Concepts was the go-to company for designers who wanted anything resembling nature concocted and executed for interior décor. A twenty-foot fountain greeting clients in a five-star hotel lobby, a veritable rain forest inside a restaurant with a three-month waiting list, a spa to appear as though it existed in the maze of a bamboo grove. Designers, they set down the mold. They decided furniture placement, fixtures, layout, and so on. Companies like Free Leaf were hired to come in after that fact and put a sheen of realism over the whole thing. Just as often, they worked with designers side by side, a coalition of paint and petals. Save that corner for an indoor tree to grow up through the ceiling with a sunroof overhead. Design a sink that fits into this pocket of hanging jasmine. Hang wallpaper to match these rare African blooms. It was meticulous, highly detailed, and expensive work.

Kay blinked a few times, let the idea settle onto her frazzled brain. Was a change of scenery enough to pull her out of her funk?

She just wasn't herself lately. The spunky, happy girl she'd always been had gone into hiding since her split from Finn. They'd worked together on a cabin with Neve last year. The place had been a total loss until Neve put her magical touch to it and created a charming, earth-meets-glamour work of art. When the owner, Gavin, decided to sell, Kay and her sexy carpenter boyfriend bought it. Together. Like idiots. Young, doe-eyed idiots. At least they hadn't eloped or done anything *wildly* stupid. Just bought a cabin together, that was all. When the relationship ended, Kay couldn't sell her half fast enough.

The break-up was proving to be a wrench in the very fabric of her personality. She was different now. She didn't know how to get back to that girl who was in love with her job, in love with *life*. She didn't think she could talk herself to the ledge of anything, let alone take an insane plunge. Neve knew that, so she'd decided to give Kay a little shove.

Kay pinched the bridge of her nose and exhaled a plume of air. "Okay. Okay." She pressed her lips together and studied Neve. She was obviously pleased with herself. Only a hint of apprehension showed in the wideness of her eyes. She'd gone out on a very precarious limb, and Kay was grateful. She owed it to her friend to at least try. "Maybe you're right. Going back to my roots. Oh, hey, get it? My *roots*?"

Neve hardly cracked a smile. "Look at you. Already getting back to your old self."

"You know, just because you and Duke can't be funny without maiming each other doesn't mean there aren't other ways to be funny."

"Oh, there's plenty to laugh at." Neve gave a breathless chuckle and looked at Kay in a way that made her skin prickle. "Like how you start tomorrow."

* * * *

Oliver Pierce stared at his boss, not caring a wink that Cappy Don was mean before his first cup of coffee. Oliver could handle mean. What he couldn't handle was another kink in the plan. There were so many hurdles, it might as well be a track meet. "Do you want to know what nobody thinks is funny? Last minute complications that look like Tinkerbell." He tossed the glossy photo down onto Cappy Don's desk.

Kay Bing looked like something out of a kid's picture book. White-blond hair cut into an adorable crop that framed a round face and big colorful eyes that weren't blue or green, but somehow both at once. Her file had her listed at a hair under five feet. Precious as pudding.

Cappy Don slurped loudly from his mug, like he took pleasure in the disgusting noise, and smacked his lips as he picked up the photo. "She won't be a problem, Pierce. She's young. Twenty-three and fresh from a stint with Neve Harper. If that name doesn't make your balls shrink, they're made of sterner stuff than mine. Girl's probably a shell of a person inside, whittled down to the marrow of what's left of her self-esteem." Spindly black eyebrows—they could never quite decide which direction they wanted to go, so they went everywhere at once—rose dramatically as Cappy Don gazed up at Oliver. "Does it bother you to take orders from a woman, is that it? Because the person who sat at this desk before me was a woman, and let me tell you, pal—"

Oliver sighed. "Of course not. But I had Kay's predecessor's file memorized. Not only that, Roscoe and me were drinking buddies, and I'd cleared him already. I'm going in blind with this little girl. Roscoe kept me busy, but not so busy I couldn't keep up with my more discreet tasks. If she's the type to micromanage, we might as well toss the whole deal in the trash. I can't do what I'm supposed to do in there if I've got a twelve-year-old hovering over my shoulder."

The captain set down his mug and sat up straighter. He slipped the photo neatly into a manila folder containing every scrap of information they'd been able to gather on Kay Bing on short notice. Cappy Don was Mr. Business now. The time for complaints had passed. "Keep telling yourself she's twelve. That way, you can't get sidetracked. If you'd gone past her picture, Pierce, you'd have read—"

"I read it all," Oliver cut in, careful to keep his tone neutral despite the frustration churning in his stomach. He didn't need to remind Cappy Don of his eidetic memory or speed-reading-to-comprehension ratio. "For example, I know her résumé was forged."

Cappy Don shrugged with a marked lack of concern. "Lightly padded."

"Her aunt's florist shop is the only real experience she has, besides a year working as the second-in-command at Harper Designs," Oliver pressed. "She's a go-getter, has a predominately positive attitude, downright bubbly by all accounts, and until recently was half owner of a cabin Neve Harper remodeled for one of Little Rock's most popular Chamber of Commerce board members, Gavin Chambers, last year. Chambers and Harper also happen to be close personal friends, which means Kay Bing has friends in high places. Could be she has some she shouldn't. Could be she's close to this. After all, Neve pulled strings to get her this job. Roscoe wasn't cute, but I can vouch he was clean."

"You also read her father is a cop. Worked burglary for years in the city before he retired. I hear he chases kids out of abandoned houses and helps old ladies cross the street these days, but he was a bulldog in his prime."

"When has being a cop ever meant anything? Charles Manson's mom was probably a devout Catholic."

Cappy Don gave Oliver an exaggerated smile, showing too many teeth. "Your paranoia is why I like you, Pierce. You've got so much going on in your brain, you're afraid of what's creeping up behind you. So, you try to look everywhere at once. Your head's practically spinning twenty-four-seven. It's a wonder you get any sleep, with the way you're always watching, looking, hunting...and usually finding, which beyond liking you, makes you my favorite. Must be exhausting in there." He tapped his temple with a thick finger. "I'll tell you, your buddy Roscoe wasn't all puppies and rainbows. That rose-colored memo the top floor sent out on Friday made him sound like he had an important date in Bali, but he got canned for sending dick pics to the receptionist. Start putting that around first thing Monday morning. If somebody else spreads the rumor before his right-hand man, it'll seem fishy, close as you two were. And don't ask where I got the information. It's need to know." The way he said it, Oliver doubted even the captain knew the identity of their informant within the ranks of Free Leaf Concepts. He picked up Kay's folder and tossed it at Oliver's chest like a Frisbee.

Oliver caught the file neatly between his palms. "This slows us down."

Cappy Don shrugged again, showing an infuriating lack of care. "So, we go back a few steps. Do what you do and *find*. Read her file again. Slow, like you're searching for a secret code. Kay Bing has survived working side-by-side with one of the biggest ball busters in this city. Between that and her license to carry a concealed weapon, she's probably going to have a few surprises for you. However..." He stopped to give Oliver a hard look from beneath the unforgiving line of his brow. "She shouldn't be a problem. Not unless you make her one, Pierce."

Oliver ran a hand over his face. Cappy Don had one thing right. It was exhausting to be him. "I'll start right away."

"Make sure you do." Then Cappy Don smiled that smile—the one that gave Oliver pause every time, because it usually meant a joke was coming, and Oliver was the punchline. "Our girl starts tomorrow."

* * * *

The Free Leaf Concepts building was a narrow silver spire that stabbed into Little Rock's hazy blue downtown sky like it was trying to pick a fight with the clouds. Aggressive, bold, but innovative and inspiring, too. Everything was chrome and shiny outside, as if they wanted to blast their clients in the face with the good stuff the moment they walked into the foyer. It worked. The lobby was a spectacle. The concrete and shiny metal of the outside world, from the dirty sidewalks to the old brick grandfather buildings lining the streets, were a million miles away as soon as Kay stepped through the mirrored doors, etched with Free Leaf's chrome leaf emblem.

Crimson chrysanthemums were arranged around copper sculptures and red velvet couches in the waiting area. The fixtures and lighting were all shades of gold and honey. It was vibrant, masterfully done, and Kay wanted to touch everything.

"I've never seen chrysanthemums that shade," she breathed to the receptionist when she came to gather Kay. "I mean, red is common enough, but that...Well, that's not red. That's fresh blood. I've seen fresh blood, I would know."

The receptionist's eyes widened slightly. Kay cleared her throat and stood up straight. She might look like a particularly wise fourteen-year-old, but Neve had taught her a thing or two about commanding herself. Kay had spent the last year taking orders and doling them out under her mentor's watchful eye. With Neve backing her, Kay had never lacked for confidence. Now, there was no mean lady over her shoulder, daring someone not to take the five-foot-nothing Kay Bing seriously. She was on her own here. She couldn't just rely on Neve—she had to *be* Neve.

The receptionist watched her curiously. Kay held back a heavy sigh. She'd never been good at first impressions. She offered the receptionist a bland smile. "Never mind. Long story. Hi, I'm Kay Bing. You should be expecting me. Or, at least, someone should."

The woman smiled back. She had on a turtleneck dress with cap sleeves in a shade near exact to the sofa, and a clear clipboard tucked against one jutting hip. "I'm Brit. And you've probably never seen chrysanthemums like that because that particular shade was manufactured in house. We have a remarkable botanist. His lab takes up the entire third floor. Please, follow me."

Kay tried hard to keep her excitement in check, but it thrummed through her like an electric guitar. "In house?" she repeated. "You have your own botanist? Wow. You know, I dig the monochrome, but a few pale yellow tulips would really—"

"No tulips," Brit interjected apologetically. "Company policy. Too common. One of the most cultivated flowers in the world. Free Leaf Concepts prides itself on 'top shelf' fauna, if you will." Then she pulled a face, sticking out her tongue in a small grimace. "At least, that's the line I feed clients. We do, of course, pander to special requests, but it requires ordering through a third party."

"Got it. No tulips." Kay's enthusiasm wilted a little as she followed Brit. She was going to work for a bunch of flower snobs. Tulips were wonderful and hardy. She hated to think how they felt about daffodils.

Brit guided her through a hallway like something out of Kay's wildest dreams. Jungle met concrete in a fantastic display of nature and man-made coming together in glorious harmony. The walls were mixed concrete overlaid with milky silver panels that cast distorted reflections placed randomly along the length of the curved hallway. Ledges cradling passionflower vines were cut into niches of concrete between the panels. The vines grew elegantly from one ledge to the next. The odd silver panels gave a strange, funhouse illusion of greenery dipping and swirling everywhere, all at once. The ceiling was low, painted a subtle sage green that reflected the industrial carpeting underfoot, and recessed lighting cast a pale light, as if the hallway were awash in lazy afternoon sunlight. The design was a marvel.

The hallway ended at a round glass-encased elevator. Brit punched a button but didn't move to step inside. "Fifth floor is all executive offices and conference rooms. Mr. Arnell, our director of operations, will probably call you in for a briefing sometime, but his calendar and working hours are hectic. Don't expect to get much advance warning. Could be this afternoon or next month. He's out of the office from noon to two most days. Complete nightmare to schedule him with clients. Your office is on the fourth floor."

Kay smiled. Just one small floor away from the botany labs. She stepped inside the cylindrical elevator.

Brit made a notation on her clipboard and grimaced with distaste. "Damian Roscoe may still have a few personal affects in the office. You can have your assistant, Oliver, clear them out for you. He and Roscoe were buddies, so don't take it personally if he doesn't hop-to on the first day, okay? He's a good guy, even if Roscoe was an idiot douchebag." She gave Kay a bright smile and a wave, then punched another button that set the doors to closing. "Your team is anxious to meet you. Have a great first day, Ms. Bing."

Kay blinked at the receptionist's retreating form, then put Brit's parting comment aside. Office gossip wasn't on the agenda.

She fixed her expression into a stone mask of observation, just like she'd seen Neve do a thousand times. It usually meant the gears were turning, calculating budget, measurements, and people all at once, deciding in an instant what, where, when, how, and why. For Kay, the stony façade would be a tool. A shield. At least, for today. Tomorrow, maybe it wouldn't be a mask, but the real thing.

She tucked her nerves and self-doubts into her back pocket. She straightened the collar of her no-nonsense black button-up. Instead of a tie, she wore a neat silk bow in a muted gray. Professional. Not overly cute.

Kay couldn't dress cute. Dressing cute meant jokes about curfew, and did her parents know where she was. Ha-ha. Yep, she got it. She was little. But she also knew if she wanted to be the queen, she couldn't dress like the jester. Anything pastel—light pink, pale lavender, baby blue—was out of the question. Hacking off her hair helped to a degree, and recently she'd began wearing heavier makeup, finding it aged her. Scrubbed clean, she could pass for a young teenager. She might be the only woman alive looking forward to a few wrinkles.

The glass elevator pinged eloquently, like someone had installed a doorbell from one of the homes in the Governor's Mansion district, when it finally came to a stop. The door slid open.

A handsome man—the kind with an eye-catching appearance that encouraged a second glance—waited just on the other side. His eyes, the same subtle green as the ceiling in the hallway downstairs, scoured her in one quick motion, literally sizing her up. He smiled indulgently, like he wanted to offer her a quarter for the candy machines. But not before she caught the gleam of calculation, there and gone in a blink.

He held out his hand. The smile lingered, relaxing into something with a little more warmth. "Oliver Pierce. But you can call me whatever you like. 'Fetch that file' is a big hit. 'More coffee,' another favorite."

Her assistant. He *would* be charming, good-looking, and not outrageously tall. A tad on the rugged side, with stubble arranged almost artfully across his jaw, and eyes the color of sage under an expressive brow. His gaze held his candid smile.

Kay took his hand without moving a single muscle on her face. God, the effort. She'd never know how Neve kept it up. "Nice to meet you, Oliver."

He seemed put off by her dry greeting. His smile dialed back a few degrees. He had the beginning of a few lines around his eyes. Older than she was. "Likewise," he said. Then he took off in a sudden energetic burst, beckoning her to follow. "C'mon, I'll show you to your office."

Kay tried not to notice Oliver Pierce had a confident stride for a man on the less generous side of five-eleven. And he did his gray dress slacks more than mere justice—he served them with fervor. He definitely worked out. And went hard on the glutes, by the look of it. His sandy light brown hair was cut stylishly, close on the sides and swept back rakishly from his forehead. The style suited him.

A sharp twang of shame hit the back of her throat like that first fizzy sip of an ice-cold soda. She dragged her gaze away from his body. *No distractions. No handsome guy butts. No dips into the past for unwelcome reminders.*

She straightened her shoulders and found something else to look at while they walked. Framed photos, editorials, and covers from esteemed magazines decorated the hallway. The hallways on this floor were less showy than the reception area, which made sense. The walls were white, the carpet beige.

Oliver talked over his shoulder as he walked. "You've heard about Damian Roscoe by now, surely. We were buds. I'm sad to see him go, but some guys never learn."

"Oh?" Kay did her best to sound disinterested.

"Yup." He came upon a door at last and turned the chrome knob. The door, plastic and high-concept modern, swung open easily. Oliver gestured for Kay to enter the room, then stepped inside behind her. "Sent nudies to the receptionist. Poor Brit. She's cool. Nudies aren't cool. Well, unless they're requested, but I don't think Brit wanted to know what Roscoe's little Roscoes looked like."

Kay kept her lips carefully pressed together. One minute in his company, and he was bringing up nudes. Her brain was not impressed. Her body was going straight for the sign marked "Forbidden Territory" in the back of her head. She didn't think she'd ever requested nudes from a man, but she *was* curious about Oliver's workout regimen.

She pulled herself together and focused on other details about Oliver. Like how he didn't seem all that torn up over his good buddy's sudden departure. And how his lips were loose as old pantyhose. She watched him open large bamboo blinds, sending slats of sunlight across white space and his own profile.

The way he observed her, half of his face slashed by yellow sunlight, the other half masked in near shadow, made her skin flush with a spike of desire. Kay might look like a little girl, but she knew when a man looked at her and saw a woman. For a full second, their gazes were locked, a smile ghosting across Oliver's wide lips.

Kay kept her features carefully slack, giving nothing away, tongue firmly planted inside her mouth instead of running over her lips. Maybe she was doomed to be a slut. It was her calling, her destiny, to be attracted to everything with nice hair and a penis. As absurd as it sounded, she was running out of explanations as to just what was wrong with her. It took some effort, but she finally broke the tension and steered her gaze elsewhere.

Her office. Boxes crowded the space. Papers, a comically oversized stapler, and a lamp with some random team logo emblazoned across the shade were scattered among the many surfaces. Roscoe's personal affects, Kay guessed. Gleaming white tiled floors reflected the sunlight back into her eyes. Every wall had a mounted whiteboard, and a litter of dry-erase markers cradled underneath. Her desk was long and narrow, with lots of drawers and a lamp bolted to the surface at one end. Tiny surface. Meant for storage, not work. The work area would be the massive, waist-high drafting table in the center of the room.

Oliver remained near the window, rubbing his hands together like he couldn't wait to get down to the real work. "How's everything so far?"

She gave her new office a final once-over. Lots of room to move about, space for creativity, a rolling chair that looked like she could dock it at the international space station. She liked everything, barring one small exception.

"Well," she admitted slowly, letting the word become two regrettable syllables. "I like everything. Except for you." She met his gaze again, certain the only thing between them this time would be tension, minus the sexual undertones.

As predicted, his pale green eyes widened, and the air between them grew heavy with an entirely different sort of pressure. "Me? Well, uh, just tell me what you need, I'll make it happen. Whatever you want."

"Great." She beamed. "Leave. You're fired."

Chapter 2

Oliver glared at Cappy Don. It was one thing to check in with the boss. It was something else for the boss to show up at dinner, help himself to the take-out, and proceed to aid in bending the hell out of a bottle of whiskey. But that wasn't even the worst part. No, the worst part was rehashing his grave miscalculation.

"I did what you said, Cap. I waltzed back in the next morning like I owned the place, much to Ms. Bing's consternation. I don't know why, but she dislikes me on principle. And in the two weeks since, she's established an iron fist of rule and eliminated nearly every ounce of wiggle room I had with Roscoe." Oliver's frustration bubbled up another layer at Cappy Don's amused chuckle. "This is bad. I can't get finished with one task before she sends me off on another. I'm so busy, I haven't had time to get into Merit's office, which I was ready to do right before Roscoe pulled his shit on the receptionist."

Oliver paused to breathe and run a hand over his face. Working for once was taking a real toll on his energy level. He'd doubled his coffee intake. "I'm terrified to make a wrong move. Kay cans me once, I come back, that's cute. It won't be cute if she fires me again."

"I handled the situation," the captain said without inflection. Cappy Don tossed back the amber liquid swirling in the bottom of Oliver's one and only tumbler. "That's what matters. Test your boundaries a little, Pierce. You're supposed to be the fiddler, not the fiddle. She fires you again, you're back the next morning. It's all a big joke if you play it right. And you have to play it right. This is the only chance we're gonna get to do things this way."

"Or Kay thinks I'm not taking her seriously and it catches Merit's attention. Mr. Arnell is the creative genius, but Merit's the one with her fingers in all the pies. Her fingers go into my pie, I'm cooked. She likes me, but she's not going to take my side over her new head designer's, especially since Kay has turned out to be the dream Roscoe never could live up to. False résumé or not, Kay's good at the job. Scary good."

Kay Bing was scary everything. Scary sharp, scary serious, and scary attractive, which only creeped him out at first. Once he'd gotten over her height, it was hard not to notice the deliberately female body making up every inch. He took a healthy swig of whiskey, served up in a coffee mug, and grimaced. He was usually a beer man, but he'd had a rough two weeks. His ego had taken a bruising. Screw the investigation, his man parts were hurting. "You tried to warn me, but you were wrong about some stuff, too. Kay didn't suffer doing time with Neve Harper. She'd been busy taking notes. She smiled, Cap. Big, happy smile on her face as she fired me. Completely unapologetic."

He'd seen it in her eyes, too, that flawless, effortless command. Her appearance hadn't mattered a lick when she'd given him that dazzling smile and knocked him on his ass in the same breath.

Except, of course, for in those brief seconds when their eyes had met, and something fiery had crackled to life between them. Kay Bing was a pair of stilettos and some hotrod red lipstick away from being a bombshell. Even the boyish cut of her buttery blond hair only made her features stand out starkly, with nothing to hide her narrow nose, lips that pursed to a perfect bud, and fathomless glare that gave nothing away.

And those indiscernible eyes. They were still a mystery. Blue one day, green the next, a variant of everything from the color of her blouse to her mood. It hardly mattered. What mattered was they had smoldered when she'd looked at him that day, and where there was smoke, there was fire. Beyond that fire? Ice. Kay had ice in her spine and wasn't afraid to use it.

"Maybe." Cappy Don's voice slashed through the moment like a whip. "But you can't afford to let this get personal. You're taking things with Kay pretty personal."

The old man was right. "A little, yeah. It's not often I meet someone I can't charm. She cut me down so swiftly at my first attempt, I'm trigger shy now."

Cappy Don tilted his head and narrowed his eyes into a calculating gleam. "Ya know, there's another way to handle this. We don't have the time for a full vet, and you can't fast-track yourself into Kay's good graces with a few dirty jokes and a bar tab, the way you did Roscoe. We're gonna have to take some chances. Leave her a clue."

Oliver leaned forward. "A clue?" he repeated, making no effort to hide the dubiousness dripping from the suggestion.

"Yeah." The captain flipped a large, weathered hand as if swatting away a fly, his lips turned down. "A clue. An open file on her computer, a note. Assuming she's ignorant of Free Leaf's scheme, leave something that'll make her say 'hmm.' If she's in on it, she'll get nervous. If she's clean and as headstrong as you say, she'll want to look into it further. I'm not saying give yourself away. She doesn't have to know who's behind these little gifts. For now, focus on getting a read on her reaction."

"And then what?" Oliver was indignant. Cap had lost his damn mind. "Make her my partner? Or just wantonly throw out I'm investigating undercover, now quit giving me so much shit to do so I can focus on getting into the fifth-floor offices in search of evidence?"

Cappy Don leaned forward. No mirth in his hard eyes now. This wasn't a negotiation. "Look, there's that fancy crap you do when you got the time, and I admire the hell out of it. But sometimes, you jump off a ledge and hope for the best. There's no indication whatsoever that Kay Bing has a dirty history, or any opportunity to ingratiate herself with whoever might be behind all this, whether it's Free Leaf acting of its own accord, or someone at Town Hall getting all fancy with the street drugs. Her association with Neve Harper came by way of Gavin Chambers, sure, but he's clean. We investigated him months ago."

"Just because we didn't find anything—"

"Yeah, yeah. I hear you. Don't mean he's not buddy-buddy with someone important in this town. But we have to place a bet, kid. I'm willing to bet on Ms. Bing."

Oliver ran a hand through his hair. He needed a trim. "I combed her file. Every inch of it. She's supposed to be exuberantly enthusiastic. Like a squirming puppy. She's not, though. If her file was correct, I might've handled her differently. Maybe it was the soured relationship with the carpenter, or whatever flavor of Wheaties Neve fed her the past year, but we shouldn't underestimate her. Her youth doesn't make her malleable."

"Listen, I only have so much pull. I can keep you your job. I can keep the investigation afloat while you dig, but if Kay presses the issue, and you hang on like a tick on a dog, it'll make her suspicious of you. Let's make her suspicious of the other guys first, huh? Fix it, Pierce, and fix it my way." Cappy Don polished off his drink and rose to leave. He turned, paused as if he changed his mind, and gave Oliver one last penetrating stare. "Here's a tip. If you say Kay ain't the girl we're seeing in her file, well, then, find that girl."

Oliver stayed in his recliner a long time after the captain departed, nursing what remained of his whiskey.

Fix it, Pierce. He was used to hearing that. Might as well shift some punctuation around, call him Fix-It Pierce. That's what he did. He maneuvered, discovered, dug, outwitted, and strung folks along for the ride. His right hand put on a puppet show, while his left broke locks and rifled through ghost files no one was ever meant to see.

Roscoe getting canned hadn't been part of the plan. Oliver had made himself indispensable to that lazy poof, and he'd been primed for a promotion. Now, Roscoe's reputation put a sour tang on their association. Oliver wouldn't be moving up the ranks anytime soon. Nor, apparently, would he be schmoozing the new head designer.

Which is what had him sucking on a bottle of whiskey. And now Cappy Don's hair-brained idea. Not that the old man was ever wrong a day in his life, but if Kay were in on the deal, they might as well fly a bannered plane over the building, announcing their investigation.

Oliver reached for his ghost cell and punched a few keys.

Molly answered immediately. "You're slipping, Oli."

Did he detect a hint of pleasure in the hacker's tone? Probably, yes. "Point to the geek squad. Listen, that file on Kay Bing is missing a few key elements. I knew I was going in blind, but if the file info is bad, then I'm really screwed."

"Oh, yeah?" Molly sounded genuinely curious. She didn't like to be wrong any more than Oliver did. Hell, any of their team. Sometimes, being wrong cost lives. There wasn't room for ego when a mistake had been made. "What have you got?"

"She's hard. Forget bubbles and bouncing around like a four-year-old on speed. She's changed, a recent thing." The buzz that had passed between him and Kay whirled through his mind again. "That cabin she sold," he said thoughtfully, "she co-owned it with her boyfriend, Finn Welk. He's a master carpenter from some speck called Red Hill. That much I dug up for myself, but the rest of the story requires your delicate touch with info gathering. I want to know what went down. Details. That and anything else you can find out about her last year with Harper Designs."

"You got it, Oli."

"I hate that name. You know I do."

"That's probably in direct correlation with why I love it."

He sighed. "Make this priority, okay? I might not have much time."

"You got it, Oli."

* * * *

Amos Winston was a diva. No getting around it. A brilliant botanist, but a diva bound to make Kay's life hell if she didn't rein him in. She'd spent the last two weeks taking baby steps in her progress, but today she was officially done tiptoeing. Time to crack the whip.

Kay and her three team members surrounded one end of her big, shiny white drafting table. Drawn plans were laid out, colors filled in with oil paints done by Guillermo Ibarra, Kay's assistant designer. He hadn't been particularly opinionated or troublesome until Jasper made a joke about burritos, and Guillermo went on a five-minute rant in broken English about his family being from Spain, not Mexico, *muchas gracias*.

Amos was still going on about the gazanias. "I didn't go through such meticulous labor for a damn bathroom. I don't care if it's in the Ritz Carlton or Alice Cooper's tour bus, y'all got that?"

"Can we please focus here?"

The request from Jasper set Kay's teeth on edge. *Says the guy going out of his way to start trouble.* Of her three co-workers, she liked him least. He was a little too together, and when he poked, there was something more than good fun behind his smile.

"Oh, *sí*." Guillermo rolled his eyes. "You want to focus now, after you ask for *burritos* from a Spaniard. You want a little ass, I can get this for you. But it probably not what you t'ink you getting, okay?"

Jasper laughed. He had a horribly cocky laugh. He also had thick dark hair, gorgeous blue eyes, and lashes Kay would die for. But because he was such an ass, none of it did a thing for her. "I was joking, Guillermo. You need to loosen up."

Neve would've never let such unprofessional, unfocused behavior go on this long. Kay stood up straight, put on her best bitch face, and zeroed in. "Jasper, a round of coffee, if you please."

Thick, lush brows furrowed as he turned to stare at her. "What? Where's Oliver?"

"Not here. And since you're more interested in loosening up and talking about lunch, I figure I'd set you to a task more your speed."

She turned her glare to Amos. She really liked him, but this was a job, not a friendly group chat. "You make the flowers. I decide where they go. If it doesn't suit you, you should've applied for my job. And you." She pointed at Guillermo, the sensitive Spaniard. "Tell Jasper what kind of coffee you'd like. Then stop getting sidetracked by his antics. I like what you've brought me, but it's heavy on the wrong shade of pink. The walls here are a dusky pale blue." She pointed to the plans, drawn near exact to the room they were putting the finishing touches on, paint signifying what they'd decided on so far. "It'll go from a beachy sunset to grandma's parlor with one wrong step in the color spectrum. Bring me another option."

All three men gaped at her. She allowed herself a winning smile. "Amos, for what it's worth, the gazanias are a bit much for this. If you want me to consider alternatives, make them good ones."

He shook his nearly bald head, one hand sassily on his hip, and whistled low, a pleased smile curving his dark, full lips. "We got us a real boss now, y'all. Playtime is officially over." He held up a pointer finger in a delicate gesture of waiting. "I do have something else, if we're moving away from the blush pink."

"Great. Until then, we'll use the gazanias for the draft."

Guillermo turned to Jasper, who hadn't moved. "I take mine black."

Jasper blinked at him, then at Kay. "You're serious."

Her stomach churned. Her natural reaction leaned toward an explanation of how his behavior was cancer to a well-tuned team. But Neve didn't suffer fools. And she didn't take any lip. Kay steeled herself, and did her best to emulate Neve in one of her epic verbal takedowns. "Do I look like I'm joking? As far as I'm concerned, you're not necessary on this particular project. Interior liaisons are needed when we're designing rooms around the plants, not plants around the room. I also happen to know you've got a project in the wings, due in six months' time. I'm not Damian Roscoe. I don't want your last-minute rough draft tossed on my desk a week before construction starts on Kind Lotus Spa. Chances are, I'm going to turn down your first several attempts, because I don't settle for anything less than perfect. My guess? You're putting off the spa plans, because it means working closely with Guillermo. So, you're going to reconcile yourself with the fact that he wasn't hired for your personal entertainment. Treat him as your professional equal, or you're going to lose your job. If you want to be considered a valuable member of this team, show me what you got. I want a sketch on my desk in two days. Wow me."

She kept her face carefully neutral, a wall behind which she suffered an onslaught of conflicting emotions. She felt good. Powerful. In control. But also regretful at the stunned look on Jasper's face. Two days wasn't enough time, and they both knew it. But she wanted to see how he handled pressure, and it was too late for her to backtrack now. If she did, her team would think she was flighty.

"You better hop-to on that coffee," she said drily, giving him a flat stare before turning her attention back to the drafting table. "I like mine hot. Double cream." She didn't look up again until the shuffle of all three pairs of feet exited her office.

She could work with these guys. They were a talented group, with the exception of the few items of Jasper's she'd found in Roscoe's old files from past projects. He gave half-assed, first-try drafts with little to no thought put into the arrangement. But he'd done some good stuff, too, overall showing promise she wouldn't mind nurturing into real talent if he'd quit being such a jerk. His employment didn't make a hell of a lot of sense, because Kay could think of three designers better than Jasper off the top of her head. He'd be the easiest team member to replace. Not that they didn't each one have their quirks. Amos, the diva, protective of his beautiful creations. Guillermo, defensive of his heritage, and Jasper...Well, Jasper Jameson was a damn racist.

What was she supposed to do with that? What would *Neve* do with that?

Precisely what I just did. Kay nodded to herself. She didn't have Neve's talent for caustic sarcasm, but she was plenty sassy in her own right. She'd done it: whipped three grown men into shape, without completely maiming anyone, and without having to dig too deep or get too nasty. Neve probably would've called Jasper out, or fired him on the spot.

But Kay had already given one employee the boot. It hadn't stuck—Oliver had strutted right back into her office the next day, with a somber apology for his gossiping—but she couldn't go around firing every designer on staff because they had a few flaws. They all had them.

Even her, evidently, because at the mere wisp of thought, Oliver came to mind. So did his tailored-to-death slacks, and his stylish hair, and those pretty green eyes, and the way they'd slammed into her on that first day, and—

"You must be having a really great day. People don't grin like that for no reason."

Kay's eyes popped open. Oliver was in the doorway, a stack of manila folders tucked beneath one arm. He seemed pleased as pie. Had she summoned him subconsciously? "Are those the files I requested? If not, consider yourself fired again, because I asked for them at eight." She glanced at her watch, her lips carefully puckered in disapproval. "It's ten to noon."

He lowered his head. Today, he wore a baby blue button up with a subtly matching tie. Very clean. Very neat. Very different from her first day, when he'd seemed a little too at ease. He grinned apologetically and shrugged. "I'll just come right back the next day. It's not policy, I'm just hard to get rid of. Like a rash." He indicated one of the chairs surrounding nearby the drafting table.

She cleared her throat, arranged her expression into one of impatience, and waited for him to sit. It was the sort of stuff that came so naturally to Neve, but Kay had to remember the steps. Taking the reins wasn't easy, but she'd spent a whole year watching one of the best. She watched Oliver, resisting the urge to blink rapidly or look away, until he fidgeted and started talking.

"My apology was a little stiff that first day, but sincere. The gossip stuff about Roscoe was stupid. I'd just found out, and you know how easy it can be to get caught up in the mill."

"Especially when you're running it. You don't strike me as a particularly loyal assistant. Why should I keep you?"

He gave her a pained look. "Because I'm part of the team. I noticed the exchange you had with the boys." He glanced at the drafting table, took a deep breath, and looked at her almost regrettably. "Guillermo and Jasper, they've been at each other a long time. Two strong personalities that can't reconcile. Amos, he's been here since the company opened. Brit, she's sort of new, but she keeps it super professional and makes the place look good. She actually dresses to match the foyer, even though I don't think anyone asked her to do that." His eyebrows drew together quizzically. "Might be overkill. But she makes it work. Of course, there's the big bosses. Brit says Merit had a family emergency out of town last week, and Mr. Arnell is negotiating with a bigwig client, but any minute, you'll be called topside. I could give you some info." He made the offer with a slight shrug.

Kay stared. "More gossip."

"No, no. Not like that. You made your feelings pretty clear." He laughed softly. It was almost a purr and sent a shiver down her back. Why couldn't he be ugly? Or so tall, that the two of them together would be unseemly? "I mean I can offer you helpful information that might make navigating a little easier. For example, I can tell you Mr. Arnell is a bit of a mystery. He's a genius by all accounts, but reclusive."

Kay grunted. Seeing as he hadn't bothered to introduce himself to the new head designer, Oliver's input was hardly a revelation.

"Merit Hollis is prickly. I heard you used to work with Neve Harper, so she shouldn't be a challenge for you, except that she's detail-orientated to the extreme. It drove Roscoe crazy, but I never minded. He just swept the extra stuff my way. Merit's assistant is Brendan Berkley. He's an all right guy. Kind of in my boat. We get coffee for the brains and try to stay out of the way."

So calculated, that charming smile of pure, sweet humility Oliver offered up. And yet, Kay saw something genuine beneath it that made her want to do a little digging. "I appreciate you trying to fix what you did wrong.

And I think you're right, you probably should get a second shot. To be fair, I needed to make an example of someone, and you fit the bill perfectly."

"You're welcome to use me anytime."

She paused and closed her eyes briefly, before the pressure between them could catch and build, like gathering smoke. It was a disease with her. "Just know, I'll let you go if you're not what I need. What this team needs," she clarified, licking her lips.

He leaned forward, and the look he gave her this time was earnest—probably the most genuine thing he'd given her so far. "I do know a lot about what goes on around here. I'm practically invisible. The lowly assistant. And I know that Jasper isn't going to take what you did today on the chin. He'll go to Merit if he hasn't already. I'd, uh, suggest a lighter touch until you get to know everyone."

Like hell. She'd fight tooth and nail for respect, and they'd damn well give it to her, or...or...she'd raze the place, shake it till they all fell. "I don't really do the 'light touch' thing," she said icily.

Oliver leaned back, the files held up like a shield. "I'm just saying, you have to do a little catering sometimes. Amos, he's in love with his own expertise. He's hoping to really impress you with his work. If he fails to wow you with his suggestion for the bathroom project, he'll sour like bad wine. He'll be grumpy and difficult to work with for weeks. I've seen it happen. He's a genius, and as his boss, your approval is what keeps his fires stoked."

Kay bit her lip. She wasn't sure what to do with that. What if the flowers sucked or didn't fit right? "That's dumb."

"Maybe," Oliver agreed readily. "I'm only telling you, I've been on the sidelines long enough to see the different approaches, and what works best. The best, most creative projects come from a head designer who's a cheerleader as often as they're a taskmaster. Sure, the guys need a stern what-for occasionally, but if you're enthused, they're enthused. They'll feed off whatever energy you put out. Get everyone pumped and excited. It doesn't feel like work when we're all amped about the job, ya know? They're eager to excel, but more than that, they're eager to please you. You were a little brutal just now. Jasper deserved it, but you have to manage everyone a little differently. Salt and pepper to taste."

Memories floated to mind. Kay recalled Neve, back when they'd remodeled Gavin's cabin. She'd spit wads to impress the general contractor, waxed poetic on history to get a rancher's cooperation, and whipped a mouthy electrician into shape with a few well-aimed jabs at what his lack of professionalism could cost him. To the plumber who'd had no issues, she'd been as pleasant and charming as a cup of earl gray tea served in fine china.

Kay deflated. She hadn't prepared for a light touch. She'd spent the last two weeks scrubbing every enthusiastic, bubbly, spastic, unrehearsed line from her tongue before it could fly through her lips.

She studied Oliver under her lashes. This time, her pursed lips were the real thing. "It's a wonder you don't have my job."

He grinned. "I'm not after yours. Actually, I'm hoping to have Brendan's one day. Being under Merit's thumb is as far as I can go with Free Leaf Concepts until I further my education. Once I'm raking in Brendan's salary, I'll do exactly that."

Kay already had a thing for Oliver's pants. She couldn't get caught up in his dreams, too. "And Guillermo? You diagnosed everyone else."

"Just don't call him a Mexican."

She rolled her eyes. "The child-sized blond bimbo managed to figure *that* out."

Oliver stopped suddenly. Frozen, his gaze locked on hers, his brows drawn slightly. A small frown put a dimple in his chin. Slowly, he cocked his head to one side and regarded Kay with undue seriousness. "I don't think you're a bimbo." He let out a soft snort, hooked his thumb toward the drafting table. "How you whipped those guys into shape? Doled out exactly what they needed, when they needed it? I mean, Jasper is a bastard who holds a grudge, and you'll have a hard time working with him now, but no, I don't think anyone in this building thinks you're a bimbo, Kay."

For a solid second, she stared. She couldn't do anything else. Even glancing away to try to hide the pink she knew had to be infusing her face wasn't an option, because they were hooked together again, her gaze and Oliver's, like unlucky fish in a tiny pond snatched from the comfort of the water. She wouldn't call the thing that pinged between them comfortable. Not even a little. It was awkward, and filled her with puzzling feelings, foremost of all was curiosity.

She wanted to know more about this funny assistant, who didn't quite seem to fit in with the rest of the crowd at Free Leaf Concepts. She wanted to know where he disappeared to on his lunch breaks, why he'd been close to Damian Roscoe but hardly spoke to anyone else on the design team, yet knew all their peculiarities like he'd taken meticulous notes on the subject. She wanted to know why their gazes kept snagging together, and what he was thinking—if her mind was tumbling, perhaps his was, too.

Did he wonder where she came from, how she'd secured the job with Free Leaf with such limited experience? Or could be he wasn't pondering anything deeper than why she took two creams in her coffee instead of three.

Oliver broke the spell with another soft laugh and stood suddenly, hopping out of the chair with a boy's careless swagger. "And while you may be on the petite side, who would I be to cast stones, eh?"

Kay cleared her throat, but couldn't dredge up a smile. Not too tall, but taller than her... He was actually kind of perfect. Suddenly, Oliver reminded her of another sweet, rakish, devil-may-care boy who'd once said nice things to her. He didn't say nice things anymore.

"Thanks for the advice. I'll make a note."

Oliver's smile turned uncertain. "Yeah, anytime. Oh, and Merit wants to see you. She's waiting."

* * * *

Oliver had absolutely no reason in his capacity as Kay's little errand boy to attend the meeting between Kay and Merit. But as her assistant, he was given access. Everyone assumed he was there doing what he'd been told to do. Amazing, the freedom he could manipulate for himself. At least when Kay wasn't coming up with a thousand reasons to keep him out of her range of sight.

Tinkerbell, Tinkerbell. She was a problem—a sexy little problem he wanted to bend over the drafting table and try to solve. He blinked the image away. Not good, not good. And the way they stared at each other, like two circling predators sizing each other up.

He'd come across energy like theirs before, the kind that crackled and leaped like flames, but never quite like this—with a sexual potency that made it nearly impossible for him to break away. Usually, the clash was the product of two minds bent on having the upper hand. Either the snaps and crackles turned into real flames, and shit got burned down, or it eventually grew into a sort of passing recognition, acceptance, and professional respect.

This was similar, while also being unlike anything he'd experienced, because Kay wasn't supposed to be this important to his investigation. She should've been nothing more than an unexpected speedbump, an easily navigated surprise.

She's only a problem if you make her one, Pierce.

Cappy Don's warning had been prophetic. Kay definitely had her eye on Oliver now. Too late to stay plastered to the background, sink into the white-washed walls of the hallway when they passed, or stay slightly distanced from her, the way he did everyone else.

He'd put himself out there, and the reason had nothing to do with his orders from Cappy Don, and everything to do with realizing that Kay was genuinely struggling inside the shell of something that wasn't her. Not according to her life's history, anyway. Just where was the effervescent Kay hiding, and would he ever get to meet her?

Oliver bit down hard on the inside of his cheek. He couldn't do much else, standing next to Kay in the elevator. Couldn't slap himself, or chuck a stapler at his own head. He should've left her alone, instead of advising her on the more subtle nuances of small office politics. After the way she'd so neatly put three outspoken designers in their place with a few zingers and some unsettlingly on-point insight, he had to acknowledge she'd do fine on her own. Besides, Cappy had asked him to bring her in with a few clues, not make himself her new best bud. And judging by the look on her face after he'd stated the rather obvious, she was probably still looking for any excuse to fire him. Or maybe the stuff that popped and fizzled every time they made prolonged eye contact put her on edge, too.

For now, he needed to shelve the personal feely stuff and focus on his other professional tasks. He had more than a few reasons to want some time to surreptitiously scout Merit Hollis's office, and this was one of his few visits his job had granted him so far.

If he'd only been able to come in a little higher on the totem pole. But Brendan Berkley had been with Merit since the inception of the company. He couldn't be easily bought and removed from his position. Merit answered only to Mr. Arnell, essentially the creative brain, who spent most of his time squirreled away in his impenetrable office, dreaming up fancy gene-swapping stuff. It wasn't a stretch Merit could be involved in any dirty activities hiding behind the company's sleek professional veneer.

Merit stood when Oliver double-tapped on the glass pane door, gave her a dull smile—really digging into that "nobody" role—and opened it wide for Kay to step past him. He patted himself on the back for only giving her ass the briefest of glances as she sashayed by. She had on a pencil skirt the color of champagne. It flared at her knees, not only giving the impression of a golden mermaid, but accentuating the shape of her hips. She was a tiny package, but undeniably grown.

"Ms. Hollis, it's nice to finally meet you." Kay stuck out her hand, kept her smile demure.

Merit returned the mild greeting and indicated for Kay to take a seat. Merit's office was the smallest room on the top floor. Two conference rooms took up massive amounts of space, and of course, Mr. Arnell had a monstrosity of an office, with a ten-foot-long floor-to-ceiling window that gave him a panoramic view of downtown Little Rock.

Everything in Merit's office was muted, as if she'd moved in but never finished unpacking. His gaze idly roamed over the fabric-covered walls, paneled like everywhere else in the building. They were mostly barren except for a few large photography shots of rare blooms set in expensive matted frames. The carpet was beige and the desk distressed oak. A mostly empty bookcase held two knickknacks and a small pile of books—all botany related at a glance.

He peeked at the two women to make sure their attention stayed focused on one another.

"I hope you're fitting in well," Merit was saying. Even the woman's hair wanted to be taken seriously. It was probably shoulder-length, a dark, caramel brown color, but she curled it into big, fat loops that circled her head like a helmet.

He let them talk niceties. He had other work to do, besides taking mental pictures of the room and soaking in every detail he could for later sketches.

The paneled wall coverings all over Free Leaf Concepts intrigued Oliver. They were little more than thin, decorative barriers, manipulated as desire or necessity dictated, like Merit's fabric-covered panels or the polished plastic in the third-floor labs. Sometimes, they were placed side-by-side, and covered an entire room. In other places, they were installed at random intervals, such as in the hallway leading from the reception area.

Or, Oliver suspected, they might be used to conceal things one might want to remain hidden. Like, say, a door.

He'd made several attempts at dislodging the panels in Amos's lab, which he thought was probably the last place someone would install a secret swinging panel. Those were practice sessions. He knew how the large pieces fit together, how they attached to the drywall behind them by a series of hooks, and how they appeared flush when properly installed. A quick inspection would tell him if he came across one that didn't seem quite right.

Merit's panels were covered by some thin wool material, and each one looked as secure as the next. He couldn't put it on paper and sign it, but he was pretty positive every panel in Merit's office was bolted into place.

He frowned. Maybe the schematics were wrong. It wouldn't be the first bad intelligence he'd come across. He cast a quick glance at Kay, who defied everything they'd gathered about her. Could be the blueprints were old and outdated, or a rejected set of plans. He'd kept their discovery a secret from the captain. Oliver wanted to locate the mysteriously hidden room and determine its relation to the investigation before telling the team, which he could've easily done by now, were it merely a matter of waltzing into the upper offices and feeling up the walls they like he'd paid them. But alas. Not so easy to do. And forget breaking into the place. Any evidence gathered wouldn't be considered legally obtained. Until Oliver stumbled upon something worthy of a warrant, they were stagnant.

Besides, they didn't want to spook Free Leaf Concepts. They might button down their secret operations. They were already hog-tied, in Oliver's opinion. A whole year he'd been undercover for the LRPD, and he had nothing but personnel documents, easily secured from the second floor, and a secret room he couldn't prove existed to show for his labors.

If he only had Brendan's job. As Merit's assistant, Oliver would have all sorts of access to interesting places and things.

Kay and Merit continued with their merry chat. He happened to glance over at the same time Merit's smile turned harsh.

She angled her head at Kay as though she were a particularly ugly daisy that had found its way into a prize garden. "Ms. Bing, I delight in your company. I truly do. You're charming as a buzzy little bee, dear. But if you attempt to fire another one of my staff, I'll have you gone."

Oliver had moved to stand against the wall, so he had a good view of Kay's profile. Her mouth popped open to respond, and he winced. To his relief and her credit, she shut it immediately. Good idea. He warned her about Merit. But then her mouth was open again, and she was responding, unsmiling and matter-of-fact. Oliver held his breath.

"I came here to do a job, Ms. Hollis." In her tone, he detected the faintest hint of a dare—she was calling Merit's bluff. "When my first interaction is with an assistant who's a little too comfy with the rumor mill, I assume he isn't a very good assistant. It's easier to train someone new than to break old habits." She shot a dark glance at Oliver, like this was all his fault.

Merit relaxed a little. She liked direct. She liked honesty. She hated brown-nosing. Shit, she was going to *love* Kay. Why hadn't he realized it sooner? Oliver almost rolled his eyes. Thank God he didn't.

Merit looked at him for the first time, bestowing the kind of proud smile that reminded him of his granny. "Fair enough. Oliver, try not to get fired again. You've got to adapt, and you've got to be able to do it on a dime. You *are* a good assistant. If Brendan ever moved on, you'd be an obvious in-house solution for his replacement. We do like to promote from within," she said to Kay.

Kay's smile was forced as she turned it on him.

"I really am a good assistant." Outside of the real reasons he was at Free Leaf Concepts, he made a decent shake of job the he'd been assigned. And when he lacked knowledge or expertise, he had a team full of people like Molly to call on for backup.

Merit stood, a signal the meeting was over. "I think you're going to make a wonderful addition to our family here, Ms. Bing. I did receive a small complaint from Jasper Jameson, but he's prone to expectations of favoritism, so I'll take no action until it proves a significant problem. We keep counselors on retainer. Hiring and firing are rather drastic actions. To hire, we need perfection. Nothing less."

Oliver couldn't help himself. A small grin stole over his mouth at Kay's stricken expression. Ah, yes. Ye olde padded résumé.

"Firing," Merit went on regretfully, her face set with distaste like she'd swallowed something bitter, "is a nasty business. High turnover rates for the company. Extra paperwork for the second floor. Especially an interior designer of some renown, such as Mr. Jameson. Not over a misunderstanding."

"You call thinly veiled racism a 'misunderstanding'? If your policies are to sweep things like that under the rug, I can resign now. I'll apologize in advance for the hit to your turnover rate."

Merit's face solidified into stone. Her eyes were two shiny polished coins as she glared at Kay. Kay didn't waver. She stared back, and Oliver waited, his chest tight with an unreleased exhale.

"Slander is often addressed during counseling sessions, Ms. Bing." Merit blinked once. Then sighed unhappily. "As are other issues. Since I've yet to hear complaints from anyone but Mr. Jameson on this point, I can assume nothing. If one were to cross my desk, I would, of course, take the proper action."

Kay nodded, seeming pleased. Oliver ran his tongue over the line of his teeth. Huh. Little girl, big stones. Bigger than he thought. To lay a whopping on people who answered to her was one thing. To call out Merit Hollis on potentially shady human resources dealings? Well, that took an altogether different sort of backbone.

Merit continued as if nothing strained had passed between them. "I have another meeting with our latest client. I'm most excited to introduce you to Capital Acres, our greenhouse compound. It covers over one hundred acres of land, with houses large and small."

Kay's eyebrows gathered in a puzzled expression. "That's...extensive."

"Not everything we grow is for Free Leaf landscaping," Merit explained. "We also do independent studies for market analysis of GMO crops, which requires growing and testing our own samples. We're a trusted source, not one of those in-the-pocket groups. Nobody can buy Free Leaf Concepts," she declared, her chin high.

Kay's mouth turned down. "I had no idea."

Merit spread her hands open and smiled. "GMOs may be the future, but so is the legislation that will govern them. We're a company the public can trust to provide accurate reports on these new crops. We publish our results annually in any number of acclaimed scientific journals. Transparency is crucial to our reputation. Unfortunately, I'm afraid my plan to show you around Capital Acres tomorrow will have to wait for another time."

Oliver sparked to life. "I could do it," he offered a bit too loudly. He cursed himself for his hasty interjection. Real smooth. Both women looked at him like he'd jumped out of a closet and shouted "Huzzah!"

Capital Acres was the big game, and he'd been a caged lion for far too long. This was his chance, and on better terms than he could've hoped for. Kay was so green, she wouldn't take any of his behavior—like searching nooks and crannies—as particularly out of the ordinary.

He cleared his throat and dialed back his excitement. "Sorry, I just like getting outside. You know how it is. We're all here because of a passion for the outdoors. Bringing it inside. And yet, I spend all my time shuffling files." He shook his head ruefully, laughed lightly. "I'd love to take her, Ms. Hollis. It'd be a pleasure. The greenhouses are always a treat. The things Amos and Tallulah can do, they just blow me away."

Kay looked at Oliver like he was shedding a layer of skin before her eyes. She'd seen right through his act. "I did want to meet Tallulah Hadley." She looked at Merit. "I heard she's the arborist, correct? We're beginning plans for Kind Lotus Spa soon. I'd love to pick Tallulah's brain."

"Oh, all right," Merit agreed indulgently. Oliver suspected she'd wanted a reason to forgo the tour. If the company had anything illegal growing in Capital Acres, maybe Merit didn't know about it after all. "You two enjoy a day at the greenhouses." She smiled warmly at Kay. "See there? Eager to please, willing to jump in to do what's necessary, a passion for the work we do. Oliver's a keeper."

Chapter 3

Lab was a relative term, Kay decided. Amos did science-y stuff with a microscope and slides and wore the white coat get-up, but in reality, the third floor was an expansive miniature greenhouse. He tested seeds, then developed and perfected their ideal growth scenarios to learn which resulted in the hardiest, most beautiful, most vibrant blooms. That way, the greenhouse would know how to cultivate the plants when he passed along the finished sample for mass production.

"Botanist is putting a light hand on it," Amos explained. He liked to discuss his work, and he held her opinion in high regard, just like Oliver said.

Kay nodded encouragingly and tried not to let her eyes glaze over. Not that the flowers weren't amazing. There were just so many of them. She tried to keep track of Amos's long string of names and descriptions, but it was useless once he started throwing around Latin terms. Her aunt's florist shop simply hadn't prepared her for this level of botany.

"What I do, it's the real science. The tree surgeon down at Capital Acres, Tallulah, she don't do what I do. She's basically a glorified farmer."

"Hm," Kay responded, trying to sound impressed.

Amos guided Kay through narrow shelves of seedlings planted in rich, fertilized soil, so dark it was nearly black. "Horticulture, you probably heard of that. It ain't exactly plant breeding, or propagation, which is what I do." He gave her a toothy grin. "All about making them little plant babies. I started out with lichenology—don't laugh, that's a real thing—and then I got interested in mycology, before moving on to orchid-ology. That's when I started getting into flowering plants. Blooms—they're at the heart of plant propagation. They ain't pretty and smell good for no reason, ya know?"

Nope. Kay didn't have the slightest. "Thanks for the tour. And for working double-time," she added, with meaning. "Those orange fire azaleas are gorgeous, and they work with the new palette Guillermo provided. The hot pink definitely resets the tone. No granny vibes. Speaking of Guillermo, I'm thinking of sending him out on his own to complete the bathroom, once your order from the greenhouse arrives."

Ordering and awaiting the arrival of the flowers seemed like an unnecessary extra step when Kay could pick them up during her visit to Capital Acres with Oliver. But Amos explained everything was logged and shipped to maintain an exact inventory. Flowers were harvested, packaged, and delivered in cooling trucks by the trained greenhouse employees, and no one else.

Amos bobbed his head. "Guillermo is good for it. He has a keen eye. Jasper, too. They both good, G and Jasper. Just can't be in the same room together."

She'd see about that. She couldn't work around those two bickering constantly. She'd whip Jasper into shape or get rid of him. Kay waved good-bye to Amos as she left his lab and headed for the elevator. Back on the fourth floor, she waved again, this time at Guillermo as he passed her.

"You staying late? Not good for the skin, ya know t'at?" Guillermo's dark eyes twinkled.

Kay gave him a wan smile. "Only for a little while. I met Ms. Hollis this afternoon, went to lunch, and then spent some time going over client files. Amos called me to the lab, wanted to show me what he'd worked on all day. I haven't been back to my office. Oliver texted me about an important e-mail I got while I was out. I'll take an extra wrinkle not to have to do deal with it first thing in the morning."

She didn't give a fig about the e-mail.

Amos was going to provide her with a smorgasbord of offerings for the spa that was their upcoming project, everything from flowers to vines, ferns and probably a bunch of other shit she'd never heard of—like the Hawaiian skeleton flower she'd dumbly asked about before realizing it was something she ought to know. If she chose one plant over another, she'd need a reason beyond color. Because the bloom didn't open at the right time, because it survived better in dry climes, and would die in a humid spa environment, because the leaves didn't lend themselves to the stylistic flow.

Normally, one might pawn research off onto their assistant, but the last thing Kay needed was for Oliver to realize she was up to her neck and one misstep from drowning.

She left Guillermo and walked resolutely to her office. She rather liked it in the quiet hours. The drafting table was still scattered with the renderings of the bathroom project. Affixed lamps burned bright over the lacquered white surface. Despite flailing like a puppy trying to swim for the first time, she was enjoying herself. She might be a little lost with Amos's homemade fauna and rare samples, but she had the drive to learn. The research was interesting, and she could get caught up in hours of study. Pinpricks of the old excitement that used to rule her world were blossoming. Her mind was re-opening, her heart expanding, and the weight of the guilt she had strapped to her back lightened marginally every day. She was coming back to herself, in bits and pieces.

At the same time, she was having a hard time letting go of the parts of herself Neve had inspired. She'd established herself as someone who wouldn't be tread on. Her team seemed to respect her. She'd even stood up to Merit. If she quit trying so hard to do things Neve's way, would everything all fall apart? Or could she return to herself and still maintain the current status quo?

Talk about an identity crisis. She went over to the small personal desk where she kept her laptop, her calendar perpetually open. Oliver filled it in with every company event, and made special notations on what required Kay's attendance or that of her team's.

Pattie Michaels, the manager of Capital Acres, had sent over an e-mail. Oliver had printed it out and set it on the laptop's keyboard. Merit had informed Pattie of Kay and Oliver's impending trip, and she'd sent along instructions on which entrance to use and where to locate her office so she could give them a proper tour.

Kay set the page aside. Beneath it was a cutout newspaper article. She almost tossed the scrap aside, but the byline caught her attention.

Strange new hallucinogen hits the streets. Fayetteville PD at a loss.

She wrinkled her nose and sat down. The clipping was exact, precisely hemming in the story. Kay flipped it over. Only an ad on the backside, bisected and incomplete, so the story was obviously the important thing. She settled back and read, frowning at the age of the paper, as well as the location. What was Fayetteville to a Little Rock girl?

Magic mushrooms aren't an uncommon drug in the university party circuit. College students often think mushrooms are more eco-friendly and cost-effective than other similar hallucinogens, such as LSD, and less dangerous than a few other alternatives.

Recently, however, local police enforcement have begun investigating what the press has dubbed 'super shrooms,' a growing epidemic of genetically modified magic mushrooms being grown and cultivated to increase their potency. With these new super mushrooms, episodes last longer, are more intense, and have new side effects, not unlike those seen in chemical substances like PCP, which is terrifying for anyone who's read the news in the last decade. Lab-produced drugs, such as PCP, MDMA, better known as ecstasy, and the fabled 'bath salts,' often have unpredictable, and sometimes fatal, side effects.

In Fayetteville's first reported case, two anonymous UA students admitted to taking the super shrooms after they ended up in the ER last Saturday night. One student regurgitated repeatedly, in an attempt to purge the drugs from his body over an incredible two-day period, resulting in dehydration. Both students claimed they suffered debilitating paranoia and panic attacks, as well as hyperrealistic hallucinations they could often not differentiate from reality, for days before they sought to call 911 and get help when they realized the side effects weren't lessening. One student is quoted as saying, they were "familiar with magic mushrooms," but that the high of these in particular was "more like an overdosing on ice [methamphetamines]... I thought we were going to die."

They very well could have.

Studies done by local police labs have come back with astounding results, matching those of other cases reported in southern parts of the state, including Texarkana. Other municipalities infected include Fort Smith, Pine Bluff, and an incident in Jonesboro, which may be the most tragic and telling report so far. Three people died—

Kay stopped and scanned the rest of the article. Since it had been cut below the title, only the tagline showed. No date. She set the article down. The story made her feel icky. Something about it, maybe the context or a few of the words, clung to her like a thin film, but she couldn't explain what bothered her, exactly. How in the hell had it ended up on her desk?

She picked it up again and stuffed it into her purse. She shut down her laptop, took a final glance at the e-mail Oliver had printed, and wondered if he didn't know something about the strange gift.

* * * *

It wasn't like she was cheating on Neve. That'd be absurd. A mentee couldn't cheat, per se, on their mentor.

Okay, so it felt a little like cheating. Neve Harper had been Kay's guiding light for a little over a year now. Her hero, her inspiration for becoming an interior designer, the woman who'd shaped Kay's future after a happenstance introduction. Neve's work had been what sent Kay to design school, steered her toward a new life. But Kay sought a different sort of guidance now.

Seraphina Fawkes's tiny studio apartment was on the second floor of a mid-town building, not far from Neve's place. Kay pasted a smile on her face as she knocked on the door. Her smile widened into something more genuine at the blank expression on Seraphina's face.

Her old friend opened the door wide. Old was kind of pushing it. At twenty-three, Kay didn't have much of anything that qualified as "old" just yet. Not even teaching assistants from college, who'd been instrumental in helping Kay become top of her class.

Seraphina hadn't changed a bit. Her hair was still pin-straight, and came to a full-stop at her chin. It'd be a drastic, sharp hairstyle for most. But Seraphina's wide cheeks, pointed chin, long slender nose, and wide baby blue eyes beneath a canopy of fringe bangs softened the severe cut. Her hair was baby-fine, the soft shade of a brand-new penny; a glorious, shiny red-blond that Kay envied with all her heart.

Neve had a certain dangerous appeal that had little to do with her appearance, yet made her attractive all the same. Seraphina, by contrast, was a marble statue—beautiful, regal, solid, and elusively mysterious.

It was that façade that Kay had come for. "Been awhile, Sera. Sorry to drop by so suddenly. I was around, and I—"

"Forget it," Seraphina said, busting into a rarely seen yet beatific smile. "I'm just glad to see you. Come inside." She spoke the soft command with the same quiet authority Seraphina tended to say everything.

Kay did as she was told, glad Seraphina was in the mood for company. But then, Seraphina's mood was always a guess. She left the people around her to speculate and gauge, without giving them much to go on outwardly.

That was the kind of power Kay was after. If she couldn't be a mallet, she'd be a drop of something more subtle but just as effective. Like an odorless poison.

The apartment was a treasure for any artistically minded individual. Seraphina had an exquisite touch, blending whimsical country charm with modern elements, like stainless steel and glass surfaces. A white-washed ladder rested against a wall near a bookshelf—no television in sight—the rungs providing shelving for an array of potted herbs and small flowering plants: ivy vines, and fat, squat vases of hydrangeas in varying colors, from pale blue to vibrant violet.

"So," Kay began, seating herself at Seraphina's beckoning on a periwinkle tweed love seat. Probably an original from the seventies given its design, refinished to appear modern. "I hear you left the university recently."

Seraphina was only four steps away, but in another room. From a half-sized refrigerator, she pulled out two expensive bottles of water and a bowl of trail mix. The good kind, Kay noticed, with yogurt-covered stuff. She could almost convince herself it was candy.

Seraphina handed a bottle to Kay, joined her, and set the bowl on the glass-topped table. "It's tap," she said, giving her own water a shake. "I reuse the bottles."

Kay waited, comfortable and at ease. Seraphina's quiet disposition could be comforting or intimidating, probably depending on whatever subtle vibes she gave out.

"I'm with Gallagher Interiors," Seraphina explained, arranging her long legs on the sofa as she sat. "Or, at least, I intend to be. I've been through a few rounds of interviewing. I'm confident I'll get the job, but their hiring process is intense."

"I imagine so. I mean, they end up with a lot of city contracts, right?" Everyone, at least in Kay's world, knew Grant Gallagher. His reputation rivaled Neve's, though it was said he kept to himself.

"The city council voted last year to build additional offices on the grounds of the Governor's Mansion, and it's no secret Gallagher Interiors will end up winning the bid. I intend to run that project."

"Wow, you really think ahead."

Seraphina's mouth curved into a small smile. "Building a résumé. We can't all be Neve Harper."

Kay had no idea what to make of the comment. Seraphina didn't sound jealous, impetuous, nor admiring. Just stating a fact, but Kay sensed something behind the innocuous statement. Before she could ask, Seraphina pinned her with an unnervingly keen stare. Her light blue eyes were the kind that seemed to penetrate one's mind. Neve could throw daggers, make a person feel like they'd run smack into a concrete wall. But Seraphina seemed to see right through Kay.

"Enough about me. I hear things, too. How're you finding Free Leaf Concepts?"

Kay unlatched the door to the dam inside her. She hadn't come here to impress Seraphina, but ask for her help. "I'm a wreck. I'm on my toes every second, because the truth is I have no formal education in this particular field. At the same time, I'm like a life-sized doll, so I have this tremendous attitude. It's so unlike me, but without some sass, I'm afraid I'll lose the respect I've earned. I'm trying to do things like I've watched Neve do them the last year, but it's impossible. Because she's Neve Harper, and I'm not."

"Small blessings," Seraphina interjected, straight-faced. "This city doesn't need two."

Surprise drew Kay's stare. "Do you think Neve's terrible? Of course you do." Everyone thought Neve was terrible. "She's not that bad, really. She's mean as a snake, but only when someone does something stupid. She's actually surprisingly thoughtful, in terms of managing people, discovering what makes them tick and how to earn their respect. And that's just the problem! I can emulate her attitude. I can slay my team with a few words, effortlessly. But what I can't seem to do is give them a reason to like me. Me. Kay Bing. They respect my authority, all right, but do they really respect me?"

Seraphina's face was impassive, but her gaze filled with pity. "You can't really believe that, Kay." She settled closer. "Do you know why Neve Harper is successful?"

"Because she's mean as a snake. She really is. I've been lucky, because I work too hard for her to find any fault, even when I screw up—"

"Being mean doesn't ensure a path to success, and it certainly doesn't buy respect, as you're finding out." Her fine copper eyebrows turned up at the corners questioningly. "Kay, what's happened? This isn't like you, to try to be someone else to achieve your goals. You don't need to be like Neve—or me," she said, quietly. Beneath the fringe of her penny-colored bangs, her stare was knowing. "You need to be like Kay Bing. That girl may not have a huge grasp of flora and fauna, but she's got spunk and drive. She's a little badass—a surprise waiting for anyone who thinks she's as small inside as she is outside. You're *big*, Kay. You've always been big to me. Just be yourself."

"I can't right now," Kay mumbled through her fingers.

"This isn't about flowers." Seraphina's tone was decisive at she arrived at the conclusion.

Kay licked her lips and blinked back emotions she'd managed to bury the last several months. "Ever do something that makes you question who you are as a person? Something that challenges your beliefs about yourself?"

Seraphina's smile was more of a smirk, and she glanced away briefly. "Everyone does. We don't know our own limits until we test them. Making mistakes is how we learn who we are, what we're willing to accept." She quirked a brow. "And what we aren't."

"Maybe," Kay begrudgingly admitted. She'd definitely learned something about herself. That much was true. "I've always liked who I am. But then I went and did something I would've sworn until that very moment I wasn't capable of. I haven't wanted to be me ever since. Worse, I feel like I've forgotten how."

Seraphina's gaze turned to concern. "Want to talk about it?"

Kay nodded, but she couldn't look at Seraphina anymore. She stared at her hands in her lap, clasped around the water bottle, drifting aimlessly over words on the label that blurred and meant nothing. "I didn't tell anyone, but after Finn and I bought the cabin, he proposed. I loved him. Or, I did enough to say yes, even though I had doubts. Twenty-two, that's a bit young, right? I think I kept the engagement to myself because, somewhere inside, I knew I wouldn't go through with it. At least, that's my theory. It was all in the back of my mind, but the rest of me just went along for the ride. Caught up in the moment, I guess. It's exciting, you know? Buying property together, getting engaged. But later, it became pretty clear I didn't love Finn as much as I thought I did, or I'd have never done what I did. I don't hurt people, Sera. It's not who I am." She was surprised by the wetness on her cheeks. She rubbed her face.

"You had a nasty breakup?"

"Finn started working for Neve when I did. A few months after Finn's proposal, Neve sent me out to spearhead my first solo project. A mother-in-law cottage in the back gardens of this mini-mansion. Neve had other obligations, ones that required Finn, but she didn't want to turn down any work starting out. New company, even with her name, means building clientele. And I was primed for a chance to lead, raring to go. You know me. I jump in headfirst. I actually did a great job on the cottage. I took a few hints from the cabin we did for Gavin Chambers, woodsy stuff and elegant tweaks, like fine china dishes and the most amazing antique brass—"

"Kay." Seraphina cut into her rambling with ease. Just her name, with no inflection, was as good as a shout.

Kay's cheeks heated, and she cleared her throat. "Sorry. The meat of it comes down to the less-skilled carpenter we hired for the cottage. Charlie Bowles. I have a thing for guys who can handle wood, apparently. It's a good thing I wasn't around in Jesus's day." She snorted softly. "I would've ruined everything for that guy." She caught a warning glance from Seraphina, and swallowed. "Charlie and I, uh... we had, um... there were..."

"Relations had?"

"I cheated on Finn." Kay ground out the words like they were glass in her mouth. "It's so unlike me, so uncharacteristic. Like I didn't know I wanted to play fast and loose until the option was taken away. And I told Finn, of course. He had to know. I couldn't go through with our engagement, hiding something like that. I'm an awful liar."

She didn't feel better after baring her soul. She felt wretched.

Seraphina wrapped a long arm around Kay's bunched shoulders. "Once, I let a student take the blame for one of my screw-ups. It was my first week, and there were at least thirty other undergrads who wanted the teaching assistant slot."

Kay had to force herself not to turn and stare. Talk about out of character.

"Today, I like to tell myself I'd be braver and take the punishment. In fact, before I left, I came forward and admitted to the professor what I'd done. He laughed and told me I wouldn't have been a good aide if I didn't let students know how it was in the real world occasionally. We don't always get the kudos we deserve, and sometimes an electrician's bad work gets blamed on the plumber, as the saying goes. I still don't feel right about it. It's not something I'd ever do again. But most importantly, Kay, I didn't beat myself up over it for the rest of time."

Kay chewed her lip. "I'm not trying to punish myself. Not intentionally, anyway. It's just this unfinished business. I thought I'd turned a corner and revealed my true nature. A girl who can't commit. But since then, I haven't slept with anyone. So, maybe it was personal, after all. In the end, Finn had so many questions. I wish I could answer them. I hate myself for what I did to him."

Seraphina gave Kay one last squeeze, then sat forward to fish cashews out of the bowl of trail mix. "You're right. It's still affecting you, all this time later. Maybe you need closure. A chance to say the things you just said to me. You should consider calling Finn. Find peace with him, find peace with yourself."

* * * *

Molly's phone number came up on Oliver's screen as a series of nonsense symbols, the way some people spelled out cuss words to avoid spelling out a cuss word.

"Hey." A beat of silence greeted him. He frowned at that. "Molly?"

"Yeah. It's me." The resignation in her voice came over the line clear as a cloudless summer day. Oliver's frown deepened, but he kept mum. "Sorry it took me so long to dig up this girl's backstory. Red Hill is really isolated. I had to send someone out to the cabin to track down Finn Welk. A discreet call to Harper Designs revealed he took leave after the breakup with Kay, then left Neve's employ altogether."

Oliver rubbed his chin thoughtfully. "Broken heart?"

"How'd you guess?" Molly sounded a little more like herself then, an eager, gleeful gossip. "We planted a guy at the local bar. Finn Welk is a swell fellow. He's got nothing but lovely things to say, until someone mentions Kay Bing. Then Welk clams up, and you couldn't pry his mouth open with a crowbar."

"Then how—"

"Whiskey keeps no secrets. We both know that."

Oliver ignored that last bit. "So, what we'd learn?"

"First, Oli, tell me, what's your impression of Kay?"

Oliver rose from his recliner and padded into the kitchen. Whiskey sounded about right. He reached for the decanter on the counter with one hand, held his phone steady with the other, and answered honestly. His answer was for the sake of the job, not personal. Keeping his opinion to himself wouldn't help the cause. "I think she's trying too hard. I also think it won't be a leap for her to figure out I'm the one who left the article on her desk. I've got nothing for when she confronts me, which I don't doubt she'll do." *I also think she has a fantastic ass and legs that make up in shape what they may lack in length.* "That do it for you, Molly?"

"As a person." Molly was impatient and gruff. "As a human being, how do you see her?"

He paused to pour a finger of whiskey and tossed it back soundlessly. "Tell me why this matters."

"It's a test. How well can you read others?"

"Pretty damn well, granted they're being upfront." He let that settle between them like a stone. "Well enough to guess Kay is probably morally sound, a decent judge of other people, and receptive. You want to get to the good part, now we're done with trivial bullshit?"

"I don't think it's trivial," Molly shot back. "I think it's damn near poetic."

Oliver squeezed his eyes shut against an oncoming headache. "Can you just tell me what I need to know? Despite all the very good reasons we aren't best friends, we still have to work together. Do you have something or not?"

Another strange beat of silence, so unlike Molly. "Fine," she relented. "Your girl is cheating scum. She bought a love shack with this dude, then went and got cozy with someone else—another carpenter, mind you—while leading a small side project for Neve Harper."

A deep sigh left Oliver's chest, and his eyes opened to slits. He could feel his lips as they twisted into a grim, sardonic smile. "Hits a bit close to home."

"Almost," Molly said with mocking sweetness. "They were engaged."

Oliver's brows went up in spite of himself. He didn't think anything could surprise him, but he wouldn't have expected that sort of thing from Kay, cheating on her fiancé. She seemed too noble, if not innocent.

He kept that to himself and focused on Molly. Her attitude made sense now. "What did you expect me to say, Molly? That I sensed Kay and I

Roxanne Smith

had something in common? I haven't got close enough to her to guess at anything in her personal life. She's buttoned down, not at all the person we were led to believe. Now, I've got my finger on why. Thanks. I have to go. Cappy Don would probably be interested to know precious little Ms. Bing has a dark side." *As do I*, Oliver thought with an eye roll as he hung up.

A year ago, guilt would've eaten him up the rest of the night. Not that he and Molly had been anywhere near engagement. He hadn't even considered what they had a legitimate relationship. Molly had felt differently. Unfortunately, she'd waited too late to make her feelings known.

Oliver sipped on a second glass of whiskey. Sometimes, people cheated because they didn't realize they were cheating, such was Oliver's case. Sometimes because they were pathetic louts with no self-control. Kay Bing didn't fit neatly into any category, and yet, she'd been in a long-term committed relationship. Hard to confuse that with a fling.

She'd cheated on her fiancé, then she'd let him discover the adultery. Why? She was smart; she could've kept her secret for eternity.

Oliver smirked into his glass. Keeping the secret would've defeated the purpose. Sometimes, people cheated for another reason—an easy break, with simple answers. A cut-and-dried end to the relationship, with no complicated explanations of emotions that defied them. It was only a theory, of course. One he might be able to prove if he could get close enough to Kay.

Chapter 4

"You're quiet today."

Oliver's casual observation woke Kay from her gloom. She'd been staring out the car window, her mind a hundred miles from the scenery flashing by. Oliver's sedan sped down the highway at a nice clip, a few notches over the speed limit. Hills dotted with rocks and trees whizzed by. She made herself sit up straighter.

"Just thinking." She forced a light tone, hoping to borrow some of his careless affectation. Thinking was her problem these days. If she was going to reach out to Finn, she needed to grit her teeth and get it over with. Wallowing wasn't her style. A ménage of frustration, shame, and despair roiled over her like bad weather.

She gave Oliver a sidelong glance. She'd have had more fun bringing Amos or Guillermo along. But Amos didn't like to leave the lab unless he had to, and she'd sent Guillermo to finish their bathroom project. She'd had to send Jasper along, too, or they wouldn't complete the work today. Hopefully, they'd didn't come back to work in pieces tomorrow morning.

"Why're you so excited to visit the greenhouses?" she asked idly.

Silence greeted her. Oliver chewed the inside of his cheek. His mouth opened twice as if to answer, only to close again.

Kay narrowed her eyes. "I don't know what to make of you sometimes, Oliver. You were buddies with Roscoe. From your own mouth, I gather the guy's a pig. You don't seem close to anyone else, not even Amos or Guillermo, who're both decent folks. The fact that you're unaccountably friendly toward me makes me curious. You're calculating, but you hide it well."

He gripped the steering wheel with both hands, and his jaw clenched. It happened in a split second, so quick Kay almost missed it. "Calculating?"

"Sure." She shrugged carelessly. "You're about making the right connections. You don't bother with people like Amos or Guillermo because they can't help your career. But Roscoe could. And I can. So what if he was a douchebag and I'm a bitch." She shook her head, unaccountably disappointed by her own conclusions.

Oliver pressed his lips together and nodded. His gaze was pinned to the road, and it gave Kay ample opportunity to take in his profile. He'd never looked more serious. He cast her a quick glance, wearing an unreadable expression. "Maybe I'm just a nice guy. Roscoe was lazy. I picked up the slack so he wouldn't get canned. And you...well, it's my job to keep track of your e-mails. Like the ones you get from the National Horticulture Society, the American Botany Society, and Purdue University's garden publications. Did you know Purdue has one of the most successful and highly regarded genetic engineering programs in the country? I bet you did."

Kay's mouth went dry. "It's called research."

"It's called not knowing your shit," Oliver shot back. He cast her another glance, this time his face was a study in annoyance. "I'm trying to help you the same way I helped Roscoe. I gave you advice about your team, didn't I?"

Kay glared at the side of his face. "You sure did. I'm still trying to figure out what the hell you gain from your little helping hand."

That tick in his jaw came to life again. He inhaled deep, exhaled loudly. Then his shoulders relaxed, and he shook his head. "I'm a calculating son of a bitch, remember? According to my math, if you suck at your job, I can't excel at mine. Let's stick with that. No use explaining myself when you got it all figured out."

Kay stared out her window and tried to ignore her clammy palms. She didn't care what Oliver said; there was more to him than met the eye. He'd figured out her deep, dark secret. He didn't seem like the type to use it against her, and she couldn't think of anything he could gain from blackmailing her with the information. A raise? Better benefits? A glowing recommendation for Merit? Merit already liked Oliver. Kay's opinion didn't factor into the equation.

But it seemed naïve as hell to believe he was just a helpful dude, with nothing riding on the return from his investment. Her dad was in law enforcement, and Oliver was exactly the kind of guy slinking behind scams and white-collar crimes all the time. Unassuming, charming, seemingly helpful. Just a regular guy. A "good guy," neighbors would describe him. Keeps to himself and doesn't bother anyone. Says hello with a friendly smile when they pass in the stairwell.

She hadn't forgotten his eagerness to visit Capital Acres, either. She spoke into the loaded silence simmering between them. "You still haven't explained why coming out here is so important. Merit sees what she wants to see, apparently. But my dad helped profile criminals in the burglary unit, and I didn't miss the gleam in your eye when she brought up the greenhouses, and you realized an opportunity."

She was going to keep digging, but Oliver beat her to the punch. "Why are you brooding like some emo kid who ran out of eyeliner?"

A lesser mind would've missed the very real edge to Oliver's sarcastic remark. Kay took note, but didn't comment. Instead, she snorted, moved by another realization. "Neve Harper would love you. She really would. Anyway, I'm not brooding. I told you, I'm thinking. Some of us have big brains, and lots going on up there."

Oliver's mouth quirked up at one corner. "Maybe my tiny brain can help your big brain."

"You think so?" She rolled her eyes. Why did men always think women needed their help? And how could he go from a snit to extending an olive branch in the space of a few minutes? Hoping to throw him off his game, she replied glibly, "How are you with boy trouble?"

"Ah. Thinking of the lover you spurned?"

She hadn't expected an answer. Oliver's took the breath from her lungs. She glared at his profile in silence, until he finally sent her a questioning glance.

"What? It was a joke. You look like I insulted your mother."

A joke. Right. A joke blithely uttered, as if he already knew the secret she'd departed for the first time yesterday. Besides Seraphina, only Neve knew about what had happened with Finn, and Neve didn't gossip. Kay's senses went on high alert.

Another clue, another not-quite-right string of words tumbling from Oliver's mouth. Kay went back to her dad's training. When investigating a crime, it was essential to let expectations and assumptions melt away. Focus on what was known, and take nothing else for granted.

What did she know? Oliver had done more than sort her e-mails for her. He'd read them and correctly guessed the truth behind her voracious amounts of research. He befriended her, and while it seemed genuine enough, he'd also befriended her dirtbag predecessor, which didn't quite explain his motives, but was evidence he certainly had some.

Neve always told her to trust her instincts, but not let herself be ruled by them. They provided information, but they didn't have to dictate her behavior. So, what next? Kay could pretend he hadn't said anything important. She smiled at her reflection in the glass. Why play along when she could blow shit up?

"It's remarkable, the way you know things. You know what I think, Oliver? I think you know all about Finn. You probably know he lives in Red Hill, his last name is Welk, and he was Neve's master carpenter. I think you left the newspaper article on my desk. And I'm damn sure I'd like to know why, on both counts. That way, when I fire you for whatever breach of privacy it took for you to gain personal information about me, Merit won't be able to contest my decision."

Oliver had pulled off the highway and turned down a packed dirt road. Signs warning that trespassers would be violated crowded on either side of the lane. He cleared his throat. His face had flushed a fetching pink, not unlike a particular group of Amos's precious peonies. Her hunch had been a wild toss of a dart into a black void. She was almost as stunned as he was to realize she'd struck something solid.

She pressed her lips together and nodded. She even turned in her seat as far as she could to face him. She wanted him to feel her scrutiny, like a bug on a slide under the lens of a microscope. "No witty explanation?"

She didn't know who he was or what he was supposed to be doing at Free Leaf Concepts, but she knew she was going to find out. If she had to kidnap him, toss him in her trunk, take him back to her place and start a waterboarding session, she was going to get some answers. Daddy would probably help her cover up the crime if she asked real nice. She glanced up as they rounded a hill, and the road spread out into a huge gravel parking area. A field of white tents in the distance marked the greenhouses. They'd arrived. She turned back to Oliver.

He'd parked and was looking at her with intense consideration. His stare was fastened onto her with unnerving stillness. A lick of sexual awareness danced up her spine as their gazes locked.

This time, Kay didn't fight the pull. Instinct always warned her to tear herself away, to shut down the connection before it sparked and caught flame. Now, she let the warmth spread between them. Oliver's eyes were a brilliant green in the morning light. They widened suddenly. He blinked rapidly, snapping the moment in two like a twig underfoot.

Kay didn't wait for him to pop off with some flippant remark. "We'll talk later." She gave him a smile to put the Joker to shame and flung open her car door.

* * * *

By some miracle, Oliver's forehead wasn't beaded with nervous sweat. His head was wrecked. Had Kay hacked his secure e-mails? Had he let something slip, burbled the captain's name while napping in the break room?

He'd expected Kay to figure out the news article. He was a prime suspect for that. But she wasn't supposed to whip the rest of the nuts and bolts together like a goddamn do-it-yourself kit. And just who the hell was she to call *him* calculating? It was his job to maneuver, manipulate, and manage.

So, why'd he keep taking Kay's opinion so personal? It didn't matter. She didn't matter. She was a tiny, annoying obstacle. A gnat. He could rally, deny she'd totally hit the bullseye. Or he could roll with the punches. Cappy Don had wanted to bring her in, and now it looked like he'd gotten his wish. At least Oliver didn't have to waste any more time painstakingly trimming old newspaper articles.

Kay marched ahead of him, toward a gate and a small outpost building. A ten-foot-tall chain link fence marked the boundary of the compound. Compound certainly did the place justice. A hundred acres, surrounded by high fences covered with black mesh fabric to keep the wandering eyes of Free Leaf's many competitors from getting a glimpse of any proprietary material.

Rowan, one of Tallulah's assistants, greeted them at the secure entrance and led them inside the small building, hardly bigger than a garden shed.

She removed a thick pair of canvas gardening gloves and offered a darkly tanned hand to Oliver, nodding to Kay. "Pattie asked me to bring y'all around. Nice to meet you, Kay. Don't see you often enough, Oli," she added with a grin. Her dark eyes flashed with mirth.

Oliver set his teeth and wrenched a grin from the depths. God, he hated that nickname. As much as other people seemed to love it. "I'm inclined to agree. Top-side execs act like you're keeping state secrets out here."

"We're keeping secrets, they got that much right." Rowan laughed, clueless at how the comment made Oliver's skin prickle.

The sensation deepened as he glanced over and realized Kay had her gaze set on him. Something worse than irritation gripped him. He was supposed to be studying her, not the other way around. He smoothed his features and followed Rowan as she led them through the gate and into a small security building.

Kay's blond eyebrows hitched when Rowan handed her a visitor log to sign. "You get enough traffic to warrant this kind of recordkeeping?"

Rowan smiled. Her teeth were brilliantly white against her tanned face. "It's not about traffic. It's about knowing which employees come and go.

If a proprietary idea ends up in the hands of one of our competitors, the company investigates."

Oliver nodded, thinking of the confidentiality clause in his hiring contract. "They do some really cutting edge stuff out here. It's not like nuclear weapons or anything, but every niche of the market has its competition, and top-rated botany projects are no different."

Rowan took the signed log from Kay and hung the clipboard on a peg near a counter littered with paperwork. She handed them their visitor tags, which were premade labels. Each employee had one, even the receptionist, Brit. "He's right. We had a rare modified tree stolen. The idea is they get the sample, then break it down to see how it was created in a lab setting. Other greenhouses are able to repeat the effects, and we lose exclusivity. Tallulah was livid about the tree. She's the one who petitioned for more rigorous security measures."

Oliver tried to hide his frown. Kay kept throwing narrow-eyed glances his way, as if trying to put together a puzzle with only half the pieces. Last year, security had been tightened. He'd assumed he'd tipped them off somehow, and Cappy Don had drawn back, forced Oliver to dial back on his investigative measures. But if it had all been over a damn tree, he could easily convince the captain to loosen the reins.

"It wasn't a tree." A low female voice snarled behind Oliver. Tallulah stood in the doorway, a sour expression ruining the effects of her nearly perfect face. He'd only met her a few times. Either she was always in a snit, or he just chose bad times to visit. "It was a flowering bush, and it put anything Amos has done in the last three years to shame. I still think the theft was an inside job."

Rowan rolled her eyes, but Oliver noticed her smile had turned brittle. "So we've all heard. Kay, meet Tallulah, our resident arborist. She and Amos have a hell of a rivalry going, as you might've gathered. Tallulah, Kay is the new head designer."

Kay handled the abrasive Tallulah with the same easy manner she'd used to earn Merit's esteem. She stuck out a hand. "I've been looking forward to meeting you."

Tallulah took Kay's hand but immediately crossed her arms after a terse shake. The sunlight from outside slanted inside the small security building and hit the wavy ringlets of Tallulah's hair. A honey-blond halo framed her face. "That right? Isn't the next big project some fancy spa? I hear fountains are all the rage."

Kay's mouth twisted into a half-grin, half-sneer combo that was stupidly adorable. "I don't think Merit hired me to roll with the tide."

"Merit didn't hire you," Oliver couldn't help pointing out. "Easton did."

Kay shrugged as if he hadn't just announced the director of the entire company had handpicked her résumé out of hundreds from all over the state. She kept her attention on Tallulah. "All the more reason to do something outrageous. I'd love to see your latest and greatest."

Tallulah gave Kay's small form a considering once-over. "Sure. Find me after your tour with Pattie."

If there was one thing Oliver didn't want, it was a guided tour with Pattie. Pattie was great. A nice lady with a real zest for the outdoors. She handled Capital Acres with the easy efficiency of someone in love with her job. But he needed some one-on-one time with the greenhouses.

Without meaning to, Tallulah came to his rescue. She hooked a thumb over her shoulder, toward the exit, and dropped a withering stare on Rowan. "Speaking of the old bat, she was looking for you. Something she wanted to tie down before guests arrived, but I guess it's too late for that." Finally, she spared Oliver a glance. It wasn't the kind of look he'd normally hope to get from a good-looking girl, but in this case, he didn't mind missing out on the attention. Tallulah wasn't the fun kind of scary. She was the scary kind of scary.

Rowan paused a beat to consider, her brows drawn as she wrestled with uncertainty. "Um. Well, I should probably go see what she wanted. You guys sit tight for a sec, okay?"

Kay mirrored the expression and angled it at Oliver.

He shrugged. "I told you security is tight."

Tallulah rolled her eyes, then turned to watch Rowan scamper away. "I'm sure as hell not babysitting you." She turned to go, and shot a parting glance at Kay. "Don't forget to find me. I have something I think you'll like."

They were alone in the small shed, and Oliver could smell Kay's coconut body spray. He had a sudden desire to visit the beach.

Kay let out a breath. "I guess we're stuck here." She leaned against the counter, settling in.

He hitched his chin at the doorway. "Door's open. I say we go peek around a little. We're not five-year-old children on a field trip. Don't you find it a little curious we need an escort?"

"No." Her stare was flat, probably meant to be scathing, but her eyes were alight with eager interest. "But I'm curious as to why it makes *you* curious."

His job required a certain degree of courage. Sometimes, even foolish bravery. It took all he had to grab Kay's hand, smile daringly, and tug her toward the door. "You'll have to come with me to find out."

* * * *

Oliver's hand was like a branding iron enveloping Kay's. She swallowed and let him keep possession. That way, she couldn't lose him as they weaved through the massive compound. She swore to herself repeatedly it had nothing to do with the heat of skin touching skin, or the languid way he moved around buildings and through greenhouses bursting with a veritable carnival of colorful flowers, or the sudden thrill of sneaking around shooting through her body, quickening her pulse.

"What are we looking for?" She put her best effort into the demand. She hoped he thought she was half as annoyed as she tried to sound, and not struggling to decide if her skin was on fire because she was excited, or merely excited by his heated touch.

Oliver didn't slow down, nor did his lightly jovial tone cease, though he pitched his voice low and quiet. Intimate. "One of these things is not like the others." He tightened his grip. "My God, your hands are tiny."

"Be a tad weird if they were large," she responded drily. "You owe me a hell of an explanation when this is over."

"Yep." He led her to a long narrow greenhouse with a thick metal painted door. "This is the only greenhouse with a padlock this close to the main office."

Kay bit her lip. "Sure, but the door's wide open."

"Probably not for long. Pattie wanted to see Rowan before we arrived. We must've caught someone off guard."

"Well, then explain proximity. There are a hundred acres in this compound. Why would this particular greenhouse be so special?"

"You answered the question before you asked it." His whisper betrayed a trace of impatience. "Proximity. If you were hiding something, you'd keep it close. Easy to dispose of in an emergency. Now, let's go."

Oliver tugged once, and Kay followed.

The air inside the greenhouse had the earthy smell of rich, damp soil. Old dirt on the concrete underfoot sounded a gravelly whisper Kay was convinced the governor could hear from his mansion downtown.

Oliver stopped abruptly when they reached the exit on the far side to peek through the cracked open door. "Look, do you see that?"

Kay peered around his shoulder and outside. He pointed to a small cottage. It seemed centrally located, with differently shaped greenhouses surrounding it and spreading outward like a game of Tetris. "The tiny house?"

"Yeah. That's Pattie's office. She and Rowan just stepped inside. We'll wait until they leave, then we'll try the lock."

Kay almost wrenched her hand from his. Sneaking around, that was one thing. Looking for hidden stuff, well, that was another. But breaking and entering had to be where she drew the line.

Or did it? Her heart pounded in her chest, her breathing was a roar in her ears. She hadn't been this fired up since she'd aim a loaded, cocked pistol at a man's head last year. Only this time, she wasn't in control. The plan wasn't hers, and the goal was fuzzy.

While they waited, and Oliver kept eyes on the cottage, Kay surveyed the contents of the low-slung greenhouse. Trailing ice plants, known to the common gardener as pink carpet, ran the length of the far side, tucked into beds along a low bench. Yellow wormwood buds sprouted from tall green stalks along the center aisle. Kay narrowed her eyes at the plants growing closest to her, along the wall. A spread of small, delicately veined leaves took up half of the benches on this side. Fittonia, she recognized, reaching back to her days in her aunt's shop. Not rare, but difficult to keep alive.

Kay assessed a plant she didn't recognize, growing at the other end of the greenhouse near where they'd entered. She wished she'd have noticed them right away, because they were the only plant she couldn't name. The flowers started as teensy little buds, with long thin filaments shooting out like a cluster of little antennae. They ranged in color from pale lavender to daffodil yellow.

Oliver tugged her hand again. She crept up beside him and peered over his shoulder. Her pulse jumped. Rowan stood next to a short old lady with a crown of fluffy white hair, like a cotton ball. "That's Pattie?"

"Yeah." Oliver snorted. "Don't let the granny visage fool you. The only difference between Merit and Pattie is one of them doesn't mind getting her hands dirty."

He spoke with such derision Kay swiveled to stare at him, realizing suddenly how close she'd sidled up to him in an attempt to stay hidden from view. His gaze met hers, and the lack of amusement made her skin prickle with unease. "What do you mean by that?"

Oliver licked his teeth and stared out at the cottage. "She runs this place. If there's anything underhanded happening out here, she knows about it. And I'm ninety-two percent sure something *is* going on in these greenhouses. Something unethical and illegal. But I need proof."

Kay blinked, her mind trying to wrap around the implications. "Are you a cop?"

Oliver glanced at her. "We need to move. They're leaving." After a hushed conference, the two women walked out of sight, past the corner of another far off greenhouse.

Kay experienced a sudden sharp jab of uncertainty. Did she need a thrill so bad she was willing to sacrifice her job? She could get fired over this. Oliver could *definitely* get fired over this.

"Why get me involved?" Her hand was clammy inside his. Some of the excitement had worn off, and she was left with humming nerves and common sense knocking around inside her head, begging to know just what in the hell she was doing.

He looked over his shoulder for a split second, one eyebrow arched. "You dropped a bomb in the car, Kay. This is the blowback."

"You mean payback."

His grip tightened as they approached the cottage. He stopped, wheeled around, and pulled Kay in close. Her heart thumped wildly in her chest as their bodies brushed together. His gaze met hers, then dropped to her mouth. "Wrong. I want you on my team. Why would I want to punish you?" His voice dropped to a low murmur. "Besides, why would I tell you when I could show you?"

Oliver's words said one thing, but his body implied a dual meaning that hers responded to without consent. The air was trapped in her lungs while she waited for what he'd do next, anticipating his mouth coming down on hers.

The kiss never came. Oliver clamped his jaw shut and whirled away. Disappointment came fast, relief quick on its heels. Was it too much to ask for one job that didn't offer an opportunity for her to prove she was a craven floozy? Together they stepped up to the door of Pattie's office cottage. Oliver's light mood returned, just as Kay's sank even lower. This was insanity. Once they broke into the cottage, there'd be no turning back. Oliver gripped the knob.

Kay leaned down, and covered his hand with her own. "You're sure about this?"

He shook his head. "If we don't find anything, you're probably going to fire me again, and with just cause." He didn't wait for a reply, but turned the knob. He scowled. "Locked. Goddamn it." He ran a hand through his hair. His lips formed a grim, unforgiving line as he turned his back to the door and stared at the ground.

Kay was intrigued by his anger, and the hardness peeking through his lighthearted veneer. She decided he was probably a far more serious person than he let on, and the whole helpful assistant routine was nothing more than a carefully crafted disguise. "Are you really surprised? Makes sense she'd lock up her office, given the security in this place."

He looked up and over her shoulder. His voice was low when he spoke. "Just disappointed. We stumbled onto one unlocked door. Couldn't help but hope my luck would hold. That makes three bad decisions I've made since we got here, and one of them is bound to blow up in my face."

Kay snorted. "Only three?"

He nodded, his gaze still hovering on a point over her shoulder. "Just three."

She counted two. First, dragging her away from the front gate, where they'd been told to stay. They'd have a fun time coming up with an excuse for that one. Second, if she had to wager, would be telling Kay more than he'd intended to tell her. "One and two have been duly noted, but what's three? If you plan on breaking a window, I want nothing—"

"They're coming."

Then the kiss happened. Delayed but inevitable. His lips sent chills racing up her spine as they slid slow and promising over hers. Her skin came alive at his touch on her waist as he pulled her into him. It began a harsh and hungry thing. Then his tense body softened against hers. His fingers pressed into her hips, and she came up on her toes to deepen the kiss. It was as if a long sigh escaped from her body. She melted into him, and tentatively opened her mouth, allowing him to fill her.

A gasp from nearby startled Kay into her senses. They'd been caught. She pulled away, covered her mouth, and glared at Oliver. She expected triumph, even gloating. He'd used her to hide what they'd really been up to. She wasn't sure if she was pissed off or not.

Instead, she was met with the same uncertainty pounding away in her chest. Oliver trailed his thumb along her bottom lip. "Three."

* * * *

Oliver pasted on his best easygoing smile. It had never before been so difficult, as unease roiled inside him. "Hi, ladies. We were looking for you."

Kay didn't turn around immediately. A scarlet blush rose from her collar and claimed her face in an adorable flush. If he were the type to blush, they'd be nearly identical, in both color and expression. Stunned. That was the word for her face, and he'd felt it as surely as she had. He just happened to have more experience with a quick recovery. They'd finally gotten a small taste of the heat that flared between them.

Kay swallowed hard, closed her eyes briefly, and bent her lips into a pinched smile before turning around. "Pattie. I'm Kay." She held out her hand.

Pattie's shrewd hazel eyes assessed them in taut silence for a beat too long. Finally, she accepted Kay's hand.

Oliver's mind was elsewhere during their short interview and the following tour. He'd been here before, although he noticed they weren't shown the greenhouse he and Kay had slipped through in order to sneak up on the cottage. A subtle hint that they'd been watched? Perhaps, but he knew there were no cameras in the greenhouses, only posted at the entrances of the compound. He didn't follow Kay when she sauntered away to find Tallulah with hardly a glance in his direction.

He turned his attention to Pattie. "Again, I apologize about earlier. We got caught up in looking at all the plants and wandered further than we realized." He gave her his most doltish grin. He didn't like dumbing down, but what else would the manager of Capital Acres expect from a mere assistant?

Pattie's hard gaze delivered an unnerving reply before her lips ever parted. "It's but one of your unfortunate missteps. I'm undecided on whether your little liaison deserves a strongly worded e-mail to Easton Arnell himself."

Oliver's stomach fell. He wouldn't get in nearly as much trouble as Kay. He dropped all pretenses of acting and leveled a pleading stare at Pattie. "What's the harm? We didn't mess with any of the plants. Kay's new, and I should definitely know better. We could both lose our jobs."

"Maybe you should."

He licked his lips nervously. "Maybe. But at least give us a fighting chance. Tell Merit instead of Mr. Arnell." He didn't know if he was doing them any favors. But Kay had earned Merit's respect, and Merit seemed to have an inexplicable soft spot for Oliver.

Pattie studied Oliver another long minute. "We'll see."

A fluffy-haired granny shouldn't strike such an intimidating figure, but he found himself shuffling his feet and fidgeting.

Back in the small security building, Oliver signed them out while he waited for Kay to finish her hushed conversation with Tallulah. The time for head games had passed. He'd irrevocably brought Kay into his investigation, and even though he could argue she had sandblasted her way in, no one told him to drag her around Capital Acres, or use the fact that they were physically compatible to escape getting caught snooping. He could've said they'd gotten turned around, claimed ignorance instead of Kay's perfectly perky mouth.

But she'd been so close, he could count the faint freckles across her nose and the lashes spanning her indiscernible eyes. A smitten fool had taken advantage of the opportunity, even as Oliver recognized the huge mistake as it happened. That kiss could ruin everything, yet he couldn't deny it had been worth it. At least for the smitten fool. Professionally, Oliver wanted his own head on a platter. He ran a hand over his face. He was so screwed. And it was too late to do anything but go further down the rabbit hole.

Kay joined him in the car a few minutes later. He looked over his shoulder as he backed out of his parking spot. "We need to get our story straight." A few seconds ticked by. "I think my story is fine, thanks."

He realized then the power she had over him. "Look, I couldn't get caught trying to break into the Capital Acres office. I didn't clear the search with Cappy Don. And another thing, Merit is going to question us separately if Pattie goes through with her threat to rat us out. We'll both look guilty if the accounts don't match up. You might have rank, but I've got seniority and a clean bill of conduct. Weren't you involved in a shoot-out on your last job?"

He could feel the heat from her stare. "It wasn't a shoot-out. Two shots were fired, none from my gun. And I saved lives. When have you ever done that?"

"Plenty of times." He jerked the car into drive. "I'll explain everything." He paused, weighed his words, and spoke carefully. "Over dinner."

Kay scoffed. "You've already signed the death warrant on my reputation. Even if Pattie says nothing, Rowan will. That kiss is going to end up on the office news blotter, one way or another. Now, I have to buy my answers?"

"That's not—"

"That's exactly what your invitation is. Pay to play."

Oliver sighed. He should know by now nothing with Kay would come easy. "I don't know the reach of Free Leaf. I'd rather not discuss sensitive information in a company car. You can meet me at Lucy's downtown if you want details. Or don't."

He wanted a chance to explain, but he wasn't going to dangle bait. Once she had the whole story, he didn't doubt she'd be willing to help out. But as long as she was suspicious of him and his motives, he had something to fear.

She could go straight to Merit, or even Easton, and his entire investigation would come to an abrupt end. Not only would he lose his fake job, he'd put Free Leaf Concepts on alert, and make it nearly impossible for his team to plant another mole within the company. Grimly, he realized he'd put both their reputations on the line.

Chapter 5

Oliver shifted uneasily in his chair and checked his watch again. He kept his gaze locked on the restaurant's entrance, willing Kay to appear in the doorway, look his way, smile and wave. Okay, so the smile and the friendly greeting were a lot to hope for. She was pissed off and had a right to be.

The waiter came by and dropped off Oliver's second beer. He threw down a ten. "Basket of fries?"

"You got it." Then he was gone, Oliver's empty beer bottle neatly swept from the table. As he departed, Oliver's stare landed on an all-too-familiar figure ducking into the restaurant. He groaned audibly as Molly caught his eye and waved, an impish grin on her wide dimpled face.

She was cute, in her way. Not petite or blond like Kay, but pleasantly round in the places that mattered. Straight shoulder-length auburn hair caught the lights overhead and glinted red. She was whip-smart, beyond average. Beyond him, even, despite his keen memory and penchant for acting a part. Her personality had once been equally pleasant, before their ill-fated dalliance. If she was smiling, it didn't mean anything good for Oliver.

"To what do I owe this distinctly unfortunate displeasure?" He hoped she'd state her business and boogie on out of here before Kay showed up.

"Kay's not coming." Molly had gone for brisk, but she was unable to hide the fine sprinkling of glee on the words. The fries arrived, and she didn't hesitate to dig in. She plucked one from the top of the pile, bit off the tip, and swung it like a miniature baton in time to her voice. "She has a date elsewhere tonight."

Oliver frowned. "You're tracking her?" He didn't recall that being part of the plan.

Molly smiled grimly and bit the fry in half. "That would be illegal. Just you, Oli. In fact, Cappy Don and I tracked your GPS coordinates all afternoon. We didn't need to follow Kay to know she was with you. Where else would she be while you snooped around Capital Acres?"

He sat back, tipped his beer into his mouth. Well, shit. He'd figured on having some time to sort things out before coming clean with the captain. "I couldn't pass up the opportunity. We were left unattended. Besides, Cappy Don mentioned bringing Kay into the fold. She's not like Roscoe, who didn't care what I did as long as his coffee wasn't lukewarm. I'm good, but she might be better. I took a chance. How do you know Kay isn't coming?"

Molly shrugged. "Some street surveillance. I pinged you at a bar and managed some very basic math, after what happened today. I'm guessing you want to explain the details of our investigation before she tries to fire you again. I kept an eye on Kay's place, but she didn't head this way." Molly stared at him, waiting. She wanted him to guess.

He didn't feel like playing games tonight. He set his bottle down with a thud. "Well? Where'd she go?"

With obvious disappointment, Molly exhaled heavily. "Neve Harper's place. They left together on foot a short time later. I came here. Wanted to catch you before you gave up and went home, because it's the most delicious fun I've had in ages. When's the last time Oliver Pierce got stood up?"

He sat forward and glared at Molly. Her bright round russet-colored eyes twinkled. The giveaway was a small dimple that appeared on one cheek, a minute detail a stranger wouldn't have noticed. Reading faces was easy, as long as Oliver had a baseline. He struggled with Kay, because none of her reactions were genuine. She wore a mask and hid her feelings behind a stark blank wall. But he knew Molly. He had all of her twitches and tweaks memorized. She wasn't surprised by his anger, which meant she was intentionally pushing buttons. He didn't want to give her the satisfaction of hitting her mark, but she'd made a potentially major error.

"You should've followed them. Kay's record might be clean, but let's not forget she has some close ties pretty high up on the social ladder. And a job she's not exactly qualified for. I tipped more of our hand than Cappy Don maybe wanted me to, but Kay and Neve could've been on their way to meet someone important. Someone tied to Free Leaf's illegal operations."

Molly rolled her eyes, unfazed, and signaled for the waiter. She waited for him to pass by and duck his head quickly to take her order. "I'll have one of those," she said sweetly, with a nod toward Oliver's sweating beer bottle. He moved along, and Molly's amused gaze moved to Oliver's face. "Kay Bing is clean, my dear. Squeaky fucking clean. Don't ask questions, because as long as it's not evidence I need to present in court, my methods of obtaining information can run a little on the fuzzy side of the law. I'm a hacker, so I hacked. There's nothing. No off-the-grid e-mail accounts, no P.O. Boxes, no mailing addresses registered to other names, no out-of-state documentation, no aliases. From college onward, everything Kay has been and done is well and thoroughly documented in the system. She pays her taxes, her vehicle registration is up to date, and she's a registered Democrat. Craziest thing I uncovered are regular visits to a firing range, and several legally obtained firearms. She is exactly who she appears to be, Oli."

Except Oliver knew she wasn't. "The breakup with the carpenter in Red Hill, that's all we've got to explain the drastic change in her personality?"

Molly's expression turned pitying. Oliver realized with some alarm that it was genuine, and Molly wasn't teasing anymore. She cocked her head to one side. "Oli, come on. You and I both know the kinks in her attitude are irrelevant to the investigation. It doesn't matter why she changed. It was a profiling mistake, nothing more."

"That's not true. If she were being coerced to work for Free Leaf—"

"But she's not."

They sat together in strained silence until Molly's beer arrived. The waiter gave them a quick questioning glance, then moved on without a word.

Molly chugged her beer and came away breathless. Her face screwed up into a grimace. "Gah, this stuff is bitter." She stuck her tongue out, then pegged Oliver with a different kind of look—the kind that made him uncomfortable before words even emerged from her mouth. She had a knack for that kind of thing. He also remembered she had a knack for reading the bottom line of a situation. The kind of girl who'd never had a problem coming up with a quirky tagline for a twelve-page report.

"I can see how you'd get hung up on a girl like that, even from thirty yards away. She's cute as a cottontail. Petite, but there's nothing boyish in how those little hips of hers swing as she walks. But you have to open your eyes. Kay is not the investigation. She's a piece of it. A piece we either move around or use to our purposes. So it's always been."

Oliver swallowed and peered hard at Molly. "You think I'm compromised?"

"I damn sure do."

He bit down on an unnecessarily rude reply. "You've talked to Cappy Don about this?"

Molly inhaled deeply and studied the table's surface. A black-painted fingernail filed nearly to a claw-like point trailed across her napkin coaster. "To a degree. I didn't—"

"You can get a little more specific, surely." Compromised agents were removed from cases. His heart galloped in his chest like a runaway stallion, and right now all that mattered was knowing just how far he'd fallen. Wasn't a long drop. His career had been dangling from a string when he'd joined the captain's task force.

She looked up, fixed an unyielding gaze onto his. "You let Kay get a bead on you. You can argue she's clever and sharper than Roscoe, but she shouldn't be sharper than *you*. Cap asked you to bring her in because he's convinced you're going to fuck up everything if you keep trying to get around Kay. She's like a wall, and you're not trying hard enough to find a way through, even though there are doors to open and windows to climb through. You're distracted, and she's the reason. Better to have her working at your side toward a common goal than keep her rooted into the opposition. Cap took a huge risk. If I had found any dirt on Kay, not a lick of it would be any good in court. But we didn't have time to wait it out. If you were anyone else, Oli—*anyone*—he'd pull you."

He sat back and crossed his arms. He might look defensive, but he was only trying to keep his stomach from plummeting to the floor. "Goddamn, Molly. That's what you're calling *to a degree*? Should I even ask what you didn't mention to Cap?"

A hurt look flitted across Molly's face, there and gone like a shadow. "I have my suspicions."

He laughed humorlessly. It came out a dry croak. "You've already thrown the gut punch, darling. Go for the kill."

She shrugged, but it was forced. "I think deep down, you're worried Kay is still hung up on Finn Welk."

The concept didn't register at first. Oliver swirled the words around his head, the way he might an expensive Bordeaux, letting them breathe and settle. He licked his lips. "You're jealous." He nodded to himself and took a slug of warm beer. "Now, shit's making sense."

Leave it to him to say the exact wrong thing. A flush of red spread up from Molly's collar. She stiffened, and her gaze changed, like soft caramel turning hard and brittle. She snorted, a soft laugh, but anger simmered below the surface, just intense enough for Oliver to feel the heat.

"I'm not here as your ex-girlfriend." She bit off the words as if they tasted foul. "I'm here as your teammate, someone relying on our guy in the field to pull this entire investigation through a very tiny window of possible success. You screwed me over, Oli. You played me. Yeah, I'm bitter about it. You were shit. But I am not the one making this personal."

"Neither am I," Oliver replied, with force.

Molly snorted again. "I call bullshit. I know you, even if you wish I didn't. Kay's new attitude bothers you, because if she were happy and bubbly, it'd mean she was free. Available. But she's closed off, and it's making you crazy. You've made this about her."

Sudden weariness swooped in and stole the indignation right out from under him. Oliver glanced around the fairly popular establishment. A couple in a dark corner were practically having sex against the wall, vaguely moving in rhythm to soft music playing overhead. Two women sat together at a table in the window, heads bent together, talking furiously as if they couldn't get the words out fast enough. Their table was littered with drink napkins. He'd switch places with any one of them right now.

Oliver tried one last time. "You don't know what you're talking about. Cappy Don is the one who suggested I get to the bottom of Kay's issues, so she wouldn't become a problem. Cap said—"

"Cappy Don is old, and sitting behind a desk allows him to be idealistic. Players in the field don't have that luxury. Does that spiel sound familiar? Because it should. Guess who said it first."

Oliver swallowed hard, knowing he wore a flush to match Molly's.

"You, Oli," she continued. "You said that, back when you weren't complacent enough to hang this investigation on Cap's idealistic methods. He solves cases, but you solve them faster. Isn't that why you joined our team to begin with? Why you fight to take point every chance you get, put yourself out in front of his instructions? In the field, you can make your own calls nine times out of ten. Cap has always had flowery means, and you've always known better than to take it for practical advice." Molly glared at him, and he felt it down to his bones. She'd exposed a raw nerve. She slid from her chair, and finished her beer in one quick, savage drink, as if she were tossing back a shot of whiskey. She gave him a wry smile, but it'd take a blind imbecile to miss the hurt lying beneath it. "Just keep in mind I adore cake and would love an invite to the wedding."

* * * *

Neve was her usual charming self as Kay practically dragged her down the dark mid-town streets. Duke was out of town, visiting a specialist with his retired show dog, Hannah, a massive Great Dane, whose age was starting to get the better of her. Neve was always a little raw when Duke left town.

"What if he doesn't come back?" It made twice she'd begged the question. "If I were him, going through the shit storm I'm currently serving him, I wouldn't come back. Hell, he's got Hannah. He could book a flight to the Bahamas and send a postcard with *no thanks* scrawled on the back. That's what I'd do."

Kay's head was narrowly surviving a traffic jam of epic proportions. Nonetheless, she tried her best to assuage her mentor's insecurities. "You know, it would help if you'd quit dragging him around by the nose. You guys were all set to move in together, and you bailed. You said yes when he proposed but refuse to set a date. Honestly, I'm as confused as he is. You're crazy about him." She grimaced at her pathetic pep talk. "Sorry, I should be more supportive. This new job has me totally distracted."

Neve shrugged and glanced around. "All the best jobs get into your head sooner or later. I don't recognize this street. Where the hell are you taking me?"

"To meet a friend of mine."

"At nine on a Tuesday night?"

Kay sighed. "I might be in some trouble."

Neve was silent as a blessing the rest of the way. It gave Kay time to rehearse in her head. She was going to sound like a delusional freak no matter how she explained the situation, and she couldn't pick and choose the advice on this one. She needed it all; the mean and the sweet, the hard and the soft. If Seraphina and Neve came together of one mind on the issue, Kay would have a definitive course of action to pursue.

Her neediness was like a puncture wound to her bubble of self-esteem. She was grown. She was talented and driven. She should know what to do. But anymore, she didn't trust herself to do the right thing. Until she figured out how to recalibrate her internal compass, the best she could do was rely on other intelligent, driven women to point her in the right direction.

Neve's patience finally bottomed out. "Okay, seriously, we're done if you don't throw me a bone, princess."

"We're here," Kay announced. She swung her flashiest smile over her shoulder. A goofy touch or an unexpected joke always took the edge off Neve's sharp attitude. Indeed, Neve smiled. Facetiously, maybe, but it counted.

A few minutes later, they were standing at Seraphina's door. Seraphina wore a slightly miffed expression that was as good as a dropped jaw as far as Kay was concerned. "Hi," Kay warbled, her bright smile still pushing the limits of her cheeks. "I know it's late but I need your help."

Seraphina's pale blue eyes widened. "Yeah, of course." She stepped back and allowed them to enter. "Nice to meet you, Ms. Harper," she added as Neve swept by.

"Call me Neve. I hear you signed on with Grant Gallagher. He's a real dick. My only real competition, but a dick nonetheless."

Seraphina smiled serenely. "Then I'm not sure why you two aren't the best of friends."

Kay's eyebrows shot to the sky of their own volition.

"The pretty flower has thorns," Neve murmured, tossing a lock of wavy chestnut brown hair over her shoulder. "You know, I want to be offended, but my reputation for being an asshole not only rivals Grant's, it supersedes it. My downfall is that I enjoy snarky people. They make me laugh. And I'm guessing you think I have something to do with Kay's sudden lack of *cajones*, and commend you for being a good friend. The first one is free, but the next one will cost you." She smiled kindly, as if she hadn't just uttered a threat to verbally shred Seraphina into pieces.

Kay stepped between them and cupped Seraphina's elbow. "She's good for it, Sera. I've seen the carnage firsthand. And no, Neve hasn't been prodding the open wound that is my shattered self-confidence."

Seraphina arched a fox-red brow. "My skin only looks delicate, Kay, but thanks for worrying about me. However, as long as you're sure you aren't being mistreated, I suppose we can call a truce."

Neve leaned into Kay's shoulder and lowered her voice, but kept her amused gaze on Seraphina. "Can I keep her?"

Kay tried hard not to grin but failed. Neve was like a cat that way, latching onto people she liked, without a care for whether they returned the sentiment. She always won them over in the end—Duke was a prime example of the feat—and Kay relaxed.

Seraphina stared for another few seconds, then turned her back and pointed toward the couch. "Get comfortable." A few minutes later, Kay sat with her legs crossed on the rug, while Neve and Seraphina carefully avoided sitting too close together on the small sofa. Seraphina had set out her go-to refreshments: bottled tap water and bowls of trail mix.

Neve picked through the offering with a frown. "If there's nothing yogurt-covered, it's just bird seed."

Before Neve could gripe about the tap water, Kay cleared her throat. "I promise I wouldn't have introduced you two like this if I had another choice. But tomorrow morning, I have to return to my job, and my job has become suddenly and irrevocably complicated."

In absolute detail, she explained her day at the greenhouses. Well, not *absolute*. She left out that damning kiss. She knew Oliver had needed to sell the moment if they had a hope of Pattie believing they were up to nothing more than stealing a few kisses. He'd sold it a little too well, because a small, terrified part of Kay wanted to believe he hadn't been faking it.

She couldn't even say why. Was a little mystery and wit all it took for her to develop an unhealthy crush?

After she finished her story, her two friends stared at her blankly.

"He's full of baloney."

"I believe him."

Neve and Seraphina locked eyes. Kay groaned. "Neve, why do you think he's lying?"

"How else would a rival company steal secrets from a major competitor if not from within? I think it makes perfect sense that your guy, Oscar—"

"Oliver."

"Olliander is probably trying to get his hands on proprietary information."

Kay sagged. "My first thought, too. Espionage."

Seraphina shook her head. "A whole year undercover? That's extreme for company rivalry. Besides, Free Leaf Concepts has always seemed a little *too* shiny, if that makes sense."

Neve popped a handful of cashews into her mouth. "It doesn't. How can you judge a company by its logo?"

"Easy." Seraphina settled back into the sofa and crossed her arms. "We're designers. Think about it from our point of view. Free Leaf is about landscaping, and yet, they give off the appearance of a pharmaceutical company. It seems to me they're appealing to clients outside of the nurseries and gardeners that should make up their bread and butter."

"It's kind of true." Kay told them everything Merit had explained. "They're involved in some deep stuff, developing their own GMO crops. They study gene-swapping. Definitely more than pruning parties going on out at Capital Acres. Amos only discussed flower propagation with me, but I gather they have him working on any number of experiments."

Seraphina shook her head slowly. "I'd trust one guy working on his own over a corporation any day of the week."

Neve chewed her bottom lip. "The clinical crap throws a healthy amount of shade onto Free Leaf Concepts. Can't ignore that big flashing neon light."

"But what if he really is working for another landscaping company, Neve? I have to cut ties immediately. That's why I didn't meet him tonight. I'll be guilty by association when he gets caught. No one will believe I wasn't in on it, too. New to the company? Check. Buddy-buddy with the mole? Check. In a position of power and relevance? Check. I have clearance to access accounting records, the executive offices on the fourth floor, Capital Acres, and Amos's lab any time I like."

Seraphina frowned. She sat forward and drummed slim fingernails on the coffee table. "Three very good reasons for Oliver to go out of his way to get you involved. Could be a blackmail scheme."

Kay hadn't thought of that. "Make me look guilty, then threaten to use false evidence against me if I don't help him. Man, that'd be some shit, wouldn't it?" She buried her face in her hands.

An arm snaked around Kay's shoulders. She looked up at Neve, who'd left her spot on the couch and joined Kay on the floor. "You have the upper hand, kid. If you come forward now with what you know, there's no way you can get waylaid by the wily Orlando."

"Oliver. And if he's telling the truth? The article on my desk about the super shrooms, or whatever, could be legitimate. What if Free Leaf Concepts, or someone working the greenhouses, is responsible? They might get away with it if I ruin Oliver's investigation."

"Yeah, but why run the risk?" Seraphina asked aloud thoughtfully. "Free Leaf Concepts is a multi-million-dollar company. They're successful. Why mess with that? How much money is there in street drugs?"

"Billions."

"Trillions."

Kay rolled her eyes. Neve always had to one-up. "In all seriousness, the illegal drug trade is easily a billion-dollar market. I gave it a cursory Google search after I read the article, because that was the first question I asked, too. Why? Evidently, there are a billion good reasons for a company like Free Leaf to want a piece of that pie."

Neve gave her another good squeeze, then padded back to the sofa and the bowl of picked-through trail mix. "You're going to have to make a decision. Believe your guy or rat him out for his shenanigans at the greenhouses."

Seraphina shook her head. "Don't jump at the simple conclusions, Kay. You've got some time before this comes to a head. Waiting a day or two won't matter, and if you're asked why it took you so long to report Oliver, tell them you wanted to look into it and be certain before you condemned an innocent man to the unemployment block. Besides, there's an easy way to get to the bottom of all this."

Neve snapped her fingers. "Make Otis introduce you to the rest of his team. If he's clean, make him prove it. Going undercover isn't something he could pull off on his own."

Seraphina pressed her lips together and nodded. She and Neve had come around full circle to find themselves on the same side of the debate. On a better day, Kay might've come up with an alternative, but these weren't better days. And this was exactly what she'd been hoping for when she'd dragged Neve away from her loft in the first place; a consensus from the two most important opinions in the world, barring her own. A whiff of despair settled over her like a delicate scent, wispy and untouchable, too vague to sweep away. What kind of loser had she become? Next, she'd be asking Neve what she should have for dinner, and calling Seraphina to help her decide between the nude bra and the black one.

Neve's gaze did an alarming thing, a quirk Kay was all too familiar with. Her amber eyes fixed onto a point in the distance, and her lips thinned as an idea took shape. Usually, it heralded a brilliant design concept. But this wasn't a scrapbooking party, and for Kay, that look was an omen.

Neve swung her probing stare to Kay and blinked. "You like him."

Kay closed her eyes. She couldn't lie. Neve would be on her like a flea on a stray dog. "He's not ugly," she admitted carefully.

"No, no." Neve smiled even while shaking her head, shifting to sit forward and look at Kay head on. "You *like* him. Kay, I know you. Under normal circumstances, you wouldn't have hesitated to turn him in immediately. You covered for him at the greenhouses."

"I did not! He—"

"You didn't give him away. It's the same thing. Silence is also a choice."

Seraphina's eyebrows were drawn in deep concern. "You must believe him. Even if you're not prepared to state your official position. You just don't trust yourself to be right."

Kay's ears were ringing. She hadn't wanted to go down this road. Not tonight, not with Neve, not with the memory so recent. "I don't trust myself not to make this about the kiss, instead of focusing on what matters. You're right, Sera, I can't rely on my best judgment, because my judgment is pure shit lately."

Neve grinned, hardly moved by her outburst. "A kiss. Ah."

This had been a terrible idea. "Not as romantic as it sounds. He kissed me to hide the fact we were trying to break into Pattie's office. I think his little bait and switch worked, but there will be a cost if Pattie reports us to Merit. I had two choices. Play along, or rear back and slap his face, and come up with some other reason we went snooping around after they told us to stay put." She rubbed her face and glared at Neve. "You're the last person I wanted to discuss this with."

Her grin widened. "Because I won't spare your feelings, or because I have a proven track record of being right about ninety-seven percent of the time?"

"Both."

Seraphina cleared her throat, somehow making it a delicate gesture. "Kay, um, I don't want to bring it up again, but have you given any more thought to what I suggested?"

Finn. She'd forgotten all about Finn. "Not really. You still think that's the answer to getting over myself? Dredge up the past with the boyfriend I screwed over?"

She lifted one shoulder. "More like explaining yourself to him might help you get over what's really bothering you."

Neve blew a raspberry and cocked a brow in Seraphina's direction. "You don't have to justify yourself to anyone, Kay. Shit happens. For all you know, Finn has moved on, and you'll just make everything worse by showing up unannounced and uninvited."

Kay sighed and crawled toward the coffee table and the dregs of trail mix. Neve was clueless. The best part was the dried cranberries she'd left sitting in the bottom of the bowl. Kay scooped them into her palm and settled back onto the carpet. At least they weren't talking about the kiss anymore. "Whether or not Finn forgives me shouldn't be the deciding factor on whether I can forgive myself. It would help, but for now, I don't know if I can face him."

"You mean face yourself."

Neve's expression had turned serious, and Kay's heart pattered uncomfortably in her chest. Neve was amusing and condemning in turn, maddening when she wouldn't take things seriously. But for all that, when she got real, Kay never knew her to be wrong. Whatever she said next would be as good as gospel.

"Kay, hon, this has nothing to do with Finn. Have you asked yourself why you took a baseball bat to your relationship? I think it's because you knew drastic measures were the only way. Finn, he's an all-or-nothing kind of guy. Say you'd simply told him you weren't happy and wanted to move on. It'd be as good as coloring your engagement in shades of gray, which is nothing shy of torture for a man who lives in terms of black and white. He'd have never let it go. Instead of being angry, he'd have spent eternity trying to fix something that can't be fixed in an effort to win you back. Then, you'd both be miserable. In the end, you did what you did for a reason. And while the method was harsh, the method almost doesn't matter, because Finn was going to suffer no matter what." She sat back suddenly and shrugged. "Life is conflict."

Seraphina was staring at Neve like she was something that had crawled out of a gutter. "Extraordinary gift you have, Neve. I bet you can explain away anything. No wonder you find it so easy to be crass and intolerable."

When Neve turned her sharp look on Seraphina, it was all Kay could do not to shield her old friend and take the bullet for her. But there wasn't any hiding from Neve.

"I'm not surprised you find my honesty distasteful. I don't dress up my words in fancy outfits, which is stressful for people who rely on them to communicate effectively, because it never occurs to them to simply say what they mean. Now, as far as making excuses, I'll be very clear...Kay doesn't need to excuse what she did. She only has to acknowledge *why* she did it. Were it me, there'd probably be some terribly selfish reason, because I'm terrible and selfish. Kay is not. And so, one must ask why someone thoughtful and kind, like our dear little pumpkin, would do something so cruel."

At this, Seraphina made quick work of a questioning glance toward Kay and bit her lip.

Neve carried on—a professor schooling her students. "In keeping with her character, only one thing makes sense. She martyred herself. She'd rather make Finn hate her than to admit to him he's just not good enough. Girl like me, I wouldn't care. I'd have crushed poor Finn's little soul and left him drowning in the knowledge that he was boring the life out of me. But Kay couldn't live with herself, because she knows that everything I've said about Finn is the absolute truth—he'd have never let her go that easy. She broke off the relationship in a clean break, if ruthless. I admire that. You don't, and it's fine that we're different, Seraphina. Or maybe it's not, since you just pegged me into a hole and slapped a label on it." She turned to Kay with a genuinely puzzled expression. "Why do people find it so hard to believe that life is complicated and painful?" She shook her head as if she could hardly stomach the disappointment and looked at Seraphina again. "Life isn't pretty all the time. And trying to force something pretty, well, it's like plucking a flower and sticking it onto a pile of steaming dog turds because you can't stand the smell. It's a disservice to humanity. We run the spectrum, and so do our thoughts and actions."

Seraphina chewed the inside of her cheek for what felt like an eternity, her thoughtful expression glued to Neve. Kay watched with bated breath for the next evolution in her life to take place. Her mentors were so different, yet so alike. They could take over the world if they joined forces, or destroy it in a fantastic clash of opposing wills.

Neve finally lost patience. "Whatever," she said, waving her hand as if batting away a response that never came. She rose from the sofa. "I don't need an opinion of my opinion. Kay, it's been interesting. Keep me updated on Omar."

Kay sighed. "Oliver."

"Whatever. Call if you need me."

"Pfft. I'm going to call all right, but only to get to the bottom of your problems with Duke."

Neve reached the door and cast Kay a withering glance over her shoulder. "Careful where you step, little one." Then she was gone.

The energy in the room seemed to have left with her, because Kay was suddenly exhausted. "So." She smiled benignly at Seraphina. "What do you think?"

"Of Neve? I think she lives up to her reputation."

"Is that a good thing or a bad thing?"

Seraphina shook her head. "I can't decide." Her wide, considering gaze moved to Kay. "Is she right?"

Kay's skin felt thin, her throat dry. Maybe it was a disservice to humanity to determinately stroll through life in rose-colored shades, believing only the good stuff. Turning a blind eye to the harsher side of humanity's nature. But Neve had struck a deep chord of truth, and it reverberated and sang through Kay like a warbling swallow. "Yeah," she admitted quietly, breaking eye contact. "I think so."

Chapter 6

It's almost over. It's almost over. Kay repeated the mantra through her morning meeting. Her mood seemed contagious. No one was particularly peppy—with a pang, she realized bringing the pep was her job. She had to set the dial for the team's energy level. She was failing them.

Guillermo and Jasper were at each other's throats again. Amos wore an expression that probably mirrored Kay's own: barely contained rage, brought on by the incessant arguing.

Amos had a cart piled high with vases nurturing cut sprigs of several flowering bushes. "These here, the yellow ones, they gonna be for this area back here." The plant he held was a long stick with tiny yellow buds running the length of the long thin branches. They were delicate yet hardy, but Kay wasn't sure about the color.

"Yellow?" She scratched her cheek and went to the wall where they'd hung up the color board. "I don't know. So far, we've got cherry blossoms and a sage background. The green and yellow together..." She couldn't compare them to puke out loud. Amos would never forgive her. "They don't flatter each other. But if we got rid of the green, I think the pink and yellow would pop on a white background."

"White?" Guillermo's plaintive voice exposed Kay's own concern. White was typical and boring. Design had to be something really stunning to pull off plain white. And they hadn't stumbled upon stunning yet.

Frustrated, Kay groaned. "Okay, let's start over. Maybe cherry blossoms are too easy."

Amos raised his thick, coarse eyebrows. "Too overdone, certainly."

She couldn't recall whose idea they'd been. Probably hers. She kept her shoulders straight with sheer will. "Nix the cherry blossoms."

Guillermo pointed at the carefully penciled plans on the drafting table. It was a layout of the spa's entrance, where a greeter would wait to jot down names and collect payment after services were rendered. Jasper's first assignment, and Kay was disappointed with the simplicity. "What about the mocha here? It's called mocha 'cause is the color of brown, you see?"

"It's not the color of brown, it *is* brown. And you can't call any shade of brown mocha because you like how it sounds. There are rules, Taco Bob." Jasper smirked, and it took everything Kay had not to backhand it right off his mouth.

She drummed her fingers across the white surface and pressed her lips together against the onslaught of a hundred choice words. Guillermo's face was reddening, and he was sucking in a big inhale to fuel his lengthy, indignant reply. Kay held up a hand to stop him, but the Spaniard's eyes glittered as he stared at Jasper, who remained delightfully amused by the scene.

Kay glared at him. "I'm writing you a pink slip for harassment. You're excused for the day, Jasper."

Just like last time, he had the audacity to appear perplexed, staring at her as if she'd lost her damn mind. "Are you kidding me? It's one thing to send me to fetch coffee, but you're actually going to write me up? For a *joke?*"

"For one joke, no. For ten, all aimed at Guillermo? Absolutely." Kay fought to appear calm and in control. Inside, she was seething. "I've already given you a verbal warning. I don't know how else to get through to you. It's harassment, plain and simple. And that's not all. Two days ago, I said I wanted a rough draft. This morning, I arrived to find an e-mail from Guillermo, explaining that you were unavailable the two times he approached you to discuss the spa." She stabbed a finger at the plans laid out before her. "You worked alone instead of coinciding your efforts with Guillermo. What we have as a result isn't the cohesive template I wanted to start with, but a boring, standard backdrop on which we're to play a game of stick and paste. Your design should inspire ours."

Jasper's face smoothed out. He stared at her blankly.

She paused and sighed. "Merit's not going to be ecstatic when she hears I've taken definitive action against you, but I'll happily stake my job on disciplinary action I believe is wholly deserved. Apparently, you're willing to stake yours on an inherent right to amuse yourself at the expense of another team member, and at the cost of quality." She snatched up the plans. "And this? This isn't good enough. I also warned you I won't settle for mediocre. You're off the project."

He stormed from the room and Kay wiped her forehead, certain there were beads of sweat forming. She hadn't intended to drop him from the job altogether, but it made perfect sense as soon as she said it.

Amos had a pained expression on his dark face. Guillermo's eyebrows were scraping the ceiling, but a glint of satisfaction gleamed from his eyes. "So," he said. "What we do now?"

Kay forced herself to straighten and put on an air of confidence she didn't feel. Just another day at the office. "We work. Amos, put together a dossier of your most unique, rare flowers. Think big. I want fireworks. Maybe putting together a color board around specific plants we want to use is the way to go." Probably not, but she had to keep her team busy.

Her phone pinged. She picked it up, and her shoulders, so carefully poised all morning, drooped at the message from Brit. *Brendan Berkley would like to see you. Conference room two. Also, clients from Kind Lotus Spa are in conference room one with Mr. Arnell. He would like you to introduce yourself.* Another ping. *See Brendan first but don't take too long.*

Kay nodded. She didn't realize she planned to visit Capital Acres again until this moment, as the opportunity was swept out from under her. The mysterious flowers would have to wait another day. Unless... "Hey, Amos. Would you be up to a visit to Capital Acres for me?"

He already had his back to her, bound for his labs. His white coat swooshed as he turned around. "I can, but you know the drill. Can't bring nothing back with me."

"No, I know. It's, uh..." Shit. She didn't have a choice but to admit to a gap in her knowledge. "Oliver and I, we stumbled into a particular greenhouse. I recognized pink carpet, wormwood, and fittonia on sight, but there were these really amazing flowers growing next to them. I don't know what the plant is, and I'd be interested to know more about them. If I knew the name, you could just tell me, of course, but all I know is where they're located. The bloom description is rather common. Yellow and lavender flowers, real tiny, with little things that are long and stick out." She held out her index fingers and wiggled them, then shrugged. "See what I mean? Totally unhelpful. Just ask about the pink carpet. Someone will know which greenhouse it was. If you can, bring back a sample."

It was a long, uncomfortable silence while she waited for Amos's reply. He appeared to mull over her request, thinking and deciding. "Sure." His smile looked forced, and it made Kay nervous. Was he going to tell Merit she was a total idiot, unfit for her job? Or maybe he was just annoyed at being sent out. "Can't promise no sample, but seeing as they all walk on tip-toe when I'm there, I'll see what I can do."

Kay beamed. "Thanks."

Her smile fled as the room emptied. Now, Brendan. What did Merit's assistant want with her, when the woman herself wasn't even in the office today? She hated the new unease in her gut. Before yesterday, she'd been nothing but proud to be employed at these offices. Now, she wasn't sure how to feel. If the company was dirty, would it ruin her career when it was found out?

If, she reminded herself. *If* Free Leaf was indeed involved in illegal activity, she'd worry about it when Oliver found a way to prove it. Or to at least prove that he was trying to prove it.

She'd missed him this morning but hadn't minded. Somehow, since the kiss and the date that never happened, she felt like her crush was written on her forehead in blazing red ink. Just like the time she'd admitted to a friend she had a thing for the gym coach in high school. By noon, the entire school knew. She survived, mostly because the gym coach was hot and she wasn't the only one who thought so. These circumstances were much narrower in scope. She didn't have ten other girls to hide behind.

She was irritated she even found herself labeling her feelings about Oliver in the first place, let alone concluding those feelings were driven by a physical attraction she couldn't seem to shake. It confused her more than ever when she entertained the notion of seeing Finn again. What if Finn thought her confession was an offer to rekindle their relationship? A part of her shied away of the idea that he might actually forgive her. She'd only hurt him again if he misunderstood her intentions—intentions that weren't entirely honorable. She didn't want to offer Finn peace, as much as offering him peace might assuage the guilt that weighed on her like a ten-pound feathered headdress.

She entered the elevator and shook out her limbs, readjusting herself and chasing away thoughts of evil corporations, shifty cover-ups, jilted ex-boyfriends, and her own questionable scruples. Chin up, shoulders square.

Finally, she'd meet the legendary Easton Arnell. Everyone seemed to say his name with a hint of reverence, but Kay could never tell if it was inspired by awe or fear. Maybe a little of both. He was, of course, a genius by reputation. Amos might be the hands that brought the company's unique plants to life, but Mr. Arnell was the big brain behind most of their cutting-edge concepts.

She exited the elevators and looked left toward Merit's office. It stood to reason the conference rooms would be in the opposite direction of the two private offices. She was rewarded immediately, and bypassed the first conference room. The door to the second was ajar, an obvious invitation.

Inside sat Brendan. His hands were set into a steeple over a single sheet of paper lying on the table. It held his attention a second longer, before he glanced up at Kay with one of those wide, close-mouthed squinty grins she was used to getting from her uncles. Also from strangers who looked at her and saw a girl too young and helpless for her own good. From Brendan, it fairly reeked of condescension, and put Kay on the defensive.

A little of her old spark warmed through her veins at the thought that she'd soon disabuse him of any assumptions about her. She almost dared a smile. But not yet.

The chairs were plush and comfortable, black leather over shiny polished wood. The table was likewise, a long skinny monster of a thing, gleaming under the overhead pendant lights, big green bulbs hanging a few feet above the table's surface. "No plants in here?"

Brendan's smiled widened. "Don't want to unduly influence clients."

Kay made no effort to hide her continued scrutiny as she took the seat opposite Brendan. His hair was a few shades darker than Oliver's light brown and styled nearly the same. Trimmed close to a shave on the sides, with a good inch or two sticking straight up on top. His long face wasn't exactly narrow, and his nose was the kind that started out slender, but came to a bulbous end. She couldn't see his eyes well behind the thick black-framed glasses he wore.

"Have I done something to offend you?" His smile morphed into one slightly less creepy. The question seemed genuine enough.

Surprised he'd noticed her reaction, she smiled thinly. She couldn't accuse him of anything more than smiling wrong. "Not yet."

"You look like I kicked your favorite puppy." His smile changed again, warming into something less forced. "I quit the practice years ago. You can relax."

Can I? She wondered where Merit was, why she was meeting Brendan here instead of in one of the offices.

He watched her carefully. "You've got questions. For now, I can't directly answer any of them, but it's important to tell you this meeting is off the books. It never happened."

"Why doesn't Merit—"

"This doesn't have anything to do with Merit." He shook his head at Kay in a deliberate fashion, as if willing her to understand. "She's out. An amazing stroke of luck. I'm going to spend the rest of my day deleting information from the company's servers, but there's no help for it." Without another word, he slid the sheet of paper toward Kay.

She scanned the page. Her heart thumped once, hard, in her chest, then scampered like a hare caught in a trap. Hardly breathing, she started over and read every word, letting them sear into her brain. She'd need to remember as much as possible when she tracked down Oliver. She took in a deep, fortifying breath and slid the printed e-mail back to Brendan. "What are you going to do with this information?"

He slid back to her. "Give it you for safekeeping. Draft a simple reply to Pattie, hopefully marking the end of the conversation, and delete every last bit of evidence from Merit's files that this e-mail ever existed." He crossed his arms and waited like he had nothing else on earth to do.

Kay read the e-mail again. This time, she didn't let herself get hung up on the personal details—how she and Oliver were caught sucking face—but the other point Pattie made.

Greenhouse Five was unlocked, and we can't trace another route they could've taken to get around me and meet up at the office. I'm launching a small investigation into the matter. As you know, Greenhouse Five is level five clearance—meaning top floor personnel only. The plants growing here are kept separate for a reason, as you well know.

Top floor personnel. Kay scratched her chin. It'd be interesting to see if Amos came back with information about the plant she'd found in Greenhouse Five. He wasn't top floor personnel, so if he was able to get in, would that imply he was guilty?

Guilty of what, Kay didn't know just yet. Nor could she fathom what was so special about the plants that they should be kept separate. Pink carpet and fittonia were both relatively common gardening plants, and wormwood was used in pharmaceuticals, but something must tie the plants together, or they wouldn't be growing side by side. Could be similar growth climate, or simply a common blooming season.

She flapped the paper at Brendan. "Thanks for this. I won't get caught macking on my assistant again any time soon, I assure you." She rose to leave.

Brendan held out a palm. "Kay, it'd be in your best interest to keep off Merit's radar. Luckily, she and Pattie aren't in regular contact. Probably not a stretch for you to imagine Pattie isn't much for e-mails, or even phone calls, so it's significant she reported the incident at all."

Kay bit her lip. "Why? Why give this to me? Why help me? And why is that particular greenhouse so special?"

Brendan sat back and shrugged. "Not a clue. I'm just doing my job, Kay. Well, my *other* job." He came out of his chair and walked around her to the door. "Pattie won't leave you unattended at Capital Acres again. Leave the greenhouses to me. In the meantime, take my warning to heart. The last thing we need is a suspicious Merit breathing down our necks." He winked and ducked out of the room, leaving her standing there with the incriminating e-mail.

He thinks it's me, she realized with a start. Brendan had assumed, probably due to her recent placement, she was working undercover. Investigating Free Leaf Concepts.

She swallowed the curse that rose in her throat. This complicated everything, and left her with no choice but to confront Oliver. And believe him. She'd be asking for that proof, regardless. She wanted facts put in front of her, not words and not conjecture. Evidence. And she wanted to know exactly what role Brendan played.

She could hardly take the print-out into the other conference room with her to meet Mr. Arnell and their clients. She folded it into a perfect square and slid it into her bra. Then she readjusted her pale pink silk blouse. The hem fell into a neat A-line pattern across her wide-legged dress slacks. The click-clack of her black peep-toe heels on the tiled hallway floor gave her a small boost of confidence with each step. She watched the dark shapes shift through the fuzzy barrier of the glass wall while she gathered her spirit, like the fraying ends of a rope.

She wanted to be a hundred percent Kay Bing, as only she could, when she met Mr. Arnell. The bounce in her step, the carefree smile on her face, her eager excitement; all traits that had made for a lifetime of easy friends and adoring superiors. She needed that now, as much as she could muster.

An instant of anger toward Finn brushed over her. He'd caused this great rift, sundering Kay from the things essential to her sense of self. Guilt and uncertainty had driven her apart. A puzzle with scattered pieces. The cloud dissipated as quickly as it had gathered. Great. Now she was passing blame. She shook her head and tried to dig deep for the girl she needed to be, because whoever she was right now wasn't good enough.

* * * *

Oliver's breathing pounded in his ears like a bass drum. What harm was one more unsanctioned peek around without the captain's permission? Besides, Oliver had slim pickings as far as favorable opportunities went, and Merit being out of the office while Mr. Arnell was tied up in client meetings was more than he could stand to pass up. He didn't think he'd be very good at his job if he did. No risk, no reward.

He stepped out of the hallway into a quiet corridor. He crept, without seeming to do so, stepping lightly to make the least amount of noise possible, all the way to Merit's door. Easton's office was the real gem. Not all risks were worth taking, however, and getting caught snooping in the top dog's private arena would end catastrophically for both Oliver and his investigation. The clients keeping Mr. Arnell's attention might leave at any minute. But Merit was out for the day. And according to Brit's message to Kay—texts were always doubled-up, a copy sent to Oliver to ensure delivery—she and Brendan were busy in conference room two.

Oliver tried the door. A grin split his face when the knob turned easily in his hand. He mouthed a silent prayer that his luck would hold. He closed the door behind him with a nearly soundless click. Someone would've had to be standing just on the other side to have heard the noise. Safely ensconced within, Oliver stopped creeping and moved with deliberate quickness.

Merit's space was as unadorned and passive as ever. No new knick-knacks, potted plants, or wall hangings. The first thing he did was check behind each hanged frame for a wall safe. He struck out. He ignored the panels, because he was certain after his last assessment that the secret compartment wasn't in Merit's office. He shuffled through the bookshelves, finding nothing of note. He checked his watch. Five minutes gone, with nothing to show. He finally moved to the desk. Desks were obvious for typical civilians: receipts hidden from spouses, photos not suitable for display.

At the moment, Oliver would call it a win to find anything. A scrap of paper with a strange plant name, an unlabeled phone number—anything he could easily take that might lead to further information. He'd have a much easier time explaining this off-the-books search to Cappy Don if he came away with something of note.

He spent another five minutes searching for false bottoms and backs, running his fingers along the underside of the desktop, and pressing knobs in the vain hope of triggering a secret compartment to spring open.

Nothing. Not a damn thing.

Oliver stood straight and glared around the office with his lips pressed tight against his mounting frustration. The pressure of a ticking clock thrummed inside him.

Kay had bailed on their meeting and hadn't bothered tracking him down today. Her next step could very well be to turn him in. Without something to give Cappy Don, it could all be over without so much as a scrap of evidence to implicate Free Leaf's involvement in the drug ring currently decimating Arkansas's major cities, from border to border.

Some city officials were happy to let druggies kill themselves off with bad mushrooms. But it wasn't only junkies who were after the fabled hallucinogens raging through these communities. College students, at-risk teens, and even the occasional recreational user were getting sucked into the vortex of the new and dangerous designer drug. And sometimes, they were users who'd been clean and considered an afternoon mushroom trip an easy break, because they weren't addictive. Addicts like his childhood friend, fresh out of rehab, who'd died because of some bad mushrooms.

Oliver had sworn he'd bring down whoever was behind the scheme. He wouldn't let one more kid linger at death's door in a hospital bed while their helpless parents sat by, drowning in grief and disbelief.

With renewed resolve, Oliver left Merit's office behind. It was time to up the stakes. If Kay was going to bring the ceiling crashing down on his head, he'd damn well get something out of the wreckage before he disappeared. The odds Easton Arnell had waltzed away from his precious office without locking the door were astronomically low. Still, Oliver had to try. He may never get another shot this wide open.

His breath corralled in his throat, unable to move in either direction, until the heavy pale oak door swung inward with hardly a whisper. He exhaled in a torrent.

The door had opened, which was amazing, but he still had to get away with rifling through the company director's super-private, highly personal workspace. Now that he was standing in the threshold, he found himself almost unable to take the next step.

Peeking through the wide slit of the doorway, Oliver's gaze was helplessly drawn to the massive window showcasing a panoramic view of downtown Little Rock. Growing bold, he stepped inside and approached the window, careful not to put his hands against the glass, so pristine his face reflected back at him with unexpected clarity. Below and in the distance, he had a clear view of the popular riverside park and Junction Bridge, where it crossed the Arkansas River.

He tore himself away from the window. No wonder Easton never left his office. The view beckoned Oliver, steel and sky stretched out forever. He could stand there and ponder any number of things indefinitely.

But not now. Now, he had one chance to make this decision—this stupidly rash decision—pay off in a big way.

He realized this may very well be the only place in the entire building where the walls weren't covered by those useless panels, not even brokenly like in the hallway on the first floor. So maybe the panels had nothing to do with the secret room. His hands curled into fists. Without the panels, an idea that made too much sense for him to ignore, he was basically blind and back to square one. How else would someone hide a damn door?

Easton kept his walls stark white and clean, only a few large photographs expertly framed and hung—a professional shoot, Mr. Arnell and the missus. Another photograph was Easton and the mayor shaking hands. Finding nothing of note behind either picture frame, Oliver moved on. The office, like many others, was split down the middle. One half for administrative business, the other half for hands-on projects.

The exception was in size. Easton's drafting table was twice as large as Kay's. Oliver couldn't resist a cursory inspection. Drawings, some colored in with pastels or watercolors, were scattered everywhere. A mad scientist's laboratory. There were rushed penciled drawings of fat roses on cattail stems and careful renderings of more realistic concepts: daffodils the same dusky shade as a thunder cloud and gray roses, edged in black, the size of dimes. There were stacks of drawings, paint spatters and pastel smears marring the table's surface.

How in the hell did Mr. Arnell keep his suit so damn crisp and clean? Oliver had never seen the man anything less than dapper. Every hair in place, a calm smile. Behind it, an apparently frenzied artist chomped at the bit. Oliver ran the tip of his finger over the tiny roses, perfectly drawn. This was where the real Mr. Arnell came out to play.

Oliver began his search in earnest on the business side of the large office. Huge bookcases lining the wall behind the monstrous desk took him several long minutes to inspect. None of the large tomes he picked up had the feel of a hollowed center. Easton's few knick-knacks were all what they seemed to be. No surprises.

The only real shock was the lack of any kind of locked cabinet. There were no files kept here. It was predominately a creative space for the director of operations, and the important files must be kept in Merit's office, which did host a locked filing cabinet Oliver had passed up, because client files were useless to him. But maybe it was worth breaking out the picks.

Oliver licked his lips nervously and moved to the desk with a small shake of his head. He was batshit crazy. Easton Arnell's desk. What in the hell was he thinking? For once, he couldn't afford to. He shut off his internal caution filters and sprang into action before his courage failed him.

One drawer after the next. None were locked, but none held anything special. An unopened set of acrylic paints and accompanying brushes. Old birthday cards, some from the employees at Free Leaf, a couple from his wife. Oliver felt immensely uncomfortable handling these. He shouldn't. He sorted through personal items all the time. The problem was he genuinely respected Mr. Arnell, a man who guarded his privacy like it were a state secret. Oliver hated when his work made him feel slimy. The inconvenient meeting of his duties butting up against his conscience didn't happen often enough for him to ever get used to the feeling. He gritted his teeth and kept moving.

He almost didn't check the shallow top drawer centered beneath the desktop. Ten times out of ten, they held the usual suspects—sticky notes, pens, paper clips, push pins—a jumble of ordinary office staples. A veritable junk drawer, but Oliver only knew that because he was thorough. He opened the drawer and froze. Then his index finger touched lightly on a small figurine nestled into a plastic bowl of paper clips.

A mushroom.

Oliver picked it up and set it carefully upright on the desk. Less than an inch tall. Possibly made of clay, with the reddish brown color of the stem. The cap was glazed white with blue and green spots. He snatched it up and rolled it in his palm as he stared out of the giant window and tried to sew together fragmented information.

It couldn't be a coincidence, could it? They were investigating psychedelic mushrooms that were killing people. What were the odds Easton Arnell had a mushroom figurine planted in his desk? If it were simple décor, why wasn't it displayed on a shelf?

By the time Oliver caught the whisper of feet on carpet outside the door, he had to choose between closing the drawer or dropping the mushroom back inside, because he couldn't do both. He slid the mushroom in his pocket, simultaneously using his hip to close the top drawer, and was standing at the window with his palms pressed against the glass when the door behind him whooshed open.

Oliver turned with a wide-open expression, launching himself into his role. "Mr. Ar—oh. You're not Mr. Arnell." He didn't have to fake his momentary surprise.

Brendan stepped into the office and clasped his hands behind his back. Tall and wiry, his black button-up and matching thick-framed glasses, and his hair sticking straight up, made Oliver think of a burnt matchstick. "Oliver. Not sure you should be in here."

"I know, I know. To be fair, I looked for you." Perfectly true. He'd peeked around for Brendan to make sure he was busy with Kay. Their meeting sure hadn't lasted long. Hopefully, this one wouldn't, either. "When I didn't find you, I decided I'd wait for Mr. Arnell here. I need to talk to him."

Brendan stared, as if hoping to move Oliver to some deeper confession by the weight of his authority. Maybe if Oliver were a legitimate employee, it would've worked. As it was, he found Brendan Berkley about as intimidating as a member of the nighttime cleaning crew.

He shook his head ruefully and turned back to the window, deliberately running his hands over the glass, smearing his fingerprints. He had something prepared, but he'd been hoping it wouldn't come to this. "I think I really messed up." He turned from the window and hurried toward Brendan, letting desperation build on his features. "If I could just explain myself to Mr. Arnell. Merit's great, but she'll never understand. But if I could get Mr. Arnell on my side, surely he'd help me out. I can't lose this job. I've worked too hard."

Brendan still seemed unsure. "So, you snuck into his office instead of making an appointment?"

Oliver swallowed hard enough to make his Adam's apple bob. He blinked several times and rubbed his hands together. Dealing with Brendan had always been a tightrope situation. Oliver was loud about his desire to move up the ranks. But to keep Brendan from feeling threatened, he played the village idiot. Hopefully not so well he wouldn't be considered for a promotion if the chance came up, but he couldn't afford to give Brendan a reason to watch him too closely.

"Look," Oliver said, lowering his voice conspiratorially. "It's extreme, but something..." He licked his lips. "Something *stupid* happened between me and Kay at Capital Acres. If I can explain before Pattie tells on us, maybe I won't get fired. Mr. Arnell seems so reasonable. He'll hear me out, don't you think?"

Brendan glanced around the office. "You could've waited outside."

Oliver had been ready for that, too. He toed an imaginary spot on the flawless carpet and smiled up at Brendan. It's a good thing he didn't blush, because inside he bubbled with embarrassment. He was a little *too* good at playing the part sometimes. "I know. But everyone knows about Mr. Arnell's window. I-I tried the door. I just meant to have a look." He brightened his expression with a full smile and hooked his thumb toward the window. "Have you been in here before? The rumors are true, man, look at that thing! I meant to have a quick peek but I couldn't pull myself away. I could stare out at that view for hours. You've seen my office, right? Freakin' mop closet."

Finally, Brendan smiled. His shoulders relaxed—only a fraction, but enough for Oliver to take note—and he walked toward the window. Oliver followed, and they stood side by side. "Tell you what, Oliver, why don't I explain things to Mr. Arnell for you? I'll wait, of course, to see if Pattie even says anything. I doubt she will. You know how much she hates the office games we all love to play."

Genuinely surprised, he looked at Brendan. "You'd cover for me?"

Brendan slipped his hands into his khaki slacks and shrugged. "Why not?"

Oliver had to make sure he wasn't being led by his ear. "I don't know. Doesn't feel right. I should take the heat myself. It's not fair to ask you to get involved." He doused each word with a liberal coating of doubt. What did Brendan gain by helping him?

Brendan answered by clamping a hand down on Oliver's shoulder and pressing his lips together in a thin, firm smile. "Look, Oli, I don't want you to get into any trouble. If Mr. Arnell had caught you in here...I hate to think. I promise, I'll let you know if Pattie says anything. If she does, I've got your back. Count on it."

It wouldn't make sense for the village idiot to press the issue. So, Oliver smiled stupidly, as if in awe of his good fortune, and shook Brendan's hand. "Even if I got promoted, I wouldn't ever fill your shoes, ya know it? I don't even know how to thank you."

"Just try to stay out of trouble."

Oliver made a beeline for the door like he couldn't get away fast enough. "I guess I owe you that much."

Chapter 7

Kay stepped into conference room one wearing her brightest smile. A smartly dressed man and woman in matching beige pantsuits—slacks for him and a knee-length skirt for her—sat closest to the door. Mr. Arnell stood at the head of the long table, leaning forward on his palms.

If she stopped and stared for a moment, it was because anyone would have. Easton Arnell was a huge man. Linebacker huge. Broad shoulders seemed to take up more space than they should, but they tapered into a trim waist and narrow hips, and thighs that fought the confining material of his slacks. As if he were used to having the impact of making new acquaintances speechless, Mr. Arnell took the lead, offering a giant muscled hand for Kay to shake and an apologetic smile. "Ms. Bing. A pleasure."

"All mine," she mumbled, watching her hand as it was swallowed whole.

He turned his smile to their clients. He wore his dark brown hair pushed back from his forehead, and gentle blue eyes held a steady gaze. He had an unassuming air. Kay liked him right away. "Ms. Bing is our new head designer. In fact, your spa is her launching pad here at Free Leaf Concepts, so I bet we can all expect great things."

Introductions were made, handshakes exchanged. It was then Kay realized Mr. Arnell had stepped back, essentially giving her the floor. A test, then? To see how she handled their precious clientele? A hell of a way to get a bead on her, but she grudgingly admitted the tactic was effective. Instinctively, Kay knew she'd get this one chance to impress Mr. Arnell, which his countenance naturally made her want to do. Trying too hard would spell certain failure. She swallowed. She had to do this the Kay Bing way or not at all.

Instead of taking a chair across from her clients, Kay settled next to Mrs. Followill. "I'm actually glad you're here. I have an idea. Not unheard of, but different from what most spas are doing these days."

Mr. and Mrs. Followill exchanged a glance. The woman folded her hands together. "We're open to suggestions."

"Free Leaf Concepts is known for fountains. That's our bread and butter. So it's given nearly every building and business we've worked on has one. The lobby of the Grand Pines Hotel, Parry Donald's Salon inside the Brookdale Mall, to name a couple. We could make your spa something magical...but more than that, we can make it unlike anything else this city has seen." Kay laid out her plan in detail.

Mr. Arnell seemed pleased. "Did Jasper come up with this?"

The idea to forgo the tropical bamboo forest concept was Kay's own, inspired by the mocha-colored paint Guillermo brought to the drafting table that morning. The rich tone had captured her imagination, inspired thoughts of fairy tales and magic. Instead of light bamboo-green, why not rich, deep pine?

She wasn't letting Jasper get a speck of credit. "No, sir. I've dropped him from the project."

Mr. Arnell nibbled his lip, while the Followills seemed uncertain for the first time, exchanging another glance.

Kay put extra warmth into her smile. "As Mr. Arnell has suggested, Kind Lotus Spa is my opportunity to prove myself here at Free Leaf Concepts. Jasper's specialty is the fountains we're so fond of. I've simply set him to another task more aligned with his area of expertise."

That seemed to put them at ease. At least her clients. Mr. Arnell had receded into himself, distracted and distant, which Kay found unprofessional, but being the director gave him leeway to act however he wanted, she guessed.

As the Followills were leaving, Mr. Followill shook Kay's hand and smiled approvingly. It was at absolute odds with what came out of his mouth. "I foresee a single problem. Our working name for the business. Kind Lotus implies something of a Far East design, doesn't it?"

I'm such an idiot. Kay licked her lips. "I was going to see how you liked our model before I suggested something as drastic as name change."

He laughed. "I guess no one filled you in on the first half of the meeting. That's why we're here. We wanted to change the business name before you started on your designs. We're calling it Sweetclover. No spa at the end, either. We're hoping curious folks might drop in to see what we're about if we don't label."

Relief flowed like a light summer breeze. Talk about stars aligning. She beamed. "That's brilliant. Great marketing strategy. I'll have it look so amazing inside, people will take any excuse to stay."

Mrs. Followill grinned excitedly behind her husband's shoulder. "We're going to have a menu of quick services just for drop-ins. Ten-minute facials, that kind of thing."

"I plan on being one of your first customers." Kay couldn't have begged for her first client meeting to go any better. She turned to Mr. Arnell, happy and flush with her success, only to find him still drawn and worried. Her initial frustration was quickly overcome by concern. "Sir? Can I ask what I did wrong?"

Slowly, Mr. Arnell's anxious gaze settled on hers. "Probably nothing. Jasper is...uh, well, he's my best friend's boy." He flapped his hand as if that hardly mattered, even as the revelation caught Kay in the gut.

Her thoughts went to Merit. "For what it's worth, it's not the popular opinion. But it is mine, and I stand by it. I had no idea of your personal connection."

"No one does. Except for Merit, of course." Mr. Arnell rubbed his jaw thoughtfully. "I've been remiss, haven't I? Jasper is okay. Not great." His gaze became uncertain as it alighted on Kay again. "I commend you, making that tough call. Not one I could make." His gaze darted away again, and his eyebrows rose slightly at the admission. "Just as bad, playing favorites, though. May I ask who you'd like to replace Jasper on the Sweetclover project?"

Kay decided Easton Arnell was a strange man. An open book, but folded into himself. It made her wary, and she could see how he kept employees in line, even intimidated them, without doing anything more than having a large body and a distant mind. She experienced a strong shot of gratitude that he asked her opinion. He was treating her like her job title, not according to her appearance.

She cleared her throat. "Well, sir—"

"Easton. You can call me Easton." His expression was still drawn in worried consideration, but the words were polite.

"Okay. Um, Easton. I thought maybe we could subsidize the job, just this once. Jasper is good, you're right about that. But he could be better. With some practice, maybe some classes down at the university, he could be great." For some reason, something held her back from confessing Jasper's talent was only half his problem.

"You have impressive friends to call on," Easton said, nodding to himself. "You have my permission to hire whoever you'd like. I'm intrigued by your vision for the Followills' spa."

"Thank you, sir. Easton. I'll do my best to follow through."

"Yes. Yes, of course you will." He glanced at his watch. "Noon already. I have an appointment. I bet you haven't taken lunch." He walked to the door and opened it for Kay. An honest-to-goodness gentleman.

"No, not yet." She smiled tentatively. "We can go down together."

"Oh, no, I..." Easton cleared his throat and straightened his tie as he walked into the hallway after Kay and closed the door to the conference room. "I take the stairs. Elevator's always occupied. And the exercise, it's good for a man my age."

Kay stared. She'd die of exhaustion, taking on five flights of stairs multiple times a day. No wonder she'd never seen him coming or going. "Okay, then. Thanks for the support, Mr. Arnell. Easton." She'd never, ever get used to that. He was simply the kind of man due a certain degree of respect. "I'm sorry, sir, I don't think I'll ever feel right calling you Easton." She laughed nervously. "But thanks, you know, for supporting me."

He smiled, but he'd grown more distant, and it was a flash, there and gone in seconds. He stared at the floor now, hands in his slacks pockets, already moving in the opposite direction of the elevator. "Best thing a boss can do is let their employees do their jobs."

She nodded. Didn't know what else to say. With a dorky little wave, she left him.

Panic consumed her immediately. She'd done it. Convinced her boss to let her bring in outside help. Not even Merit could override her, now that she had Mr. Arnell's blessing. Securing it had been easy compared to what came next.

How would she ever choose between Neve and Seraphina?

She rushed to the elevator, suddenly desperate to escape the building. A brisk walk in beautiful downtown, a latte, and something loaded with calories would do a lot to clear her head. If choosing between her mentors wasn't stressful enough, she had an e-mail stuffed in her bra that could bring her short-lived career to a dead halt.

She came around the corner and almost went back to the stairs. She'd almost rather deal with sweat stains for the rest of the day than face Oliver just yet. But she didn't have time to sit on the damning e-mail.

She took a deep breath and forced herself to march forward. Because the elevator was glass, she saw him clearly. But he couldn't see her. He leaned against the elevator wall, holding his head gingerly. Maybe his morning had been as bumpy as hers. She pressed the button to open the elevator doors and slipped inside.

Oliver barely spared her a glance, then grunted.

For some reason, the greeting rubbed her the wrong way. She was good enough for a brazen distraction but didn't warrant a simple hello? Slightly miffed, she shuffled to one side and crossed her arms. "What are you doing?"

"Sulking. Everyone knows elevators are ideal for sulking." Oliver groaned and stood up straight. "The boring answer is I'm on my way back to my office. I, uh, wanted to meet the Kind Lotus folks, but I was too late."

"They're calling it Sweetclover now. And we need to talk, but not about the spa."

He rubbed a hand over his face and peered at her. "You made it pretty clear there's nothing to discuss. You stood me up. I wasn't waiting for you in here, you know. I can take a hint. Just...just let me do my job, okay? My other job. That's all I ask."

"You don't want me involved anymore?"

"I didn't say that." He parked his hands on his hips.

Kay tried really, really hard not to notice the sharp figure he cut, and how his weariness made her want to bring him back to his flirty cheerfulness. She could do it, too. She gave a mean back rub. She hated that she felt partly responsible for his wan mood, then hated that she cared. "Seems neither of us has a choice anymore." She reached into her bra and flung the folded paper at Oliver.

He caught it against his chest with one hand, the other still resting easily on his hip. Why did the simple way his body moved, graceful and easy, grab her attention so forcefully? With a look not unlike Mr. Arnell's constant expression of consternation, Oliver scanned the e-mail.

When his jade eyes made their way to Kay, they were wide and worried— almost frightened. "Where did you get this?"

"I'll tell you." She licked her lips. She wasn't done gambling today, apparently. "If you can prove who you really are and what you're really doing here."

He took a step closer. He'd never looked at her like that before, jaw tight, glaring. "You read the article, Kay, and managed to guess everything else. You know what I'm doing here."

"I know what you've told me. I want proof, Oliver. More than some ancient newspaper article from out of town, more than your special knowledge of the private details of my personal life."

He shook his head. "What more can I do?"

"Introduce me to your team. You work with people. You've mentioned names. I want to know your reasons for being here are what you claim."

He tilted his head slightly and studied Kay with an openness that startled her. For the first time, she felt like she was seeing Oliver in his entirety. All of him, not just the flashy parts he used to run his little investigation, or the careless way he tried to seem unobtrusive around the other designers, like he was just another useful piece of office equipment. A copier, maybe.

A stark intelligence glimmered in his quiet stare. "What reason have I given you not to trust me?"

She snatched the e-mail from his hand. "For starters, you could've gotten me fired with that little kissing stunt."

It was as if mentioning the kiss were some kind of code word. A smile broke out over Oliver's face. He was his usual self again—his real self or not, she still had no clue. Playful smile, dancing eyes, quick decisive hands as he retook possession of the page. "A stunt, huh? That makes it sound pretty exciting. Must've been a great kiss."

If she were Neve, she'd say something cutting. If she were Seraphina, she'd rattle off something wise. Instead, for a fleeting moment, Oliver's teasing coaxed Kay from her hiding place. She was gloriously herself as she burst into laughter.

* * * *

Oliver had no idea what the hell had been so funny. He was half-offended, half-delighted. Kay seemed weirdly upbeat as they walked together toward a café two blocks from work. Okay, maybe not *weirdly* upbeat. Maybe *finally* was the word he was looking for. Could it be he was meeting the genuine, real-deal Kay Bing at long last?

Last night, he'd gone back to his apartment and came to some rough terms after Molly's intervention. She was right, of course. He was obsessed with Kay. Caught up in trying to figure her out, captivated by the struggle of self she endured. What was she fighting so hard against? He wanted to name her demons, and if she'd let him, help her conquer them. It made her laughter a little easier to swallow. He'd done something right, even if he had no clue what.

They settled into a table for two outside, ordered their drinks and food. Kay revealed a sweet tooth. She asked for two blueberry scones. Oliver went with a deli sandwich. While they waited, he crossed his hands, hoping to appear serious. In reality, he tingled with anticipation. Finally, he had Kay all to himself, with every reason to ask nosy questions and press for answers.

"You realize," he began, carefully trying to avoid accidently being funny again, "that the risk here is all mine. It's one thing to paint you a picture. But you're asking me to connect you to the very people running my operation. Little Rock is a big city with a small-town attitude. I'm from out of town, so no one is likely to recognize me. But the others, they're all from here. Cap's been in the paper, been interviewed on local television, stuff like that. If either one of us is seen with him, it could blow the whole thing right out of the sky."

A queer light sparked in her canny gaze. Her eyes still bothered him. Blue, then green, back to blue again. "Is there another informant working inside Free Leaf Concepts?"

An odd question. "No. At least, I doubt it. Cappy Don—that'd be Captain Donald Cappricci"—recognition widened Kay's indiscernible eyes—"would know if another state agency got involved. Or the feds." Oliver picked up the printed e-mail and shook it. "This is sloppy work, wherever it came from."

"How so?" Their coffees arrived. Kay didn't wait for hers to cool before taking a sip, wincing, and taking another.

Oliver pushed his aside for the moment. "Tell me who. I'll explain. Come on, Kay. At some point, we've got to establish trust. I promise, I'll set up a meeting. Cappy Don won't like it, but I'll convince him. But I need to know who gave this to you and why."

Kay pressed her lips together and studied him. Since Oliver no longer had anything to hide, he almost enjoyed the scrutiny. Nothing like attention from a fierce woman to get his blood going. "Don't make me regret this, Oliver. I can rustle up some trouble for your investigation."

The threat put a sour note on the moment. "I'll do what I think is best, and you and your implied blackmail can take a hike. People have died." He stopped, not trusting himself to go on. For a long minute, he waited, sipped coffee, and corralled his fraying patience. At least Kay had the grace to appear stricken. "Sorry," he mumbled at last. "But this is much larger than you. And if you knew what we were up against, you wouldn't make empty threats."

They both knew they were empty. Kay might be laboring under the mantle of a hardass, but he'd read her file. If she thought innocent people were coming to harm, she wouldn't do Free Leaf Concepts any favors. If he thought she were that kind of person, he wouldn't be sitting here now.

Kay watched him for what felt like an eternity. She didn't mask the array of enlightening emotions that ran the gamut across her features. Anger, acceptance, curiosity, a hint of guilt.

"Brendan Berkley." She waited less than ten seconds to continue. "What's wrong with him giving me the evidence to hold onto? He thinks I'm you. One of Cap—what do call you him? Cappy Don? One of Cappy Don's inside guys. I'm guessing because I'm so new to the company, and on my first visit to Capital Acres I waltzed right through a secure area."

Brendan?

If Cap had someone else inside, why wouldn't he tell Oliver? Could be Brendan's job was to investigate from another angle. Or worse, the feds had gotten involved. But that didn't make sense, either. The DEA had been informed of the statewide investigation. For now, as long as the problem stayed within Arkansas, it was a state matter. Surely, if the magic mushrooms had cropped up in Louisiana or Oklahoma, someone would've alerted the captain when the DEA took over. They'd ask Cappy Don to disband their investigation before they set up an operation of their own. It only made sense.

Then again, Oliver was a beat cop. Or had been. What the hell did he know? He couldn't help feeling that something seemed off about the connection, but couldn't pin down what made him uneasy. He mulled it over as their food arrived. Kay asked for butter and cherry preserves to go with her scones. They smelled amazing. He probably should've ordered one. He took a bite of his sandwich. Turkey bacon wasn't horrible, turned out. Oliver waved away ketchup for his fries and a coffee refill. No more caffeine. He wouldn't be able to focus.

"Brendan should know better, regardless, if he's one of ours. Whether he's a fed, reaching out to the local informant, or one of Cap's. He should've never approached you. It's a security breach. Shit. I don't even know if I should report it." He shook his head, annoyed. When this was over, someone would get an earful. And not just from Cappy Don. "Brendan could've simply deleted the e-mail. There was no reason for him to tell you anything. And to have that meeting in one of the conference rooms? Crazy. For now, I like the idea of letting him think you're the mole. It gives me some wiggle room."

Kay's blond eyebrows, perfectly arced, drew together. "Something is bothering you."

Oliver nodded. "Yeah. Something doesn't seem right. But until I can better put my finger on what, I'll play along."

She pushed the e-mail toward him. "Take it. For your team, or whatever."

"Thanks." He'd planned on asking, so it was a relief to have her give up the e-mail without an argument. Maybe Molly could pull something from the print out. Maybe not, but regardless, it was legally obtained evidence.

More so, it was a big flashing arrow. He tapped the paper. "Greenhouse Five. You recognize anything in there?"

"We both know I'm only half as good as my résumé says I am."

He shrugged. "Less smart isn't stupid. I saw you checking out the plants. Any of them familiar?"

Oliver knew the second she opened her mouth she was holding onto information. Instead of answering his question, she asked one of her own. He let it go. The trust had to go both ways, after all. If she was sitting on something, maybe she had good reason. He'd give her some time before he asked again.

"What's your impression of Easton?"

He tilted his head, wondering if he'd heard correctly, and smirked playfully. "You're on first-name basis with the director of operations within five minutes of meeting the guy. You continue to amaze me, Kay."

She didn't even smile. "You could've told me Jasper was practically the guy's nephew."

Oliver quit chewing. "I didn't know." More bad intelligence? Or lazy work, from whoever Molly had doing the background checks. That made twice reports were either off, in the case of Kay's dossier, or missing important information.

"Yeah, well." Kay stabbed into her scone and took a vicious bite. "Jasper is his best friend's kid. Which, had I known, probably would've stopped me from kicking him off the spa project this morning."

Oliver set down the remainder of his sandwich. "You dropped Jasper?"

"Like a hot potato. What's amazing is Easton didn't seem shocked. He gave me free rein to hire whoever I want. At least, temporarily. A sub deal, for the spa. I'm actually ecstatic about the new name. Works perfectly with the new direction I'm taking the design."

"You're jumping in with both feet." It was a nice change to hear her sound like he'd imagined she would in the beginning—excited, decisive, and sure of herself.

She gave him a flat stare. "What else can I do? If I keep up my tepid approach, afraid to put my mark on things, I'm going to get canned. I get one shot to make this work. Anyway, I asked about Easton. Is he always so distracted?"

The tiny mushroom figurine burned in Oliver's pocket. But if Kay was going to keep secrets, he should probably hold onto a few himself. "Yeah, I guess so." He thought of the frantic energy of Mr. Arnell's drafting table, the strange yet glorious drawings. He tapped his temple. "I think the boss has a lot going on up here. Probably why he needs someone like Merit around."

Kay's stare grew distant. She glared at her remaining scone like it had grown feathers.

"Thoughts?" At this point, he'd said all he was willing to say about the investigation. Before, he'd planned to keep Kay's involvement his little secret, revealing only what was necessary to Cappy Don. But he didn't want her going into a meeting with his team with a pocketful of hard-won intelligence.

Her gaze slammed into his suddenly, a question burning bright. "You've ferreted out all my secrets. You know who my friends are."

Oliver pushed away the remainder of his sandwich and the untouched French fries. "We had to make sure you weren't part of the ring. Your friends are important people in this city. People who, if involved, would want their own inside man. Woman. Whatever. If I'm a mouse, you could've easily been the cat sent in to hunt me down and push me out of hiding. Even after digging into your background, I still wasn't convinced. Gavin Chambers. Neve Harper. I hear your other mentor is going to work for Grant Gallagher. That man is terrifyingly influential. In fact, he's straight terrifying. So, yeah, there are some questionable connections a guy like me would feel compelled to check out."

"I don't know if I feel totally violated or super special."

He winced. "You should probably feel a tad of both. You're young and talented. Doesn't hurt to have friends who can back up a padded résumé." He grinned wide when he scored the smile he'd been aiming for.

It didn't last. Kay sobered and pushed her food away, too. "Seraphina and Neve are both really important to me. Neither one of them will hesitate to launch themselves at this project if I ask."

"That's not bad news. Why the droopy face?"

He earned a flash of annoyance for his trouble. "Because," she said, with some heat, "they both kind of suck, too."

This time, Oliver was the one moved to hysterics. When his laughter ceased, he was pleased to note there was at least a glimmer of amusement on Kay's face, in the tug of her lips and twinkle in her eyes. "Caught me off guard." He chuckled again and tossed back the rest of his coffee, now cooled.

"Yeah, well, you're not the one who'll get bulldozed by Neve or perpetually schooled by Seraphina. They're both strong personalities. I don't know if mine can stand up to either. It's one thing when they're guiding me. But this is my job, my project, my lead. Could they follow it?"

"I think..." Oliver paused, giving weight to his words. He reached across the table and took possession of one of Kay's hands. He smiled at her, hoping his own certainty would shine through. "You're bigger than you look, Kay. I've read your file. I read the report from Lady Killer Ranch last year. Neve's got her mouth, Seraphina's got poise, but you're the girl who goes in, gun drawn, hammer cocked, and saves the day. *That* girl doesn't have a damn thing to worry about. Be that girl."

Chapter 8

The tension threatened to swallow Oliver whole.

For the first time in his partnership with Captain Donald Cappricci, he might have gone too far. His instincts were gold, and he knew it. His capacity for recalling small details, without equal. Even though drawing wasn't necessarily his greatest talent, and he had no names to label, he could still sketch every plant he'd seen in Greenhouse Five. He knew he'd need at least one shiny offering to help smooth things over with Cappy Don.

It wasn't enough.

The captain wasn't raging. He was deathly silent at his desk, which was way worse in Oliver's opinion. He'd never driven Cappy Don to speechlessness before. Exasperation, great harrowing sighs, a few growls, sure. But never this. The silence was so thick Oliver could stick a fork in it. The captain planted his hands on either side of the report Oliver had typed up in the late hours of the night. He stared at the pages with a fierce frown, soaking in every detail of Oliver's off-the-rails investigating—every breach of protocol, every rash decision.

Molly sat in a chair positioned to face Oliver, next to Cappy Don, physically indicating whose side she intended to take in the debate to follow. She must've been worried, because there was a marked lack of gloating in her troubled expression. She watched Oliver with a mixture of sadness and chagrin.

For some reason, that alone almost made his rebellions worth it. For the time being, he'd smothered Molly's hostility. He'd take concerned and disappointed over wounded and acerbic any day of the week.

Finally, Cappy Don threaded his fingers together and glared at Oliver over the ridge of his knuckles. "Any other explanations you'd like to offer at this time?"

Oliver shifted uncomfortably in his chair. He didn't mind the spotlight as long as he was a star. He didn't feel like a star. "Just one. I found out someone broke into Capital Acres and stole a rare tree. Or a flowering bush. Whatever. That's why they tightened security. It had nothing to do with me. I felt this gave me some breathing room. Other than that, I've got nothing. I'm not going to hand over a pile of excuses, Cap. But we were stagnating before Kay came along. She's the catalyst."

"Apparently so." Cappy Don's response was gruff. "Ever since I asked you to bring her in—slowly, I believe I said, with a sprinkling of clues, not a goddamn dump truck full of our most valued intelligence—you've taken several unauthorized steps."

"They were steps that needed taking. Sir," he added hastily.

Cappy Don leaned forward, the movement undeniably threatening in nature. A menacing light flashed in his cold, dark eyes. It was then Oliver knew just how far he'd pushed the captain. "They were risks that could've fucked everything." He glanced at Molly. "Sorry."

Molly rolled her eyes. "Please. I dated this jerk." She hitched her chin toward Oliver. "I've heard much worse."

"You've said much worse," Oliver countered, unable to keep the touch of bitterness from his tone. He screwed up, but to gang up on him was totally unfair.

The captain's hard stare didn't waver. "You promised if I let you in on this task force, there'd be no more rogue bullshit. I saved your ass back in Jonesboro, stuck my neck out to keep you on the job. Instead of letting you face disciplinary action, I brought you in, put you on my team, and gave you the most important job in the whole damn investigation. We had a deal, Pierce."

"Cap, give me some credit here." He felt he had guilt pouring from every hole he had. "Every time I've acted, I've done it within the bounds of reasonable odds of success and walked away with valuable information." He pointed to the mushroom figurine, perched next to his report. "That's no coincidence."

"Oh? And if Easton Arnell notices his little trinket is missing? And Brendan reports seeing you in his office?"

Oliver almost broke cover. Almost admitted he knew Brendan wouldn't do that, because Brendan had outed himself. But Cappy Don didn't appear to be acting. He looked genuinely panicked at the thought, which gave

Oliver pause. Maybe Brendan *wasn't* in on the investigation...but that didn't make sense, either. How would he have known the e-mail was significant? He tucked Brendan's involvement away for later study.

"I'll admit I took it. I'll tell him I wanted to sketch it as a gift for Mr. Arnell. I'll say Brendan is the one who told me about the mushroom. They'd buy that story. Brendan might even play along, just to avoid the shadow of doubt. Trust me, I've got the dopey nice guy routine down."

"Now, why doesn't that surprise me," Molly said drily.

An intense wave of dislike rolled over Oliver. He'd be hard-pressed to recall what had ever drawn him to Molly in the first place. Definitely not her sense of humor.

"If you're going to make jokes, try to make them funny." He went back to ignoring her and turned an imploring face to Cappy Don. "The methods were touch and go, but you can't deny my results. I've got a personal item linking Mr. Arnell to the drug ring, we have an exact location in Capital Acres to investigate, which was always a needle-in-a-haystack situation, and Kay is as good as recruited once you agree to meet with her. I don't have to tell you how many doors she can open. She has direct, unquestionable access to Amos's labs, the accounting floor, where files are stored, and Capital Acres itself. She's the only way I'll get back in."

He planned to absolutely ignore what Brendan had told Kay about taking care of the greenhouses. Until word came from Cappy Don himself, Oliver would continue to do everything he could to gain access. Especially now that he had a solid bead on what he was looking for. Or rather, *where* he was looking.

Cappy Don's lips were pressed together so hard, the skin around them turned white. Oliver could tell the man was torn between protocol and results. "You seem to have an answer for everything. Tell me, what's your plan when rumors start flying about you and Kay?"

"Rumors? There are no rumors. With the e-mail deleted, no one in the building knows about the kiss." Oliver had carefully kept mum on how, exactly, Kay had come by the e-mail.

"Oh?" His bushy eyebrows rose a mile. "Tallulah Hadley and Rowan O'Connor don't have friends in accounting? And Brit Lars, the receptionist, doesn't sell secrets for gourmet coffee? Such as you and Kay leaving together last Friday?"

"I, uh..." Oliver sat back in the chair and rubbed his chin. He hadn't thought about maintaining appearances. "I'm her assistant. I went out with Roscoe all the time."

"Ever get caught sucking Roscoe's face?"

Oliver sighed at the unforeseen complication. "Can't say I ever had the pleasure."

Cappy Don didn't smile. "Any attention is bad attention, Pierce. You're supposed to be nobody, a fly on the damn wall. You and Kay becoming the latest hot topic is definitely not helping the cause."

He shrugged. "I don't know, Cap. Maybe it doesn't hurt, either." Oliver didn't miss Molly's second eye roll or her pinched lips. "I'm just saying, a hot woman in a thong bikini has a better chance of picking your pocket than an average Joe in a pair of khakis. Why? Because you're not looking at her hands. And you don't mind if she comes close."

The captain blinked at Oliver. "Misdirection. You think if people are watching you and Kay, they aren't watching you and Kay? Where's the logic in that?"

Molly stood up suddenly. Her eyes were hooded, her jaw locked. "Leave it to you to bring sex into this, Oli. You know you don't need an excuse to get it on with the little girl."

The spiteful tone and the unveiled reference that an attraction to Kay was somehow creepy and scandalous because of her size made Oliver see red. "I get if you're jealous, Molly—"

"I'm not jealous, you idiot!" Her hands fisted at her sides, and her face flushed red. "I can live with what happened between us, because that's personal. But you're taking my one refuge, my job, and trying to make it painful and unbearable." She cast a desperate glance at Cappy Don and grabbed for her purse. "I don't think I can do this."

She fled from the captain's office without another word, leaving Oliver struck dumb by the outburst, and Cappy Don wearing a mask of disappointment bordering on contempt.

"What?" Oliver demanded. "What do you want me to do? Go back in time and fix shit? I'm not trying to do anything to Molly. That's ridiculous."

The captain shrugged. "You're not trying *not* to."

Oliver gritted his teeth. "I'm doing my job. I can't operate around Molly's feelings. Or my own. If letting people believe rumors gives me greater access, I say let them fly. No one will question Kay dragging me along everywhere she goes. Places like Capital Acres and the top floor of Free Leaf. Hell, Kay doesn't even need to know we're playing that angle, unless she hears the rumors herself."

Finally, Cappy Don fell back into his chair in defeat. He rubbed both hands over his haggard face. "You really do have an answer for everything."

"You pay me to."

"I know. Tell Kay on Monday to expect instructions soon. You're out of the loop on this one, kid."

"What? Why?"

Cappy Don rose from his desk, the signal the meeting was over. "I want to talk to Kay Bing. Not her mouthpiece."

* * * *

Kay wasn't prepared for the gloomy atmosphere that greeted her inside Neve's loft. The curtains were drawn, the lights turned down. There was hardly evidence of human habitation. Just the lump on the huge white sectional sofa.

A mound of blankets guided her to where Neve lay huddled, hiding from the world. Discarded granola bar wrappers and empty Dr. Pepper cans littered the floor, which made Kay cover her mouth to stop a startled gasp from escaping. From the state of things, she couldn't hire Neve if she wanted to. But not choosing her seemed equally as cruel. Like kicking her while she was down. Kay gently shook her shoulder.

Neve pulled the blanket down from her face. She couldn't even manage her hallmark glare. She gazed at Kay in an empty way that made Kay's stomach feel weird. She stilled when she saw the mascara smears beneath Neve's amber eyes, so old the black stuff was coming off in flakes.

"Neve," she breathed, wedging herself next to Neve and brushing back strands of hair from her friend's face. "What happened?"

Neve buried her face again. For a long time, Kay sat there, unsure of what to do. Probably leave. If Neve wanted to talk, she'd have gotten in touch. Kay rose to leave when the memory of Oliver at the café yesterday sprung to the forefront of her mind. Oliver, holding her hand and reminding her of the girl who'd once brandished a loaded gun to save the life of a couple of dogs. That girl was fearless. That girl wasn't afraid to take charge, and she definitely wasn't afraid of a surly Neve Harper.

Kay gripped the blanket and wrenched the entire thing from Neve's body. She was curled into herself, like a cat. She even sprang up and hissed at Kay, grabbing for the blanket. Kay danced out of reach. "You want the blanket? Start talking."

Okay, maybe she was a little afraid. Neve's face contorted into a mask of rage, but behind it Kay recognized the telltale signs of pain. Real pain.

She waited for Neve to get herself under control. When it felt safe, Kay sat next to her and spread the blanket over both their laps. "I'm not leaving here without an explanation."

Neve's lip curled. "You didn't call, and I didn't invite you. Tell me what you're here for, Kay. We both know you want something. Can't remember the last time you stopped by without a reason."

Kay scanned Neve's face, wondering at the acid in her tone. She'd do them both a disservice by lying. She swallowed, prepared to find herself unceremoniously booted to the curb. "I came to tell you to your face that I'm asking Seraphina to be my interior design liaison for a spa I'm working on. I know you'd do the job if I asked. But I'm afraid my team will be so mesmerized by your presence, they'll forget I exist. It'll be my work, but in everyone's mind, it'll have been you leading the project. This is my one shot to make a name for myself at Free Leaf Concepts. I can't afford to let you end up with the credit. I'm sorry, Neve."

Neve's stony expression made Kay's heart falter in her chest. "My famous personality strikes again. Amazing. I didn't even have to be in the room this time."

Kay narrowed her eyes. "Stop feeling sorry for yourself for two seconds. What happened? You can take your problems out on me all day if you want. I'm made of some pretty thick stuff."

"Oh, ho! Look at you. Remembering who you are finally? Isn't that swell."

"Keep it coming. Be as nasty as you want. I'm not going anywhere."

Neve jerked and stared at Kay with an intensity that was frightening. And then the unthinkable: tears brimmed the bottom of Neve's wide-open eyes, then fell and rolled down her cheeks. All the pain Kay had seen beneath the surface rose up, washing over Neve's anger in a cleansing tide. "That," she said through trembling lips, "is all I needed to hear Duke say. I know he can handle me. But will he always want to?"

Kay's heart contracted. Neve's refusal to set a date for the wedding or move in with Duke..."You were testing him?"

Neve brushed the tears from her cheeks and looked away. "Not on purpose." She sniffed. "I couldn't help myself. I just kept pushing and pushing. Testing the boundaries. Seeing how far I could go before he had enough. But now, he thinks I don't want to marry him. He canceled everything. He said to let him know when I decide what I want."

"Oh, Neve." Kay scooted closer and wrapped her arm around her mentor's shaking shoulders. "He wants you to prove that you want this. And all along, that's all you've wanted from him. You two are impossible." Kay held her while she cried.

It took most of the afternoon, plus liberal amounts of threats and cajoling, to convince Neve to lie down in her bed and rest. Kay cleaned up the trash, took Darcy the Pit, Neve's rescued pit bull, for a walk, and washed the dishes piled in the sink. Once she started, she couldn't seem to stop. She found cleaning supplies under the kitchen sink and set to work, losing herself in the mindless activity.

An hour passed before there was a knock on the door. The tap was so quiet, she almost didn't hear it over the swish of her rag as she polished Neve's giant glass coffee table.

Kay had a moment of uncertainty when she opened the door to reveal Duke.

He was as darkly handsome as ever. He hadn't grown back his long beard, but kept a five o'clock shadow over his dimples. His dark blue eyes were lined with enviably long lashes, and his long, black rock-n-roll hair was tied back in a low ponytail. "Hi, Kay. You're not Neve."

Kay didn't move to let him enter. "I'm certainly not. To be Neve, I'd have to be recovering from a mental breakdown, brought on by a broken heart, courtesy of a boy who doesn't seem to know me at all." It took seeing him to realize how angry she was.

She glanced over her shoulder, made sure no sounds were coming from Neve's bedroom, and stepped outside into the hallway, closing the door behind her. She ignored Duke's attempt to speak. She poked him in the chest. He was tall, so she felt a little ridiculous, like a child scolding a parent. But her emotions were true enough. As was Duke's failure. "Did you forget who you fell in love with?"

"No—"

"Did you expect her to grow puppy tails where her claws used to be? You didn't change her, Duke. She didn't become someone different because you love her. She just wanted you to prove you could handle her, for better or for worse, otherwise those vows would never mean anything to her. All you showed her was how right she was. I'm not saying she's easy to love. But you're in or you're out, Duke. You can't change your mind when she stops playing nice. It's not fair. You love her for who she is—all of her—or you don't."

"I know."

Kay shook her head. "I've already said the things she was waiting to hear from you. You missed your moment."

Duke met Kay's gaze and held it. He didn't try to hide the guilt singing from his face. But there was hardness there, too. "Kay, please. You know I'm not afraid of Neve's bite. Or her bark. But she kept getting worse. She's been virtually hostile the last week. I thought...shit." He ran a hand over his hair and stared at the floor. "I thought she was regretting everything."

Kay's anger dialed back to a simmer. "Duke, I don't doubt you love her. But can you live with her? Forever? As she is? She's always going to be abrasive, demanding, even unkind, because sometimes the truth isn't nice. And we've got to have someone in our lives willing to tell us the truth."

His dark blue gaze turned earnest. "I can't live without her. But I can't stand to have her hate me, while I'm over here begging her to move in with me and set a damn date, already. Aren't there other ways to test a guy's devotion?"

"Think about it. She's used to being a novelty for men. They like her until they see the worst of her, or until she turns that brutal honesty on them. Because of that, she's been driving them away her whole life. It's what she does. She's waiting for you to decide she isn't worth it, because in the end, they always do. Better to force the issue now than to figure it out later, after she's made her entire life about you."

It was Duke's turn to display some temper. Where Neve was flash bombs and violent explosions, Duke was a steady burn. "I've been Neve's enemy. I've seen her at her absolute worst, and bore the full weight of her terrifying arsenal of insults. If I had doubts, I wouldn't be standing at her door, prepared once again to battle it out with the queen of smack talk just to convince her to marry me. You can't blame a guy for drawing a line. But I'm hardly giving up. Neve can do this little dance the rest of our lives if that's what she wants. But she needs to know it's not enough to get rid of me. She'll have to do better than that."

Kay bit her lip. "You came to talk to Neve, didn't you? Convince her?"

Unsmiling, Duke made an affirmative noise. "Only there's a tiny person blocking my way."

Feeling somewhat abashed, yet proud of herself for standing up for her friend, Kay stepped aside. "I should probably leave, anyway, before I start dusting the rafters." She stepped around him, ignoring his momentarily confused expression, and started toward the elevator. "And Duke? Prepare yourself. You know how to deal with a pissed off Neve. But you've never dealt with what's waiting inside that loft. Good luck."

It took Kay fifteen minutes to get home on the city bus. She could probably walk to the Governor's Mansion district in less time than that, but the evening commute in the relative safety of a crowded bus had become part of her winding down ritual.

The bus dropped her two blocks from her Victorian-style three-level house. It was about ten times more house than any one girl needed, but need had never factored into the equation. The place had been falling apart when she bought it three years ago. Most of it was still in pretty bad shape. Self-renovations weren't anything like paid jobs. Supplies cost money and repairs took time. Daddy had tried to talk her into a chic studio apartment like Seraphina's, and then a stylish midtown loft like Neve's.

But no, not Kay. She'd dreamed of living in one of the historic Governor's Mansion homes all her life. So, when her parents offered to co-sign on a mortgage, she didn't hold back fighting to get exactly what she wanted.

No kids, no pets, no boyfriend, owner of a manor in one of Little Rock's most iconic neighborhoods, and absolute creative control over the renovations. Her dream, and she was living it.

Sometimes, on a bad day, just walking up the wide steps flanked by big white pillars, and doing a lap on the five-foot-deep wrap-around deck was enough to restore Kay's spirits. Or she'd go through each level of the house, up the ornate walnut staircase, peeping into the rooms, touching the original fixtures, and wondering at the things her house must've seen. Then she'd eyeball the plans she had drawn out and taped to the doors. She'd be lucky to complete the house in this decade, but when she was done, the old manor would be a stunner. Themed guest rooms, a full library, a media room—the list went on.

Kay bounded up the front steps, not feeling much in awe of anything today. She stopped short when she reached her front door, one hand jammed into her purse, fingers searching for the hard metal of her house keys. A note, square and pink, stood out like a pimple on the ancient wood. An inch of tape secured the paper.

Noon tomorrow. Walk to the café where you had lunch with Oliver. Take a cab to Riverside Park. We'll find you.

So very cloak-and-dagger. Would they recognize her? She supposed if they knew her private details, they likely had a photograph. Maybe even her horrifying picture taken courtesy of the DMV.

Kay glanced around as if she'd catch the note sticker hiding in the azalea bushes that stood sentinel on either side of the broken concrete path leading up from the sidewalk. She shook her head, her mind escaping to familiar concerns as her gaze roamed over her property. How much would it cost to rip up the cement and remove the tree roots that had pushed up and cracked the old path? Would it kill the oaks? Could she do the work herself? With everything else suddenly piled on her plate, she didn't know when she'd have time to look into expensive landscaping repairs, let alone get her hands dirty.

She wrenched the note from the door and threw herself inside the long, wide foyer. Her feet made loud work of the plastic sheeting underfoot. Beneath the film of plastic, the narrow planks of the original hardwood floors, scuffed and marked by age, gleamed with polish and protective coating.

The long hallway was devoid of any furniture, and nearly half the wallpaper had been painstakingly removed. What remained stuck to the walls was jagged, ugly, and stubborn. The bare spots revealed old crumbling plaster. The whole area required brand-new drywall before Kay could put up new wallpaper, or paint, or decide if the crown molding was reusable.

She and her old house had a thing or two in common. She could see a reflection of herself in the work being done. The original shiny part covered for the sake of protecting what precious little could be salvaged, the rest in the messy process of being stripped and remade. Maybe, like this house, holding onto everything in its original form was impossible. Maybe Kay could never go back to being the girl she'd once been. But she could still make herself into something wonderful.

She glanced down at the sticky note in her hand. Was forcing her way into an ongoing investigation new Kay or old Kay? A small smile forced its way onto her lips. It felt lovely if a little foreign. Definitely old, uncompromising Kay, shining through.

* * * *

Oliver had the horrible and utterly certain feeling he was making a huge mistake. But the phone was already ringing. If he hung up now, Molly would just see his number and call back. Better to man up and get the awkward conversation over with.

She answered on the fourth ring, seconds before the call would've gone to voicemail. "What do you want, Oliver?"

He stroked his chin. "No nickname? You must really be ticked."

"Not mad. Hurt. And you know what? It's stupid. I know it's stupid. You didn't have to call me up to rub my overreaction in my face. I took us more seriously than you, and it's a roundhouse kick to my pride, nothing more. I'll get over it."

"Um...I was, uh, actually calling to talk about something else," Oliver admitted slowly.

Molly had nailed it, but the last thing he wanted to do was rehash old issues, or discuss conclusions he'd come to long ago. He'd considered their hookups a fling; she'd labeled them something far more important. Feelings got hurt. He'd moved on, content to call the whole thing an unfortunate misunderstanding, because that's what it was, while Molly clung to the injustice like her life revolved around losing Oliver. Sometimes, it struck him that Molly must've had feelings for him long before they got together—some damn strong ones.

He didn't want to go there. "Have you set a meeting time with Kay yet?"

"Oh." Molly went from vulnerable to sarcastic in an instant. "Why aren't I surprised your twelve-year-old obsession is once again the cake topper of the conversation?"

Oliver cleared his throat and carefully kept his voice in neutral territory. "She's not twelve. Don't be an asshole. I'm just calling to ask if Cap is taking point, or if you're the go-between. Because if you are, I have a favor to ask."

"You're unbelievable, Oli."

"I'm serious. Molly, come on. I know you're pissed and hurt and—" He stopped shy of accusing her of jealousy. It seemed like the wrong thing to say. "And you have every right to be. But try to remember what's between you and me has nothing to do with her. She hasn't done anything wrong. Just promise you won't take your anger out on her."

"Are you questioning my professionalism?"

Oliver recalled the memory of Molly hacking his phone to get information on the girl he'd slept with. "Definitely."

A long pause. "Fuck you, Oli." The phone beeped in his ear as the call ended.

He groaned and stared at the screen. He'd probably made things worse. Molly had that special ability to sound spitefully gleeful, and she'd employ it to its fullest degree if she were the one in charge of delivering Kay to the undisclosed meeting place. He could hear Molly's contemptuous voice comparing Kay to a child, making her feel small.

Kay didn't deserve to be stripped down. She wasn't the enemy. She was on their side. Hell, she was probably going to be the thing that cracked the whole operation wide open for them. But Molly had a cruel streak, and something about Kay brought it out of her.

Oliver launched himself out of his recliner and was in the back of a cab before a minute had passed. If Kay was going to run the gauntlet, Oliver would make sure she went in armed.

Chapter 9

It took the cabbie ten minutes through traffic to reach Kay's house in the Governor's Mansion district. Oliver paid the driver and climbed out, his neck bending to take in each of the three stories of the massive house.

House? Not even. It was a veritable mansion in its own right. What in the hell did someone as small as Kay need with a home so big? She had a huge family, or a lot more friends than their background check had dug up.

The sun was setting behind the Victorian as Oliver approached, casting the white clapboard in sharp relief against an orange sky. A string of pale white lights followed the porch as it wrapped around the exterior. The image was so deliciously Southern, he had a sudden hankering for lemonade and pecan pie. He had a single thought as he climbed the stairs and approached the front door.

Home.

Not his, no. But this was the sort of home the South was known for. He felt welcome, taken in by the sweet scent of honeysuckles and blooming azaleas. The sun was almost down, and lightning bugs glittered like stars across the yard and in the boughs of two ancient oaks. He decided the only thing missing were a few rocking chairs on the porch. In fact, the porch could stand a little TLC. He noticed a few holes in the old wood, spots where planks had warped from humidity and poor maintenance. He used the big brass knocker to announce his presence.

Kay opened the door in a rush, concern etched onto her face beneath a thin sheen of sweat. She had a red headband pushing back the hair from her face. It stuck up and fanned out like a jagged blond halo. She blinked four times before finding words. "How in the hell do know where I..."

Oliver smiled as she caught on. "Your address was probably one of the first things I learned about you."

"Right." Kay nodded. "You know my ex-fiancé by name. You probably have my driving record and college transcripts memorized. Among other things."

Yes, he had them memorized, but only because he remembered anything he read in great detail. "If it helps, I think that speeding ticket was a bum rap. Everyone goes eighty on the freeway."

Her eyes widened. "That's totally creepy."

Oliver glanced at his feet, wishing he could take back the bad joke. "Yeah. Sorry. I told you why we looked into your background, but I guess it's weird no matter what."

"It is. It really is." She didn't make any move to invite him inside. "What can I do for you, Oliver?"

"Let me come inside. Offer me sweet tea and homemade lemon bars." He shrugged. "Let me give you the scoop on what to expect when you meet Cappy Don."

"I've already got my instructions."

Oliver frowned. "I figured. But there's more to the process, and it's only fair that after everything we know about you, you should know a little something, too, going in. I'll skip the tea and snacks. Just give me five minutes, and I'll let you get back to your treadmill." He pointed at his own forehead, indicating the sweat on hers. "Or whatever you do for fun after work."

She smiled humorlessly and rolled her eyes but opened the door for him to enter. He curiously scanned the plastic covering on the floor.

"Taking down wallpaper," she explained, closing the door behind him and guiding him down the hall. "Come on. The kitchen's nicer. You can do your little song and dance routine in there. No sweet tea or lemon bars, but I've got ginger ale and maybe some leftover Girl Scout cookies."

He wouldn't complain about Girl Scout cookies but couldn't resist teasing her. He'd known her address was in the Governor's Mansion district, sure, but he had imagined a small cottage, maybe an old carriage house, nestled in between monster Victorians, updated and ultra-stylish. "You'd better step up your game. If you're going to live in a place like this, you've got to meet the Southern hype. Homemade peach cobbler, fresh squeezed orange juice, pies cooling on a windowsill, and tea steeping in the sun on the back porch."

"Yeah? Guess I should round up a few slaves while I'm at it." She rounded the corner before he could cry foul.

"Oh, hey, come on. I'm teasing." He reached the end of the long hallway and followed her around the corner. "I just expected—" He stopped dead in his tracks, and his mouth popped open.

Kay stood against the white speckled granite bar with her arms crossed and a smug smile.

"I expected *this*," he confessed, walking slowly into the huge kitchen. "Exactly this."

"The first room I renovated. Took me nearly all of the past three years. Not just because I did the repairs myself, but also the insane cost. Daddy helped me get started, but even with a boost, this kitchen almost broke me. It's one of the only rooms I intend to fully modernize. The rest of the house I'll at least try to keep close to the original. Kitchens are a bit different. No one actually wants the novelty of a kitchen built in the 1800s."

"You did this?" Oliver turned in a circle, taking in the entire kitchen, the bar, and the small breakfast nook nestled beneath a huge window overlooking the side yard, with green hydrangeas growing up against the glass. "All by yourself?"

It didn't seem possible. The floor was the only thing that made sense, because he recognized the same hardwood from the foyer. The rest was catalog perfect. Silver knobs and handles shined against stark white cabinets. A mosaic of tiles in every shade of pale blue, from sky blue to periwinkle, ran beneath the cabinets, a lovely complement to the countertops, which were the same speckled white and gray as the bar. Overhead, baby blue pendant light fixtures cast a pale glow over the surfaces. The refrigerator and stove were gleaming stainless steel. It was like a chunk of the sky and clouds had fallen and disguised itself as a kitchen.

Kay ran her finger along the bar, then walked around it to a narrow door on the far wall. She opened it to reveal a nearly bare pantry. Apparently, eating wasn't high on her list of priorities. She pulled out the promised cookies. Thin Mints. His favorite.

"Mostly on my own. One piece at a time. Appliances were purchased on credit, but one more year and they're paid for." She shrugged, pulled open a cabinet on the other side of the refrigerator, and brought down a glazed pearlescent plate. Even the dishes were in sync with the design. She arranged the cookies like he was a guest worthy of the consideration.

He studied her, taking in every angle of her face like her appearance alone held her secrets. This was a new side of Kay's personality. A view of what went on behind the curtains.

With her hair back in a headband and dirty jeans, she didn't fit the scenery. But that was okay, because she wasn't meant to. She was the architect, not one of the fixtures. The painter, not the medium. He had no idea she was this talented. Or dedicated. And the sheer patience, to spend years painstakingly devoted to her passion, revealed facets Oliver had only been able to guess at. His respect for her rose several degrees.

Enough to make the hot room seem a little warmer. "It's gorgeous. Like Heaven."

Kay smiled, obviously pleased, then pressed her lips together like she wished she hadn't and looked everywhere but at Oliver. "You know, it's funny. I don't like light blue. Any pastel color, really. It's too cute for someone who looks the way I do. Makes me think of baby dolls and children's clothing. But that's the magic of design. Sometimes, the best ideas aren't personal. Can you imagine if I went around making everything my favorite color?" She gave a little snort that was absurdly cute. "You have to open yourself up to different styles, and the emotions they can evoke. You're right. It is a little heavenly in here."

Oliver watched her. She was scanning the kitchen as if seeing the room for the first time, her eyes big and a smile playing on her lips. Proud but trying to hide it. "What is it?"

Her gaze jumped to his. "What?"

"Your favorite color."

"Purple. Not soft or pale. Lavender is awful. But real, deep purple, like the sky right before it turns to total dark."

He grinned. Such a complex answer to such a standard question. It would never be as simple as just a color with Kay, any more than she was as simple as a single shade. It was fine details, the twists and the turns that kept him guessing, and she still surprised him, even when he thought he had her all figured out. She walked around with a loaded Glock in her purse. Singlehandedly did the work of a whole crew of men. He couldn't lie to himself and deny the physical attraction, either.

Unfortunately, it all quickly added up to a very serious problem. Molly was right.

He liked Kay. *Liked* liked her. The stupid kind of like that made him want to write her a silly note. *Will you go out with me? Circle Yes or No.*

He rubbed a hand over his face and stopped himself from saying something stupid by shoving a cookie in his mouth. She hated him. He'd snooped into her personal life, turned her new job into a nightmare, and almost gotten her in trouble with a badly timed kiss. He didn't have a single good thing going for him. He didn't expect the realization to weigh so heavy, but it was like a sack of grain dumped on his shoulders. The unforeseen train of his thoughts sobered him like nothing else but a bucket of ice water over his head could have.

He waved a cookie at Kay and spoke though a mouthful. "Thanks."

She smirked, probably at his bad manners, and poured ginger ale over a glass full of ice cubes and set it in front of him with a plunk. "Just trying to live up to that Southern hype."

He chewed and swallowed, gulped enough ginger ale to be able to speak clearly, and brought up the one thing he knew was guaranteed to make shit uncomfortable. If he didn't break up the cozy feeling in his chest every time he looked at Kay, he'd have to get the hell out of here, and forget the warning he'd come to offer. "Did Finn help with any of this?" He waved his finger in a circle around the kitchen.

Kay's reaction was about what he expected. Her gaze darted away, and the soft smile she'd been wearing since they started talking about her amazing accomplishment fled like it'd been chased away by ghosts. "Weird question, but no."

"He's a carpenter. I just thought."

"I told you I did it myself. Took me about ten times longer than it would have with some help. But he never offered, and I never asked."

"Oh." Oliver slipped another cookie into his mouth and forgot the reason he'd brought up Finn Welk in the first place. What kind of carpenter doesn't offer to help out on his girlfriend's huge renovation project? "I'm not surprised you didn't ask for help, but I'm kind of miffed he didn't offer. You ever need someone to slap on some paint for a six-pack, I'm your man."

Her grin made a triumphant return. Oliver felt like an ass for making it disappear in the first place. "Thanks, I guess. I'll try to remember that."

"It's cool what you're doing here. You're not hanging out on your phone or staring stupidly at the TV, you know? But seriously, if this is how you relax, I hate to ask what you do for fun."

She tilted her head. "Then don't ask. Instead, why don't you get started on that very important thing you came to tell me?" She glanced at her watch. "I've got another hour of wallpaper yanking to do. It's a loose schedule as far as renos go, but I do try to keep up a certain level of production."

Oliver dusted his hands together. "I'll help."

Her eyes went round. "What?"

"I said I'll help. I'm your assistant, after all. I can flap my gums and use my hands at the same time. Just don't offer me a piece of gum."

That earned him a small laugh. "Fine, but I don't want to hear a single complaint about sore shoulders on Monday."

From another room, she produced a second stepladder and set it up on the other side of the hallway. They'd work back to back, but Oliver figured it might be easier to talk if he didn't have to face her. Coward. He shook his head. He didn't wait for a prompt or permission. He stood on his ladder, began peeling ninety-year-old wallpaper, and started talking.

"On Monday afternoon, you'll be asked to get into a cab. You'll have instructions to go somewhere specific, but what you won't know is that the driver is one of us. Sometimes, it's a dude. Other times, a woman. Her name is Molly, and she knows everything about you. She knows about Finn and about Neve. She's, uh...well, she's less than charming, and I have a feeling she's going to go out of her way to put you on the defensive. Get under your skin, piss you off. Emotional battery."

From behind him, Kay made a rude snort. "Sounds like a nightmare."

"It will be," Oliver admitted. "So, I thought you might like some ammo of your own."

He waited for what felt like an eternity.

"And what constitutes ammunition?"

Oliver glanced over his shoulder to find Kay had done the same. They stared at each other. "Information."

* * * *

Questions piled up on Kay's tongue, but the one that meant the most to her was also the hardest to voice. *Why?* Why would Oliver go out of his way, against his own people, to help her? For the first time, she had reservations. "You're making me nervous."

He shredded another strip of wallpaper. "Not as nervous as I am."

She was more than nervous now. She was concerned. They worked a while longer, until Kay was satisfied with her quota for the day. Then she jumped down from her stepladder and turned to Oliver. She tugged his dress shirt where it had come untucked from his slacks. "Come on, I need to sit for this."

She led him back to the end of the foyer, but not back into the kitchen. Instead, she turned right and opened latched double-doors. They opened into a large parlor. One day, this would be a formal living area. For now, it was mostly used for storing reno supplies. An old plaid sofa was pushed against one wall.

She sat and beckoned for Oliver to do the same. "No more cookies, no more wallpaper. Talk." She folded her hands together and leaned forward to listen with her forearms planted on her knees.

His sigh held an undeniable note of misery as he unleashed it and slumped back on the sofa. "Molly. Right. Well, she and I have a history.

A short but evidently powerful one. She's going to give you hell, Kay, and it's my fault. I'm sorry. The story isn't unlike what happened between you and Finn, with the exception of motive, I guess."

Kay's sharp intake of breath rang in her ears. "What the hell do you know about my motives? What kind of thing is that to even say?" Jesus, were they eavesdropping on her conversations with her friends?

"Only what I can guess." He raised his eyebrows as if to challenge her. "You sabotaged your engagement. Nothing else makes sense. Everything I've learned about you, and I'm not just talking the details of your file, tells me you're not the type to slip up like that. Besides, you're ridiculously smart. Clever. You could've gotten away with the indiscretion." He didn't give her a chance to respond. Just sat back and launched into his own tale. "We weren't even dating, Molly and me. At least, I didn't think. We hooked up a few times. Never went on a legitimate date, never discussed the details. She read more into the relationship than I did. When I went out with someone else, it blew up in my face. And I couldn't just avoid Molly, because we work together. She's been systematically punishing me for the last year."

Kay scratched her head and tried to piece together a coherent picture from the information. "And she's going to give *me* hell?"

"*Yeeeeah*," he drawled. "Basically, yes. So, we'll have even more in common. Cool, right?"

She tried to swallow the indignation that rose in her throat but failed. "You call being a cheater having common interests?"

"Not interests. Just history. And I think you had the right idea. Had I realized how deeply Molly committed to the idea of us, who knows? I might've still done what I did. Clean break. I mean, I didn't consider what I did was cheating at the time, because I had no idea she thought we were exclusive, but Molly did."

Her pulse skittered. "How did you manage to unearth my motives behind cheating on Finn before I had them figured out myself? Did you bug my friend's apartment? Tap my phone?"

"No. God, no. Come on, Kay. I told you what I know about you. Besides, I couldn't take surveilling you any further at this point. I feel like I owe you better than that. You can see why the department frowns on getting romantically involved with anyone closely tied to a case. The truth is I figured it out as soon as the information came in. Do the math. If you got cozy with the other carpenter, but were deeply in love with Finn and determined to marry him, you'd have never said a word. But you're Kay Bing. Accidents happen, sure. People screw up. But not people like you.

Not in that way. You didn't 'accidently' have a good time behind Finn's back. Not saying you instigated the dalliance, but I don't doubt for a second you had the power to stop it and chose not to. Wasn't a leap and a bound to come to the conclusion I did."

Kay peered at him. She didn't know much about what he did as a detective, but she was now pretty sure he was damn good at his job. "Funny, that doesn't make me feel any better. And I'm still confused. You're going to have to do better, Oliver. How does your misunderstanding with Molly have anything, literally *anything at all*, to do with me?"

He scratched his cheek and studied the far wall intensely, even though Kay knew there was nothing all that fascinating about the old crumbling marble fireplace. "You might say she's a smidge jealous."

"Uh huh. Jealous. And she'd be jealous of me because of a certain fake kiss?" Kay didn't get the relieved nod she expected.

Oliver met her gaze squarely and licked his lips. He was still holding back, still resisting, but Kay wasn't going to let things go at that. She'd get answers if it was—

Her thoughts ended abruptly as Oliver's gaze slid to her mouth and his hand came up to take gentle possession of her chin. His lips were soft as they met hers, smooth and pliant as they teased hers apart. He broke away and almost looked frightened by his own actions. "Of a certain kiss," he breathed, hardly meeting her eyes. "Nothing fake about it."

A sweet rush of heat raced up Kay's body and through her limbs like fire catching. She didn't stop and think. She let the desire brushed in broad strokes on Oliver's face be her guiding light. He watched her with a soft, searching gaze, as if he were looking for something in her own expression. She grasped his shirt collar and pulled him to her.

His mouth crashed against hers. Like blood in the water with two sharks, it sparked a frenzy. Kay's hands trembled as she fought the buttons on Oliver's shirt. Her fingers brushing against the rough cotton of his undershirt seemed seductively intimate. His tongue stroked hers, his hands found pressure points and sensitive skin as they roamed over her. Her body came alive with a few clever touches.

In the distant corners of her mind, alarms sounded. But they were far, and Oliver was near. It didn't matter if they worked together, and it didn't matter if they got caught; nothing mattered as long as he could light her up from the inside out. Maybe what she needed was a fling...

The word, once thought, echoed in her head until it became a roar. Kay inhaled sharply and broke off the kiss.

She was on her back. At some point, Oliver's dress shirt had come off entirely. Kay's hands were splayed across his chest right along with the taut fabric of his undershirt as his body hovered over hers. She'd managed to wrap one leg around his torso. He had one hand holding himself up, the other tucked neatly along the curve of her ass.

Her throat was impossibly dry as she forced a swallow. "I can't."

What had she expected? She didn't know. Maybe for Oliver to seem disappointed, angry even. Call her a miserable tease and bolt. In the name of keeping her constantly guessing, he smiled sweetly, planted one more kiss on her lips, and removed himself from the warm cocoon of their embrace.

He sat on the other end of the sofa as if to show he had no problem giving her space, then ran his hands over his head and took a deep breath. "I'm shocked you let me kiss you at all. But you're right. You're my boss." He gave her a teasing grin.

Actually, she wasn't. Not really. And besides, that hadn't been enough to stop her. "It'd be really interesting gossip, but I'm not sure Merit or Easton would care. There was no fraternization clause in my hiring contract."

"Funny. I actually tried to convince Cappy Don that a relationship between us wouldn't hurt the investigation. It would give us an excuse to be together all the time, beyond the usual. A little misdirection to keep people's attention occupied. Anyway, I guess the big brains at Free Leaf expect designers to aim higher than their assistants."

Kay raised her eyebrows. "Well, they shouldn't hire hot assistants," she murmured. "It's entrapment."

Oliver scooted closer until their thighs touched. "Then you're not mad?"

She laughed softly. "No. My body is shaking like it's filled with gelatin, and I probably won't be able to sleep until I masturbate, but those aren't reasons to be upset."

"Wow." Oliver took a deep breath and grinned. "I think I just caught a snippet of what you're like when you're not turning yourself inside out with guilt. Or trying to be Neve Harper's clone."

Kay couldn't help it. She smiled. He was right. For a second there, the filter she'd strapped on to curb her impulses had slipped away. And with it, her ability to not fall in bed with the closest male. She shook her head. Either she had to accept this was a new facet of herself, or accept Neve was right. And if Neve was right, it didn't mean Kay was a hussy, but genuinely attracted to Oliver.

"I'm not a 'fling' kind of person." There. She said it, made a definitive statement. "There was the thing with Finn, obviously, but yeah, you're right. The affair served a purpose. A bullshit purpose, but there you have it."

He seemed taken aback. His mouth opened for a few seconds, then closed while he searched for words. "It's not like that. With you, I mean."

"Then what's it like? As of tomorrow afternoon, we're going to be working undercover together. And maybe the job with Free Leaf Concepts isn't real for you, but I still have spa owners expecting me to come through on their dream. This is very real for me. What do we do with this...this *thing* between us? What do we make of it? What do we call it?"

Oliver's eyebrows came together as he considered. "I don't know. We need to give it a name, like a puppy or something?"

"I just mean I'm not real sure about myself these days. I think I like you. Quite a lot. But also, I thought I loved Finn. Soon, there will be two layers to our relationship, and that'll make all this twice as confusing. So, I don't know, let's..." What? What did she need? What was she afraid of? Oliver confusing her feelings the way he'd confused Molly's? "Let's make a pact. No lies. We're going to be partners in more ways than one until your investigation is sorted out, and what I need more than anything else is honesty. I need someone I can take at face value."

"What makes you think you couldn't trust me? It may seem like I came all this way for cookies and sex, but—"

"Yes or no, Oliver. Can you be upfront with me, always?"

"Yeah, of course."

Kay grabbed his hand and waited for his flat gaze to meet hers. "I mean it. Don't let me think there's something here when there isn't. Don't do me like you did Molly."

"Oh." He pressed his lips together and nodded. "Now, I see. Sure, Kay. You got yourself a deal. But, hey, while we're doling out requests, don't do me any favors like the one you did Finn. If you're out, just tell me you're out."

The truth could bite like a snake. "I guess I deserve that."

Oliver squeezed her hand. "I'm sorry. I didn't mean—"

"No. No, you're right. We have a deal."

She laughed when Oliver held out his hand to shake on it. They made their pact official, then sat, holding hands, their breathing the only sound in the quiet room. Kay didn't know what was running through Oliver's mind, but hers was racing through an obstacle course, knowing she'd eventually pummel into something she'd never see coming.

Chapter 10

The set-up wasn't ideal, but it was better. Much better. If Kay could get Guillermo to quit gawking at Seraphina, they might actually achieve something today. Jasper glowering from his stool in the corner didn't help, but was at least amusing. All he needed was one of those pointy dunce caps to round out the image.

Merit had been poised to rain hellfire first thing that morning. But Mr. Arnell stepped in and saved Kay's ass at the last second, vouching for her assessment of Jasper and even offering a solution guaranteed to make everyone uncomfortable.

Seraphina was brought in, and Jasper was told to sit in on the ensuing meeting. He was banned from participating creatively in any way. His job was to take notes. Not on their designs, but on how a high-functioning team operated and achieved fantastic results when everyone committed to being a team player. If the lesson didn't soak in by time the next project hit the drawing board, Jasper could very well be looking at getting the can.

Kay's esteem for Easton rose a thousand degrees, even if his solution meant Jasper sat glaring for the next couple of weeks. If he learned something, it'd be worth the awkward discomfort they would all suffer.

Seraphina hadn't hesitated to take on the project when Kay called Saturday morning. She'd given her the basic dimensions they were working with, and Seraphina, like the beast she was, arrived with a rough draft. Super rough. Pencil scratches. A sketch of nothing but the bones, but they were damn good bones.

Kay tapped an odd corner of the floor plan, where a good five inches of wall was recessed from floor to ceiling. "What's this? Do we have wires we can wall up right here, get rid of the funky space?"

Guillermo sighed like a lovelorn puppy when Seraphina grinned. Kay had to admit it lit up her serious face prettily. "Actually, that's intentional. You said we're going for a woodsy forest vibe, and I had this idea about string lights. A whimsical touch, but also essential lighting. I got the idea from one of the resorts at Waikiki. They have this gorgeous courtyard, with big round kind of old school lightbulbs hanging from the trees. You know the clear ones, where you can see the yellowish filament inside?"

Amos snapped his finger and gave Seraphina an exaggerated head-to-toe appraisal. "Now *that* is style, y'all. I got ideas poppin' left and right. Now, we talking about fairies here? How whimsical is whimsical?"

"Not fairies," Kay interjected with a quick headshake and a soft laugh. They really didn't have time to go down any more wrong roads. "The whimsy will come from the flowers and plants we choose. No tropical stuff, no ferns. No rainforest vibe. Okay, think the setting of *Bambi*. Or, uh, *Snow White*. It's a tightrope between invoking a sincere woodland feel, keeping the elements in tune with the theme, and at the same time not taking them to extremes."

Seraphina tapped the plans and looked at each of them in turn. "Kay's right. This is a touchy theme. It could go from magical to tacky with one wrong detail."

"Yeah, like a school play production, with paper leaves and cut-out butterflies."

Guillermo nodded. "I did the butterfly once. The wings, the...uh...*come se dice papel mache*?"

"Paper...mâché?" Kay ventured.

"Ah, *sí*. Paper mâché." He flapped his arms like chicken wings. "I almost die from embarrassing."

Jasper snorted in the corner. Kay took her time swiveling her head to face him. He had the good grace to look away, any trace of amusement wiped clean from his face.

Amos stroked his chin thoughtfully, smoothing down the wiry black curls of the goatee he was growing. "Yeah, okay. I have some stuff, but see there?" He pointed to the blank white board behind Kay. "Wiped the color board clean. I need a starting point. I can give you a mess of color, but you gonna be wanting to rule some out. Save me time knowing what we're working with going in."

"You're right." Kay bit back a long, tired sigh. A color. She needed a simple color. Choose the wrong one, they'd be set back weeks if she changed her mind later. New color board, new flower choices. Damn near back to square one.

"Purple."

Kay turned around. Oliver stood in the doorway of her office, relaxed and smiling. How could he be so calm when the sight of him sent her heart thundering in her chest? Her cheeks flamed. Everybody at the drafting table would probably take one look at her face and know...*something*. That she liked Oliver. That she'd fed him stale cookies and they'd fooled around on her old couch.

Oliver took in her face with a slight smile and shrugged as if telling her to relax.

She took a deep breath and tried to sound like her usual brisk self. "What?"

"Purple," he repeated, striding closer to the drafting table in his slow careless way, bringing unseemly thoughts to her mind that had no place here at work. "Not soft like lavender. Deep, rich purple. Like the sky just before total dark."

The words did something funny to Kay's stomach. She couldn't name the sensation, but she knew she'd spoken true Friday night—she'd never be able to handle a fling with Oliver. Not when he had the power to make her skin tingle just by remembering her favorite color. And bringing to mind images of naked bodies and sweat, just by the way he walked toward her with slow purpose. She'd leap in headfirst or hightail it from the bank, but there would never be any in-between or gray area with him. Now all she had to do was pray he didn't ask how she really felt about him, because she was determined to keep her word on their pact to tell no lies. And she'd stumbled onto a truth she didn't know what to do with, let alone how to voice.

Guillermo made an appreciative hum in his throat. "This guy, he knows. Tha's good idea, no? Come, that's good idea! Anything sounds like a poem, must be good idea. I think we go with t'at."

Amos nodded his agreement. "I can run laps around purple. Just say go, little mama. I mean, ma'am. Sorry, got them creative juices taking over my brain. What do you want? Shades of purple, or contrast?"

Kay made herself stop and think. Deep purple. With white. Paint? No. No paint. Something to reflect the light from the hanging bulbs. Glass tiles. Purple, white, and lavender. Small, like pebbles, but uniformed. "Yeah. Yeah, okay. Shades for design." She pointed at Seraphina, then at Amos. "Contrast for foliage. We can work with that, right?"

"Totally." Seraphina's eyebrows were raised appreciatively as she studied Oliver. "That's your assistant? He's a keeper, Kay." Then it was back to business, in her typical way. "Now, the centerpiece you mentioned?"

Thanks, Kay mouthed to Oliver before turning her attention back to the drafting table. "Yes, about that. From old files, I know we just love our fountains here at Free Leaf Concepts, but I want to try something new." She made a point to avoid looking at Jasper. "When I went to Capital Acres, I met with Tallulah and had her show me some of the trees that are known to grow well indoors. There's always the option to put a skylight overhead, but that's going to kill some of the intimacy we'll get from the hanging bulbs." Kay opened a drawer beneath the drafting table and pulled out the renderings she'd sketched last week. She slapped them onto the table and waited while her three team members shuffled and sorted through them. "So? What do you guys think?"

Amos blasted Kay with a grin and a keen stare. "Tallulah. She told me she was working on something special. I'd say this is qualifies. A decent choice."

"A *smart* choice," Kay added, unable to stop a satisfied smile stealing over her lips. "For a hearty indoor tree, my options were pretty limited. A ficus is what I had in mind, and Tallulah recommended a fiddle-leaf fig, which is in the same family. She showed me this, one of her pet projects. She figured eventually someone would have need of a tree with pink borders on the leaves. You should see it in person. Makes the green just pop. Best of all, it's ready for transplant."

Seraphina's blue eyes were alight when she smiled up at Kay. "Stunning. And no one has ever seen anything like it."

Amos grudgingly nodded his appreciation. "Ficus trees tend to shed and they can be annoying and take significant upkeep. A fiddle-leaf fig requires less maintenance, and I have to say, the leaf structure and color are ideal for our theme. You nailed it, Kay."

Kay smiled at her team. "We've got our launching pad, guys. Now, we just have to make Sweetclover soar. Guillermo and Seraphina, let's get some real measurements on these rough sketches. Sera, feel free to find a few more crannies where we can string lights without the bulbs sticking out. Utilize corners as best you can. Guillermo, focus on operations of the spa. Labeled spaces for specific areas, and see about a source for the bulbs we want. If we have to alter the lighting, the whole design could change. Amos, can you hang back for a sec?"

When they were alone, Kay came closer and lowered her voice. "So, did you find out anything when you visited the greenhouses? About the plant I couldn't identify."

"Glad you asked. I went, and I asked about pink carpet. It's in Greenhouse Eight, by the by, you ever wanna check for yourself again, but they wasn't nothing else growing in there with it. Maybe they moved the flowers you wanted to know about, but you have to ask Pattie. Rowan didn't have a clue what I was talking about."

Interesting. "Amos, can I ask...um, well, I noticed you kind of looked at me funny when I mentioned the fittonia and the pink carpet, and asked about the mystery plant. I'd give you a dollar to hear what was running through your head."

If he were involved in Free Leaf's shadier activities, she wouldn't get much out of the question. He might even deny the strange look he'd given her. Either way, his answer might provide an important clue.

Amos nodded as if to himself. "Now, it ain't my business to say what qualifications a, uh, person like yourself should have. But it seems to me like someone in your position ought to know when they askin' about some psychedelics."

Kay blinked. "What are you talking about?"

"Pink carpet and fittonia. They both psychedelic plants. My guess, they growing all together for a reason. For safety. Say we were landscaping a day care. You'd be wanting to avoid anything poisonous, right? Same for them other plants. Don't want no little kids tripping balls while Mommy's at work. We'd get sued real quick. Knowing what's toxic to animals is important, too." He lowered his voice and leaned toward Kay. "Look, I ain't saying we ain't all got some gaps in our knowledge. But you might wanna read up on that stuff." He bobbed his head once, smiled, and dashed away.

Kay tucked away the information for later. She had a feeling it would mean more to Oliver, but the significance of the greenhouse in question wasn't lost on her. Someone had sent Amos to the wrong one.

* * * *

Playing with fire. It was one of Oliver's newly acquired hobbies, apparently.

For starters, there was Kay. She was bright, hot fire, and he was all but begging to handle the coals. He wasn't ready to face the reason behind his strong desire, but his mind kept wandering back to Finn Welk.

Kay had made a villain of herself to save Finn from having to face the fact she wasn't really in love with him. She basically took their engagement outside and shot it, rather than let the dying thing linger and suffer and make everyone miserable and unhappy. Oliver understood what she'd done, but he didn't want it for himself. It was Kay's idea to be truthful with one another, but would their truce override her instinct to protect his feelings if she decided she didn't want to get involved with a beat cop gone rogue?

She didn't have the whole story yet, but by this afternoon, she'd have more than she wanted. Oliver wiped the beads of sweat from his brow, glanced up and down the hall, and tried to focus on the lock pick. He didn't know if the pressure was an effect of trying to break into Merit's office in the middle of the day—more tempting the flames—or because he could hear Cap's voice in his head, spilling the last of his secrets.

A *snick* whispered into the coldly quiet hall, and Oliver's breath caught as the handle turned silently in his hand.

Merit's swift and sudden departure thirty minutes ago, resulting in a bulletin from Brit that she'd be gone from the office for a few hours, meant Oliver had a tiny window, and Cappy Don simply hadn't given him the right incentive to avoid taking chances. Not when Oliver's last unplanned foray had proved relatively fruitful.

No client meetings were scheduled, so Mr. Arnell would be shut up nice and tight in his office until lunch. Oliver only had to worry about bumping into Brendan, and right about now, he wouldn't mind a chat with the guy.

He stepped inside Merit's office. With the door closed, he didn't waste any time. Panel to panel, Oliver pushed, pulled, and tried to pry panels from the wall. Twenty minutes later, huffing and frustrated to the point of anger, he dropped into Merit's chair and made himself think.

Math wasn't Oliver's favorite subject, but he was pretty damn spiffy with numbers, and shit wasn't adding up. A room existed somewhere on this floor. He had the plans in his apartment; he knew it existed. Maybe he could ask Brendan. But what if he wasn't actually playing for their team? A mole's mole.

He leaped from Merit's chair and slipped outside, while trying to smother his internal caution lights. They were flashing yellow, but Oliver was already here. Snooping through Brendan's small work area—a hobbit-sized room hardly bigger than Oliver's own office—was half as risky as going through Merit's.

So long as Brendan wasn't in it. Oliver crept down the corridor, past the conference rooms, and stopped just outside Brendan's door, next to the stairwell. He tapped lightly. No one answered. Oliver tried the knob, which turned smoothly, and he let himself inside.

Oliver grimaced as he took in the small square room. Bigger than his office, but the difference was in inches. The room felt smaller, though, because Brendan was a slob. The waste bin overflowed onto the floor, a stack of magazines had toppled and spread like a smear across the carpet along one wall. Oliver groaned as he took in the desk, jumbled with crap and piled high with junk food wrappers. He was about to leave, already shaking his head in disgust, when it hit him.

He surveyed the room again. A crumpled ball of paper was on the keyboard. A magazine was on the floor just behind the wheels of the rolling chair. Discarded chip bags and soda cans littered the desktop over manila file folders.

These weren't random pieces of trash; they were booby traps. To open the drawers, read the files, log on to the computer, or to even sit in the chair would disturb an article, and give away that the office had been searched. That alone was evidence as far as Oliver was concerned. He grinned to himself and turned to leave. He'd come back another time, prepared. He'd take notes on positions of everything, and painstakingly return each item after a detailed search.

He pulled the door open, almost stepped out, and froze at the sound of voices in the stairwell. The door leading out to the stairwell swung open, and Merit burst through seconds before Oliver swung Brendan's door almost closed—he left a crack and pressed his ear against it.

"Easton, please, don't be paranoid," she whispered urgently. "I checked with Brit, the floor is empty."

Easton cleared his throat nervously. "I shouldn't have left. I shouldn't have gone out."

"You're right," Merit agreed. She was exasperated. "I don't know what you were thinking. It's so important that you stick with your routine, Easton. Noon to two. The rest of the time, you need to be here. *We* need you here."

Easton's breathing seemed labored. Oliver strained to hear him as the two headed away, down the hall toward the conference rooms. "I know. I know that. I just feel so out of the loop. I want to engage. I want to be involved."

Oliver had no problem catching Merit's placating voice. "I know you do. I know. But you have to have faith in the system we've established. You have to trust me. I'll handle it. Just leave everything to me, Easton."

They moved too far for Oliver to catch Easton's reply. He leaned against the door and scratched his head. He didn't know what to make of the conversation.

Objectively, without context, the exchange could be perfectly innocuous. But Oliver had plenty of context, and nothing could be taken for granted here at Free Leaf. For a long time, he thought Merit might be Cappy Don's anonymous tipster. Now, he'd bet money on the exact opposite. And another thought came to mind—Brendan's office was next to the stairwell, which gave him instant knowledge of Mr. Arnell's comings and goings. The day Oliver had been caught in Easton's office, had Brendan seen him enter? Or had he heard Mr. Arnell leave, and gone to do his own search, only to find Oliver had beat him to the punch?

He made it safely back to the fourth floor using the stairwell and went to his own office. It really was about the size of a janitorial closet, but he had very little of his own work to accommodate. Mostly, his job was to facilitate Kay's job.

He paced the small area and went over everything he knew—as well as what he didn't. He came up with one small, untapped lead. Kay knew which plants were locked in the special greenhouse, and it was time for her to contribute to the team. He took out his cell phone and tapped a message.

Whatcha doin, Boss?

Color board. What do u want?

Oliver smiled. He could see her face screwed up in concentration. What colors went well with purple? He thought about offering more help, but what the hell did he know about the color wheel? *Since you ask...What plants were in grn hse 5?*

Her reply was almost instant. Finally, some trust. *Fittonia, pink carpet, and one plant I couldn't identify. Sent Amos to ask and it's gone now, pink carpet, Fittonia separated, moved to new greenhouses.*

Oliver had his laptop booted up and was logging into his profile when another message popped up.

Amos says both are psychedelics. Coincidence?

Well, someone was having a productive morning. *Doubtful*, Oliver texted back with a frown. His heartbeat picked up speed. This was significant information. It could be the break they were looking for, or at the very least, a hardcore lead.

Oliver already knew a term like "edible psychedelic garden plants" would ping on the company's servers. He logged into the private mobile Wi-Fi network Molly had so graciously provided and plugged "fittonia" and "pink carpet" into the search engine. Boom. Three results down, an entire web site dedicated to the topic.

The fittonia came up first. *Fittonia albivenis*, an evergreen perennial native to rainforests, was also known by the names nerve plant or mosaic plant. Labeled ornamental. No special permits were required to harvest or purchase the plants, but in large, dried quantities exceeding a certain limit, some states considered it possession of a narcotic or controlled substance.

"Said to produce visions of eyeballs?" Oliver shook his head. Didn't sound like a good time at all, but indigenous tribes were also known to use teas made from the plant for treating headaches. "I think I'll stick with Tylenol."

A few entries down, pink carpet, or *delosperma cooperi*. Another perennial evergreen. Also called an ice plant or a trailing ice plant, and well known to contain tryptamines. Oliver recognized the term. They were psychoactive compounds.

His pulse quickened. This was the most firm lead he'd stumbled upon in the year he'd been at Free Leaf Concepts. He didn't think it was good enough for a warrant, though. They operated greenhouses, and these were common ornamental plants. The evidence was circumstantial at best. He had to find the link, tying the plants to the mushrooms, but so far, the street team had no luck posing as buyers. Sellers were paranoid and beyond discreet.

"Pink carpet, not a bad choice. Better than the fittonia. Not sure if the Followills are up for that level of maintenance, even with our landscapers on retainer."

Oliver almost jumped out of his skin. He whirled around. "Brendan. Hey." His mind raced. Did he confront him? No. No, Oliver couldn't do that. He was already pushing the limits of Cappy Don's patience. He threw himself into his usual song and dance, distancing himself from the uncertainty that might've nakedly crossed his face when he saw Brendan. "Kay wanted me to research some stuff for the spa." It was the best excuse he could come up with and had the benefit of sounding totally legitimate. He closed his laptop and pasted a proud smile on his mouth. "I made a pretty significant contribution earlier. Maybe they'll invite me to pull up a seat at the drafting table one of these days. Hey, you catch that new girl? She's Kay's friend. A big deal, I hear. About to go to work for Grant Gallagher."

For several seconds, Brendan stared, but Oliver had the feeling he wasn't the object of scrutiny. Finally, Brendan snapped out of it and raised his eyebrows slowly and deliberately, in a show of appreciation. "Gallagher? Really? That's impressive. Hey, Oli, do you happen to know if Kay's got anything on her calendar for lunch today? Plans, meetings?"

Oliver kept his jaw from clenching with brute determination. Why did people keep assuming he liked that nickname? It should be standard social practice to ask first.

Hey, Richard, mind if I call you Dick?

Why, yes, actually. I absolutely mind.

Secondly, say Brendan was on the up and up, why was he deliberately breaking protocol by making contact with Cappy Don's other informant? Oliver carelessly cracked his knuckles and opened Kay's calendar file. "Nope. Looks clear. Should I pencil something in for her?"

Brendan smiled wide, showing off a mouthful of too many teeth, and winked. "A lunch date with yours truly."

Oliver didn't fully grasp the statement at first. But when he did, he was damn near certain that Brendan wasn't one of Cap's. Contact between informants was prohibited, in case someone watching closely put two and two together. Trying to date one of them? Plain fucking stupid. But Oliver couldn't dismiss it as a ploy, either—a bone to throw Kay's clueless assistant, easily explaining away why he wanted to see Kay.

He carefully composed his features into a mask of indifference. It was twice as difficult as it should've been, because he was wrestling with twice the emotions he normally would experience. First, alarm that he might have a fake mole on his hands. Second, the rampant jealousy charging like a bull though his veins.

He cleared his throat, keeping tight control over his nonchalant grin. "Sure. I'll get on that right away, Brendan." He made his own stomach flip by returning the wink.

* * * *

Orange was out of the question. Halloween wasn't what Kay wanted clients to think of when they stepped inside. Green would already be a prominent color. Red was too strong. It might clash with some of the flowering plants, or overpower the purple. She needed what she called a threading color. It was responsible for binding all the elements together. A touch here, a shadow there. The word *tacky* floating from Seraphina's mouth kept taunting Kay, dancing in and out of her thoughts. The fear of screwing up was keeping her from making what should be a pretty simple decision.

A text vibrated the phone in her pocket. Oliver's message made her skin crawl.

"Oh, shit," she murmured. Both plants were definitely psychedelics. He was going to send the results to Cappy Don. Until then, identifying the third plant in Greenhouse Five was high priority. Also, don't trust Brendan. She bit her lip. She'd be curious to know how Oliver had come to that last conclusion.

"Bad news?"

Kay gasped and turned around. Brendan grinned like he thought she'd find being startled utterly charming. "I almost pissed myself. Please refrain from sneaking up on people. It's rude." Hopefully, the imagery would be enough to turn him off the habit.

"Apologies. I didn't realize I had. I, uh, stopped by to ask if you had plans for lunch."

"Oh, shit." Lunch. She checked her watch. She had eight minutes to catch her cab at the café. "Shit, shit, shit."

"You keep saying that."

Kay ran to her desk and snatched her purse. Stupid, stupid color board. "I'm sorry, I have an appointment. I have to run."

"Funny, Oliver didn't mention you had plans."

Of course he hadn't. She'd kept the details of the meeting to herself. "Well, that's because my lunch plans are personal, not something I felt compelled to pencil into my work schedule."

"Gotcha." He shot his fingers at her like a pistol. One eyebrow quirked playfully. "I had this most amazing salad last week from a new place down the street. I was going invite you to come along, but maybe another time. We'll talk later?"

She paused. Was Brendan *flirting* with her? Was this why Oliver told her not to trust him? She knew she was probably looking at him like he was something floating in her water glass, but she didn't have time to smooth things over just now. "Um, sure. We'll talk this afternoon. About salad." She fondly recalled a time when she'd excelled under pressure. Of course, that had been when the drama belonged to someone else.

Brendan beamed and gave her a cheery wave. "Cool. See you later, then."

Thank God she'd worn flats instead of heels today. Kay didn't even wave to Brit as she raced through the lobby and outside. It took her four minutes to reach the street, and another three to jog to the café. She stopped, breathless on the corner, and stuck her thumb out. A black-checkered cab with its light off pulled to the curb, and Kay triumphantly threw herself inside. She closed her eyes and leaned back against the headrest, thanking every god she knew for blessed air conditioning. They veered into traffic and Kay collected herself. Her breathing evened and she took a few tissues from her purse to wipe away the sweat gathered at her temples. There was no salvaging her makeup.

"This had better be worth it," she groaned at the auburn-haired woman behind the steering wheel. "You must be Molly."

It was immensely satisfying to see the woman's face jerk to stare at Kay in the rearview mirror. She whipped off her dime-store aviators, and a pair of dark amber eyes met Kay's. They reminded Kay of Neve's, except they were like dark honey and carried the subtle hint of hostility.

Molly hid her emotion well when she finally spoke in a neutral tone. "Off the rails again. Not that Oli's ever been good at sticking to the book. Yet I still find myself wondering what it is about you that makes it so hard for him to play by the rules."

Kay had no idea what to say to that. What other rules had Oliver broken? "You'd have to ask him. Look, I just want to meet the guy in charge and know who exactly I'm working with, and why. I'm not here for the small talk, so we can skip the hazing." She'd give anything not to have to hear Molly's side of her relationship with Oliver. There was no way he came out sounding like a prince from her point of view.

"Shame." Molly's tone was conversationally polite. "After learning about Finn, I confess I'm deeply curious. You look so innocent. Like a lost little lamb. And yet, you're about as cruel and heartless as they come."

Kay's mouth popped open. She shut it. She'd never had a perfect stranger pass wide-open judgment on her character. She made herself remember Oliver's warning, but she couldn't help herself. Molly struck a nerve. "You know the bullet list of what happened, not the story. The real shame is how bitter you are because Oliver didn't return your feelings. And you somehow feel justified taking your bruised ego out on me."

A long silence reigned. Kay would've been perfectly happy to have the last word, but Molly wasn't content to let the confrontation die there. "I guess there's always unintended side effects when we play with someone else's emotions. Finn's become Red Hill's most notorious drunk. Did you know that? Amazing, the power we can wield without realizing it. I have to say, that was a surprising departure from the rest of your file. How's being the villain working out for you, doll?"

It's not, Kay wanted to say but she wouldn't give Molly the satisfaction. Her heart twisted into a pretzel. She didn't want to believe her, but somehow she didn't think they'd lie to her about this.

The only power Kay had left was refusal to play the game. "Are we there yet?"

Molly drove in circles for fifteen minutes. A squeal came from the front seat, and Kay realized it was Molly's phone. She picked the phone up and waved it in the air. "Oh, look, your boyfriend's calling me. He does that a lot. Oli, my love. How can I help you, babe? Yeah, of course we can meet somewhere. I'll be right there."

Kay shook her head. This was some psychological warfare crap. She knew Oliver didn't have feelings for Molly, but her easygoing familiarity with him sat like soured milk in Kay's gut. Had he intentionally waited until Kay left the building to call Molly? She didn't want to do this anymore. Screw Cappy Don, screw the investigation. Kay wanted out. She was about to open her mouth to say so when Molly slammed on the brakes, and Kay clutched the passenger side headrest to stop herself from hurling into it.

"Here you are. He's the old man drinking Sprite in the corner. In there, he's Uncle Tom. Someone else will take you back to the office when the meeting's done. Tata, darling."

"Whatever," Kay muttered, pulling herself out of the cab and slamming the door with everything she was worth. The cab peeled away from the curb with an awful shrieking of tires. Kay choked on the stench of burning rubber.

Molly might be unreachable, but Uncle Tom was about to get his ass handed to him. The old man drinking Sprite turned out to be the most innocuous fellow in the drab rundown diner.

Kay didn't bother with pleasantries but dropped herself into the chair across from him and crossed her arms.

He tipped the can toward her. "Ms. Bing. I'm glad you came. The ride can be a little rough."

She shrugged. "I didn't notice." She tried to mean the words, but they were weighted with bitter sarcasm. Cappy Don was kind enough not to point it out. "What's with the secrecy? Are you FBI? CIA?"

"Retired military." From his shirt pocket, he withdrew an ID card, showing his photograph next to the full name Oliver had given her. Captain Donald Cappricci. "Active captain on the Little Rock police force, and a familiar figure in the local media. If someone from Free Leaf saw you with me, they might get the wrong idea—that you're an undercover cop. Or the right idea—that you're helping us bring down a bunch of brains selling genetically modified drugs that are killing people. Better for everyone involved if we're not seen together." He reached beneath the grubby plastic table and withdrew a familiar newspaper clipping. He slid it toward her. "Reread that last bit for your old Uncle Tom, will ya? The part about folks dying. Eyes aren't what they used to be."

Kay believed him. The captain's hair was stark white, but his eyebrows clung to their deep black roots, sprouting out of his face like gnarly poisonous caterpillars. She sighed and read the last portion of the article aloud. "Let's see...one isolated incident in Jonesboro, which may be the most tragic and telling report so far. Three people died—"

"There. That's it." He wagged a finger at her, tucked his identification away. She had a feeling he was deliberately exaggerating his age. "One of them happened to be the troubled childhood friend of our boy, Oliver. I like to call him Pierce. Sounds cooler."

"Cooler. Sure." She glanced around. No waitress came to ask for a drink order. Kay assumed he'd asked their table remain undisturbed, but she could really go for a coffee.

The captain sighed and settled his hands together on the tabletop. "There's a lot riding on this investigation, Ms. Bing. More than tracking down some dirty drug dealers. It's personal."

She tapped the article. "For Oliver. I get it."

"Maybe you do. But I'd like you to know what you're getting into here. Oliver's friend, he did a stint in rehab two weeks before his death. Oliver swears on his mom's grave his boy was clean as a nun's diary. Besides that, Manny—that was the kid's name—had a taste for uppers, not hallucinogens, so it came as quite a shock for Pierce. See, he and Manny went separate ways after making some bad choices in their youth. Couple of delinquents all through high school. Oliver eventually got his shit together and joined the Jonesboro PD. He was regularly arresting good old Manny on petty drug charges. He was a beat cop, Oliver was. Too young to make detective yet, when this crap here hit the streets." Cappy Don sneered at the article. "The department had a few cases tied to the mushrooms. Pierce knew about them, but they weren't his cases, and he never expected Manny to get into that sort of stuff. Or he might've warned him. Alas, Jonesboro PD kept the incidences out of the local media. At least, until people finally died. Manny being one of them, well, that got Oliver's attention. He had questions, but the drug enforcement unit wasn't handing out answers. It was an ongoing investigation, and Oliver's attempts to join the task force were denied. He began to suspect the police chief and the mayor were covering for something."

"Were they?"

"No. Oliver was emotional. They saw him as a potential liability, not an asset. And he was powerless to do much about it. He took it personal."

Kay shook her head. "Seems like a good idea to have one super motivated cop on the team."

Oliver, a cop. She'd asked him once, and he'd dodged the question. While it made sense, it was still hard for her to coincide the image of him in a uniform with the careless, charming guy she knew. Or thought she knew.

Cappy Don grinned. "My thoughts exactly. When the first case hit Little Rock, we kept it under wraps for the same reason the Jonesboro PD did—we don't want the people running the drug ring to know we're circling. Little Rock is special. Intelligence tells us the drugs are coming out of our town, but the super shrooms, as the media so delightfully coined them, didn't hit the streets here until recently. Almost as if the other cities were trials. The governor assigned my precinct the case, and I put together a team from the best the city has to offer."

"And you adopted Oliver. Did he transfer?"

"Kind of." The captain shrugged. "Pierce took leave. Well, that's stating it rather broadly. Oliver essentially went rogue, determined to investigate with or without the support the of local police authority on his hip. He crossed our path while hunting down a lead. I could've turned him over, but we went through the proper channels and had him recruited instead. Like you said, it's good to have a highly motivated man in the field. Besides, I was pretty damn impressed that he'd matched us while working on his own, without a fraction of the resources. He's got some very useful skills."

Now, there was something she wouldn't mind hearing more about. "Oh?"

"Eidetic memory, or very close to it. Extreme detail recall. If he's read it, he can remember it with ninety-seven percent accuracy in standard tests."

Kay nodded. "That's why he's your inside man. If he were to come across any pertinent documentation, he wouldn't need to copy it."

"He would, actually, for us to have viable evidence. But yes, the skill makes him a good plant. He picks up leads other informants would miss. Unfortunately, he's got other problems. Rogue beat cop. That's not exactly resume material, is it? It makes the kid unpredictable. Effective, determined, but he's not opposed to going off the books if he thinks he'll get something out of the risk." The captain shifted and leaned in closer to Kay. "Now, I tell you this for a reason. When we took Pierce in, he was lost. Grieving and pissed off, it's an ugly combination. Like I told you, there's a lot riding on this investigation, and Oliver's future is one of those things. We might be able to salvage his career on the force if we nail these sons of bitches. Success means commendation. If we fail, well, I don't know what he'll do. But I know he won't be a cop again."

"Why?" Kay couldn't believe they'd hang a man's entire career on a single investigation. "You said he's skilled beyond your average cop. He should get promoted regardless."

"Failure means the feds take over. Local law enforcement will need a scapegoat. A rogue cop is an easy target to hand over to the media."

Kay sat back, astounded. Politics were like poison in the air, seeping into places it was never meant to inhabit. She drummed her fingers and tried to figure out where she fit into the landscape. She didn't need long to figure it out. "You think I can break the case."

Cappy Don whacked his fist on the table and laughed. "Ha! You're quick. I see why Oliver likes you. You two are a fine match. Yes, I think you're key. Now, did I want you *this* involved in my investigation? Hell no. It's messy. You're not trained, and I can't tell if you're all that committed to bringing down the company that just handed you a cushy job at the top of the ladder. By the way, smooth work on your résumé. As long as no one watches too closely, I think you'll fly right under the radar."

"Thanks," Kay mumbled, uncertain if she'd been complimented or insulted. "I think."

"Look, Ms. Bing, it's entirely up to you. If you're loyal to Free Leaf Concepts, I can order Oliver to cut you out of the loop—"

Kay's hand shot out. "No. No, I don't want that. I just wanted to know what I was getting into. For a while, I thought Oliver be might be trying to steal ideas for another company or something. I mean, Free Leaf is like the space station of modern interior landscaping. They're next level. It's stupid, but the whole drug thing seemed really farfetched."

"Not stupid. Espionage is a viable concern, especially with Free Leaf's considerable government subsidies."

"So, what brought your attention to Free Leaf Concepts, specifically? What evidence have you got implicating them?"

The captain glanced around the room. It seemed like the careless action of a bored old man, but Kay didn't miss how his sharp eyes scanned each face in the diner. He studied her for a second, judging and weighing. "You go right for the goods. I can't tell you much, Ms. Bing, but I guess it won't hurt to answer one of your questions. We have an anonymous source inside Free Leaf Concepts. They contacted us."

"Us as in...?"

"As in, they informed the governor of their suspicions. And before you ask who it is, key term here is 'anonymous.' That was part of the deal. I have a decorated military record and experience in espionage, so I was handpicked to handle the investigation. Soon after, Oliver Pierce became Free Leaf's newest employee." Cappy Don grinned, reached into his pocket, and withdrew a five-dollar bill. He dropped it on the table. "I don't expect to see you again, Ms. Bing, but I'm glad we met. You're as interesting in person as you are on paper. Try to keep Pierce in line, will ya?"

Chapter 11

Oliver watched Molly take a dainty bite of salad. All he could think was it didn't smell nearly as wonderful as his blueberry scones. He skipped the preserves and set aside one of the scones to take back to the office for Kay. She'd deserve something nice after what Molly probably put her through. He checked his watch. How long would the meeting last? How much would Cappy Don tell her?

"Relax." Molly shot him an annoyed look from beneath her lashes. "Cap warned it might take longer than usual."

"I'm relaxed." He wasn't actually. He was hot and bothered, but not in the fun, sexy way. "How thick did you lay it on, Molly?"

"Ha." She smiled and popped a crouton into her mouth. "Your girl gave as good as she got. Cap's going to be pissed you coached her on protocol. Gave away my name."

"Only if you tell him."

"Of course I'm going to tell him. One of us actually follows the rules."

Oliver harrumphed. "If I followed the rules, I wouldn't be here, and we wouldn't know half the shit we do."

Molly's eyebrows went up. "Taking credit for your girlfriend now?"

He sighed and gave up. "I'm the one who dragged her into this, so yeah. A little."

She tilted her head to one side. "Interesting."

"What?" He didn't like when Molly got coy.

"She didn't protest, either."

He blinked at her. No telling where she was going with this. Obviously, it had to do with Kay, so against his better judgment, he had to ask. "What are you talking about?"

"Kay. When I said you were her boyfriend. Not a peep."

Oliver slumped in his chair and didn't do a damn thing to hide his dwindling patience. "Come on, Molly." He groaned and pushed aside his last scone, his appetite withering. Kay could have them both. He needed this investigation to be over, because as long as Molly was in his life, he'd never live down their short-lived relationship snafu. "It's childish to even go there. If Kay had argued with you, it'd be 'oh, the lady doth protest too much.' What's this then? 'The lady doth not protest enough!' There's never a right answer with you."

Molly's lips were pinched. She focused on her salad, stabbing at the purple bits of radicchio with her fork. "You're the one who called me, Oli. What did you want, anyway?"

"Besides a normal working rapport between two professionals on the same team, striving toward a common goal? Information. What do you know about the lab tests on the super shrooms?"

She stared at him for a beat before answering. "Not much. I mean, I know they don't have a complete sample. Obtaining one is difficult. Dealers know the product is hot, so the samples have all been from users who end up in the hospital. But by the time they pump their stomachs, the material is too degraded to get a full DNA profile."

Oliver wished he'd have paid more attention in chemistry. "What if they had a sequence to compare it to?"

Molly didn't look optimistic. "I don't know. I can ask. It's not my area of expertise, but I think...well, it seems to me like they should be able to compare two samples for specific markers, maybe. The problem is we're dealing with a genetically altered sequence. Why? Do you have something?"

"Maybe." He took a small note from his pocket, with the scientific names of the two psychedelic plants written in his chicken scratch. "These are grown in a locked greenhouse, with top-level security. Only Merit Hollis and Easton Arnell have access, besides greenhouse employees. There's another plant, but Kay couldn't identify it."

"High-security greenhouse and they aren't growing pot? Sounds suspicious as hell. I'd make finding out what the third plant is my top priority."

Oliver rolled his eyes. "Ya think?" He signaled the waiter and asked for a doggy bag. "What about your end? Anything good from our mysterious insider?"

She smiled sweetly. "Nothing that concerns you."

He frowned at that, thinking of Brendan. "Molly, I'm going to ask and I need to know. Did the captain send someone else in? Or is there another outfit investigating?"

Molly set down her fork and scanned Oliver's face like a concerned mother. "Are you kidding me? The feds wouldn't move in without warning the LRPD to get their men out. Would they?"

"Maybe. I'm not exactly an expert on DEA investigative procedures."

"I'm sure they don't involve hoodwinking state law enforcement. It's dangerous to go in without knowing who has your six." Molly scoffed. "Plus a total loss of resources to accidently investigate a DEA agent or have them investigating a plainclothes officer. They'd inform the governor. So, no, there's no one else in there, Oli. Just you."

"Not just me," he argued. "There's our anonymous informant."

"Yeah, but they're not one of ours. They're a civilian volunteer, someone who legitimately works for the company. And you should know, they do the bare minimum to keep from garnering or inciting suspicion and are resistant to giving away anything that may reveal their identity. It's understood that's to be a last-ditch resource. You not getting fired was one time Cap had no choice, and it wasn't pretty, Oli. Cappy Don was warned there were limits."

Oliver went over the dossiers in his head. Every employee at Free Leaf Concepts had one. Easton, Merit, Brendan, Jasper, Amos, and Guillermo. Even Brit, though Oliver had to confess hardly scanning hers. She was too new to the company, and too low on the totem pole. But maybe in the other files, he'd missed a detail, a link drawing the clues together. File clerks and accountants on the second floor had been cleared. The company's financial records had come back clean as newly minted money.

It was possible Brendan was their informant. He had some degree of influence with Merit, could've put in the word that helped Oliver keep his job. Plus, he'd covered for Oliver when he'd been caught in Easton's office.

Shit. Oliver shook his head, frustrated, and snatched up the to-go bag, now holding two untouched scones. "Not good enough, Molly. I don't have time to spend investigating who's throwing Cappy Don crumbs."

Molly grimaced and returned to her salad. "Why is it so important, anyway? You could screw up everything trying to figure out who it is."

"I don't need to discover who it is," he explained, throwing down a bill for their meal. "I just need to rule out one guy. Forget whatever else the captain has you doing, and get me everything you can dig up on Brendan Berkley."

"All of the employees have files," she argued wearily. "You've got Brendan's memorized, I bet."

Oliver's jaw ticked. "Look harder, Molly. Dig deeper, find what's missing. If Kay's profile was wrong, maybe it wasn't the only one. Actually, I recently came across one other lapse in our data. Easton Arnell and Jasper Jameson have a personal connection. I don't know if you assigned a rookie to their cases, but there's enough missing information that I can't take anything we've got on faith. And I promise you, there's more to Brendan than what we know. If he's not Cappy Don's anonymous tattletale, then we're in trouble and running out of time."

"Why? As long as he hasn't made you, we're good."

"He's made us, all right. He knows there's an agent inside. He just happens to think it's Kay. We're hell and gone from good if Brendan's one of the bad guys. She's either enlisted a strong ally inside Free Leaf Concepts, or—"

Molly's face paled. "Or she's in serious danger."

Oliver nodded, glad to finally see Molly care about Kay in a good way for once. "Could be. I advised her not to trust Brendan. That should put her guard up, at least. But I need to get to the bottom of his motives while I still have the upper hand."

All the way back to the office, Oliver's mind ran through a reel of possible outcomes. If the people running the drug ring out of Free Leaf thought they had fingered the agent working on the inside, what would they do? Feed Kay false information. Get rid of her. For now, letting them think it was Kay didn't sit well with Oliver—she was essentially bait. But the sleight of hand kept him free to watch as circumstances played out. For now, he and his team had the advantage. He'd warned Kay not to trust Brendan but worried it might not have been enough. She'd be safer if she fully understood the position she was in.

Kay hadn't returned from her meeting with Cappy Don by the time Oliver made it back to the office. He left the baggie of scones on her desk with a note. *Enjoy*, he scrawled. After a moment of hesitation, he added a heart and immediately felt ridiculous. He left it, anyway. He didn't mind feeling stupid for something done with sincerity. She could take it however she pleased.

Seraphina surprised him by poking her head through the doorway. "Hi. I've been looking for you, Oliver."

Oliver squinted at her. "Me?" He pointed at himself. Seraphina had the vibes of someone held together by mortar. An earthquake couldn't shake her. He found her oddly intimidating.

She beckoned him with a hooked finger. "Please, come with me."

Compelled to obey from her tone alone, Oliver did as she asked and followed Seraphina down the hall. He cast a suspicious glance at the back of her head when they passed Guillermo's office. At the end of the hall, she opened the door to the stairwell and waved him inside. The stairs were dark gray with black handrails. A gloomy space. He rocked back on his heels and waited for Seraphina.

Not the coy type, she launched the moment the door clicked shut. "You're almost exactly what I expected."

He raised his eyebrows questioningly.

Seraphina peered at him. It was unnerving, the way she kept her face devoid of emotion. "Neve's too caught up in her own personal affairs to be bothered with what's going on here, but I haven't forgotten that Kay only told half the story. You see, she didn't know whether you're friend or foe. I would hazard a guess she's decided you're the former."

Another unforeseen complication. He'd have to have a talk with Kay about discretion. "I'm one of the good guys, if that's what you mean."

"Hm. I suppose you would be, or she'd have disclosed your curious actions at the greenhouses to upper management by now."

"Wait. She was going to turn me in?"

"When she thought you might be working for another company, yes. Apparently, you've provided enough evidence to make her believe otherwise."

Oliver straightened and cleared his throat. Part of his brain was convinced he owed Seraphina answers. Something about her commanded cooperation. She could give the captain a run for his money—and his job. "Look, all I'll tell you is the information is classified—"

"I have no interest in your investigation," she cut him off smoothly. "But I have a deeply vested interest in Kay, her wellbeing, and her happiness. I'm aware you've looked rather thoroughly into her background."

"I have." He held his chin high. He'd done his job. It was easy to feel like a jerk now that he knew Kay, but he couldn't let himself forget she'd been a person of interest at one time.

Seraphina nodded slowly. Even in the low light, her blue eyes were almost too blue. Oliver could see why Guillermo found the woman visually intriguing, but she was cold. He much preferred Kay's warmth and vibrancy. He supposed he liked his women a little on the unraveled side.

"Then you'll know she's still healing." Seraphina managed to inject the perfect note of warning into the statement. "And if courting Kay's affection is an avenue of gaining information, you'll have some very important people to answer to when this is said and done. She's a girl. Not a tool. Convince me you're not using her, and you'll never hear another word from me about any of this."

He'd take the typical pot-bellied dad sitting on a porch with a loaded .22 over a concerned mama friend any day of the damn week. He didn't have to ask Seraphina to clarify her threat. He could tell by her tone she'd easily find ways to make trouble for him if he screwed with Kay's heart. He wanted to be pissed off, because he had no intention of misleading Kay, but he couldn't deny using her at the greenhouses. His conversation with Cappy Don ran through his head, uninvited, as he recalled claiming an office romance would be a nice, convenient cover.

He rubbed the nape of his neck. "The truth? I can't convince you of anything, because I don't know what's going on myself. But Kay and I made a deal to be upfront with each other. That's the best I can offer you in terms of guarantees. I'll keep my word or I won't."

The perfect stillness was almost inhuman. Seraphina blinked slowly, like a big cat languidly sizing up its prey. "You will, Oliver."

He was suddenly sure he would. "You're a creepy lady."

She shrugged. A slight smile played on her lips as she opened the door. Bright white light washed into the stairwell. "At least I use my powers for good."

"Silver linings." He shrugged, then chewed his lip. "Since I'm here, I think I'm going to head down." If he timed it right, he could catch Cappy Don before he snuck back into the station and avoid seeing Kay for another few hours.

Next time they met, she'd know his backstory. A guy on the edge. The department's psychobabble lady had claimed him unstable. Hell, he might even call it a day and go home, wait until tonight to visit Kay. She might take it easy on him if he showed up with pizza and willing hands. Pulling wallpaper would keep his hands busy and his mind numb. Besides, he liked Kay's old house, full of promise.

He grinned at Seraphina. "Think you can handle the boys?" Oliver recalled Guillermo's drooling and Jasper's hostility.

Seraphina brushed a fine stray hair from her shoulder and smoothed it in place before stepping through the doorway. "I've got plans for those two."

Oliver lingered in the stairwell when he reached the main floor and pulled his cell phone from his pocket, quickly dialing Cappy Don.

The old man answered with an impatient grunt.

"Wondering if you've touched base with Molly yet."

"Are we talking about your hunch concerning a particular assistant? Yeah. I cleared two men for the field. We're going to interview Brendan's mother and his college roomie. If our guys come back with nothing, that's the end of it, Pierce. We don't have infinite resources."

Oliver inhaled deeply. At least now he knew for certain Brendan wasn't one of the captain's. "Trust me. We'll learn something, one way or the other." He hoped like hell those words wouldn't come back to haunt him.

* * * *

Kay didn't go straight back to the office. A new driver, a man, received her in a different taxi and dropped her at an Italian restaurant several blocks away from the café where she'd been picked up. A coffee still sounded like just the hero to swoop in and save her day, so she stepped inside the restaurant as if it had been her destination all along and smiled at the hostess.

Her table for one was wedged into a remote corner of the dining room, flush with a low-slung window that ran the length of the restaurant. Cozy, gloomy, and perfect for Kay's current mood. She ordered a cappuccino and skipped the offer of bread for the table. She didn't think she could stomach anything just then.

The captain's revelations about Oliver weighed on her, and she couldn't put her finger on why. Because they'd vowed honesty? He could've told her his whole story that night. Maybe he'd known his captain would lay it all out for Kay, and do a better job than Oliver could. And true, the captain had been pragmatic, informative, and to the point.

No, Oliver's history didn't concern her. He was struggling through grief, a system that was failing him, and justice for his friend dangling enticingly just out of reach. That would make anyone crazy.

Molly was the real issue. In all Kay's life, through high school sweethearts and college boyfriends, she'd never had a run-in with another girl over a guy. Molly wasn't her friend. She didn't owe the woman anything. But she clearly had some unfinished business with Oliver. Lingering feelings, perhaps, or just a simple lack of closure.

Any other time, Kay would've walked away from the situation. If it sorted itself out, maybe Oliver would be more available down the line. If not, then she'd wisely avoided stepping in something smelly that would cling to her shoe and follow her home.

Things were different this time. Kay didn't want to let go. She didn't exactly want to get embroiled in whatever was between Oliver and Molly, either, but her time with Oliver felt like it had an expiration date. He'd root out their bad guys, bust up a dangerous drug ring, then go back to Jonesboro and rejoin his old department a hero. Kay would end up a footnote on this page in his history. And still, she didn't want to let go.

She shook her head and blew on the hot drink the waitress had delivered. Every day, she was less herself. Old Kay, she'd have shoved Oliver from her mind and focused on her work. New Kay considered jumping into a love triangle for the sake of a few weeks' worth of good feelings. And that was what this whole thing boiled down to—Oliver made her feel good. He smiled at her like she was the most special, clever little thing to sprout from Little Rock in a hundred years, and something in his smile made her want to believe it, too.

By the time she realized she was having an old-fashioned pity party, her drink was gone and she'd grown restless. Finally, her brain managed to wander back to the important stuff—like the Sweetclover spa. She didn't want to waste any more of her day than she already had, so Kay hopped into a taxi for the several blocks back to Free Leaf.

She waved apologetically at Brit on her way to the elevator. "Sorry if I was rude earlier. Nearly missed an appointment."

Brit smiled carelessly as Kay sauntered past. "All is forgiven. You're too cute to be annoyed with for long."

Kay sighed and punched the elevator button. Nothing for it. She'd be cute until the day she died. Might as well stop fighting a losing battle.

The fourth floor was strangely quiet as she stepped out of the elevator, angling her head for the soft Spanish folk music usually flowing from Guillermo's office. Today, only silence. Kay checked her watch, a little shocked to realize it was nearing four o'clock. Boy, the time could really fly when you were feeling sorry for yourself.

She stopped short at the sight of food on her desk. She frowned at the garden salad in its plastic container. Brendan. Great. Already leaving unsolicited gifts. Although, the tomatoes did look particularly swollen and juicy, the lettuce vibrantly green and crisp. The pile of shredded carrot, beefy mushrooms, sliced Kalamata olives, crumbled feta, and ribbons of prosciutto had her mouth watering. She wished she'd have had that bread basket back at the restaurant. Next to the salad, a paper bag had a recognizable café logo. She peered inside and inhaled the buttery sweet aroma of blueberries scones.

A wide smile took over her face. Oliver.

Well, crud. Now, she really had a dilemma. Healthy salad or delicious scones? She'd had scones for lunch earlier in the week. She'd be loosening her belt a few notches if she kept that up. Feeling like a responsible adult, she rolled the bag of scones up tight, annoyed with the smile that wouldn't seem to fade—a cute boy had bought her scones!—and tucked it away in her bag to carry home for later. She'd have them for a reward after she finished another section of the foyer's wall.

She wanted the salad to be gross, because she'd taken Oliver's advice to heart and didn't want to trust Brendan, but it was exactly what she needed to recharge. She used the black plastic fork to shovel bites into her mouth, while her other hand shifted through the papers on her desk. Mostly plant stuff she'd printed out. She stabbed a big chunk of feta, pinned down an olive to cap it off, and pulled the information sheet about the fiddle-leaf fig from under a pile of other similar sheets.

A small square of paper fluttered to the floor.

She took another bite of the salad, frowning at something chewy clinging to her teeth, then bent to retrieve the note. Her heart fluttered, and the stupid smile came back full force.

Enjoy. She'd recognize Oliver's scrawl anywhere. Just beneath it, a hastily drawn lopsided heart. Kay pressed her lips together. What did the weird vibes between them mean? It all started when they couldn't seem to look at each other without getting caught in a staring contest. Now, a budding warmth blossomed inside her when she thought of him. If Oliver had a team, there was something promising about being invited to join it. Their little oath, the one they'd shook on like kids in a schoolyard, felt important to her. Like Oliver had her back and she had his. Maybe the little heart meant he felt the same. Or, she decided with a wry grin, someone had knocked his arm as he'd scrawled his initials.

She got another unsavory bite out of the salad and pushed the rest away. The flavors were great, but the texture left something to be desired. Maybe some kind of green olive hiding in the lettuce, something faintly bitter and unpleasant. One of those "acquired taste" foods, which was code for gross.

She'd tell Brendan so the next time she saw him, too. In fact, her stomach was starting to feel oily and weird. A headache sprouted at the back of her neck, and she blinked through a small wave of dizziness. "That'll teach me to skip lunch."

She wouldn't get any more work done today. Besides, the place was a ghost town. Either everyone had their heads bent to their desks, or Seraphina had cut them loose for the day. Whatever. Kay had left her in charge, so she couldn't rightly complain. She grabbed her things and headed for the elevator. She'd never noticed before, how the buttons were tiny silver balls. She smiled and ran a curious finger over every single one of them. The smile left when she realized she'd been waiting a long time for the car to meet her floor. She shook her head, trying to clear away cobwebs of exhaustion.

Even her usual bus ride made her feel funny. She was basically riding a big metal boat, floating over an asphalt ocean. Strangers kept coming and going. Every time someone left the boat, she wanted to stop them, to warn them. They couldn't swim in asphalt. Nothing good would come of it. Nor was floating possible.

She laughed softly to herself. She was losing her mind. Obviously, they wouldn't float along without help. She had to propel them with her feet.

Her feet made a gentle *tap, tap, tap* on the floor as Kay pedaled dutifully, keeping them adrift and pushing them forward. She hummed while she propelled them on the familiar route. Weren't the other passengers lucky she knew the way?

The way home from the bus stop seemed fraught with unspoken warnings. Her instinct told her not to travel her usual route, but to chance a path she'd never taken before. Concern filled her, even as she turned away from the road she knew so well. She didn't know how far she'd have to go, or what to expect.

If the trip took too long, she'd starve. Two blueberry scones weren't going to cut it for days of traveling. It made sense to go straight home, pack a respectable amount of food like the intelligent person she was, then come back and try the journey again, better prepared. In front of her house, she paused and smiled, soaking in the grand presence, the sad history. Built by slaves, all of it. The whole South, and everything worthwhile in it, built by slaves.

A disgrace. She glared at the house. It was a testament to the worst of humanity. Built on blood and hate. Even the narrow concrete path wanted nothing to do with this house. It had split itself in two trying to escape. And there...the tree roots, trying to wrangle the path back to where it belonged. An overwhelming sadness settled on Kay like a heavy woolen cloak. She walked slowly to the tree, feeling its sorrow, how desperately it clung to the concrete path. She wrapped her arms around the massive trunk.

A car horn blasted into the air. A shout through an open car window rattled Kay into coherence. She gasped and stepped away. What...what was she doing? Hugging her tree? Why...

Her mind whirled. She ran inside and slammed the door behind her, breathless. She dropped her bag to the floor, and she pushed the hair back from her forehead.

Hot. She was hot. Hot and *starving.* She laughed. No wonder she felt awful! She should eat. Blueberry scones sounded like the best thing in the world. They *were* the best thing in the world, because a boy she had her heart set on have given them to her. Because she was special, and pretty, and hungry, and had the most astute taste in scones.

She dug inside the bag and pulled out the salad in its container. Her gag reflex kicked in and she tossed it like a Frisbee down the long hallway, grinning and retching. The Devil was in the salad. She didn't know how she knew, but the idea was ironclad in her mind. She withdrew the deli bag and then the scones, breathing in the sweet scent. She inhaled them both, hardly stopping to chew. A polite cough made her look up.

Oliver stood in front of her.

"Funhouse Oliver," she murmured through a mouthful, grinning. Boy, he looked funny today. His head was like a balloon, batting around in a light breeze. "Whatcha doing here? If you've come to help with the wallpaper, I believe it's covered."

And indeed it was. Strips of the wallpaper were working themselves from the wall. Kay sighed blissfully and worked the final lump of food down her throat. "I always wanted to be in a Disney movie. Animals that clean your house, dishes that talk and are always nice and understanding. Teapots could teach people a thing or two, ya know. If we weren't too proud to listen," she admonished.

Oliver's balloon head nodded agreeably. "You have to go into the greenhouse, Kay," he warbled. His voice sounded like cheerful cardboard.

Kay smiled through her confusion. "But I'm pretty sure I don't want to."

"I know, babe. But you have to. I can't find you on the other side if you don't go in. It's the only way."

Kay's heart started to drum in her chest. Oliver *had* to find her. But she couldn't go in there alone. In the distance, a dark black shape shimmered like asphalt on a scorching day. "Oliver, please," she whispered. "Come with me, at least."

"Can't." His head bobbled in the breeze, but the look on his face was so full of sorrow, it broke her heart.

"Okay," she breathed, inhaling great gulps of air. "Okay. But you promise you'll be on the other side?"

He held up three fingers and grinned in a way that made her heart skip a beat for a whole different reason. "Scout's honor."

Kay closed her eyes, then opened them. She'd made it to the greenhouse. The door was awful and foreboding; paint peeled from unforgiving iron. Brittle glass panes were fogged with age and grime. A vine with spiny leaves twisted around the door and the latch. Kay grabbed the handle and shoved. The door made a terrible screeching noise as she pushed it open. She sagged with relief. Neve was inside, crouched atop a growing bed. "What are you doing, Neve?"

Neve didn't answer, but swiveled her head in short, jerky motions to stare at Kay. One hand was stuffed with bunches of the flowers from Greenhouse Five. Neve shoved the handful of toxic flowers in her mouth, glaring at Kay all the while.

"Neve...you shouldn't. Those are bad, okay?"

Neve responded with glowing red eyes and another fistful of poisonous plants.

Before Kay could say another word, a loud wailing began, like the tornado warning drills the city ran every few weeks but right up close. She covered her ears and looked to the sky. Jagged edges of glass rimmed a hole punched through the ceiling of the greenhouse, and a stone tower loomed overhead.

Seraphina stood on a portico at the top of the tower. Gray clouds gathered and swirled, wind picked up and rushed through the greenhouse, baying like dogs on the trail of their prey. Seraphina's hands were a visor over her eyes as she searched for something...

With a lurch in her chest, Kay realized it was *her*. She dived onto the floor and skidded beneath one of the tables like a baseball player sliding across home base. Fear snaked through her limbs.

Seraphina's voice boomed overhead. "You'll answer for your crimes, Kay! You won't leave here before you meet justice."

Kay's heart thumped wildly. *Escape.* The word repeated on a loop in her mind. *Escape. Escape. Escape.* She closed her eyes and fought for calm. Oliver...Oliver had promised to find her, but first, she had to get through the greenhouse. She peered around the leg of the table she'd ducked under. The door on the other side of the greenhouse seemed miles away.

She fixed an image of Oliver in her mind and held tight—then she rolled from under the table, gained her feet, and ran for her life. The door loomed suddenly, and Kay had no time to stop. She crashed into door, and the crack of splintering wood filled her head, and she pitched forward into an endless fall.

Falling, falling, falling...and screaming. Kay screamed until the tinge of blood coated her tongue. And then she was floating. Still falling, but softly, a gently rocking from side to side. Arms, warm and solid, came around her, holding her like a baby.

She sank into the embrace. "Oliver?"

"I promised I'd find you."

Chapter 12

Oliver ran his hand through his hair and paced. He could explain himself a thousand ways, and Kay's overprotective friends would never understand. Still, he had to try before they blew everything. "She's going to be fine," he pressed.

Neve's glare could break glass, and Seraphina's disapproval was like a fourth person in the room.

"I swear. Trust me. She's going to have a murderous headache, and she'll need to spend the next several days in bed, but she's okay. We can't call 911 unless you want whoever did this to get away with it." He crossed his arms and waited for the inevitable rebuttal.

Kay was unconscious in her bed, curled up under a mound of blankets. Sweat beaded on her face, even as she trembled with chills. They were the symptoms of coming down, and since Kay could've only ingested the super shrooms sometime that afternoon, it meant her dose had been next to nothing. A nibble at best. For average magic mushrooms, anything a gram and under was considered a light dose.

But these weren't average, and Kay's symptoms were only considered mild when compared to the users who'd taken several grams and ended up in the emergency rooms days later, still tripping their faces off. If she'd eaten more than a gram, she'd still be in the throes of wild hallucinations. Like the one she'd been experiencing when he'd arrived shortly after dinner. He kept that to himself. By the time he'd called Cappy Don, found Kay's cell phone and dialed her friends, Kay had become coherent enough to say his name before passing out. Her vitals were steady and she murmured when anyone shook her, a good sign. The captain had been the one to stop Oliver from dialing emergency services.

Neve sat on the corner of the bed and watched Kay through worried eyes. "Explain it again, Olaf."

She'd been calling him every name but his actual name since she'd shown up. He figured the obstinacy was intentional and ignored it.

"It looks like she hardly ate any of the salad, so she probably ingested less than a gram. She also ate two blueberry scones, which would've slowed the absorption, lessening the effects." He'd found the salad container on the floor at the end of the hall, flung wide and far, as if Kay had hurled it like a football. Apparently, her subconscious had picked up on the foul nature of the contents.

A muscle twitched in Seraphina's jaw. "The science isn't what concerns us. I'm fairly certain Neve wants to know why your investigation calls for denying Kay proper care. She should be in the ER right now."

Oliver rubbed his face. "The amount in that salad—" He stopped and swallowed. "Whoever did this probably expected her to eat the whole thing. Let's just say if she had, she'd be singing the Spongebob theme song in her underwear on Main Street for two days before her conscious mind kicked back on and she wound up in the hospital." Or worse. The dose could've killed someone her size. "If she's out of her mind, she can't tell us where she got the salad, right? So it makes sense that if our culprit finds out she only ate enough of the mushrooms to give her an interesting night and a hangover, he'll run. We don't want that. We want to lure the douchebag who did this into a false sense of security. We're going to set him up. Look, my team is on the way. We've got med staff coming. I promise, Kay's going to be okay."

The wait for Oliver's team was long and laden with dirty glances and unhappy sighs from Kay's two best friends. The three of them together would make a hell of a team, Oliver decided. They could fight crime with sheer intimidation.

Finally, a boom echoed through the old house from downstairs. Cappy Don didn't wait for anyone to answer but let the team inside swiftly.

Oliver left Neve and Seraphina to tend to Kay and ran down the stairs. "What the hell took you guys so long?"

Molly answered with a dirty look, and the captain spoke while directing men and women with his hands. Point and click. "Wanted to wait for cover of darkness. Whole plan goes kaput if the baddies are watching Kay's place to see what she does. We parked the van a few blocks away and all took a different route. The nurse is coming in the back. Where's the evidence?"

Oliver led Molly and Cappy Don to the end of the foyer and pointed at the scattered remains of the salad. "She must've lobbed the container down the hallway. I found her just a few feet past the front door. I noted a few garden-variety mushrooms. But I believe the ones we're looking for are the shriveled greenish-brown bits. They smell sour."

"Holy shit," Molly gushed, dropping into a crouch and snapping blue medical gloves onto her hands. From a pack at her waist she withdrew a small plastic bag and large metal tweezers. "Oli, you know what this means? We've got a sample. We can run a full DNA profile."

Oliver couldn't bring himself to return her giddy smile. The cost had almost been Kay's life. The thought made him feel cold all over. "Let's hope we can do something with the information."

Cappy Don scoffed. "You kidding? We can trace the mushrooms to their source. We'll know which plants are being spliced and diced, and we'll have means for a search warrant. Together with the e-mail Kay provided from Pattie concerning their special greenhouse, we might just be able to get in there legally."

"What's the plan here, Cap?" Oliver rubbed his hands together. He felt antsy. Something wriggled in the back of his mind, a nugget of information or the bud of a new idea unfurling, but he couldn't quite grasp it yet. He needed to cool down, rest, take some time to stew over events.

Cappy Don hitched one of his out of control eyebrows. "Kay was dropped in front of an Italian place after our meeting. When she's awake, we'll work out any kinks in the story, but the way I see it, she had some questionable puttanesca. Food poisoning. As for the salad, never touched it. We'll let our would-be executioner think his plan simply failed."

Oliver nodded. It was what he expected. From a room he hadn't explored yet, two men appeared. They wore navy carpenter pants and collared shirts, and carried small black duffle bags. Oliver breathed a sigh of relief and pointed them toward the stairs. "Medical. Finally. She's up there." Wordlessly, the duo made for the stairs.

He watched Molly carefully pluck mushrooms from the pile of lettuce and random ingredients. After several minutes, she sat back on her haunches, and whistled at the pile she'd gathered. "That's a little over two grams, says my eyeballs. I'll have the lab confirm, of course. You know the guys who were in that article you keep shoving under Kay's nose? This is about the dose they claimed to have taken. And they were big guys. Athletes. Muscled and in top shape. If Kay had—"

"I know." Oliver pinched the bridge of his nose. He'd pieced it together already. Teeny-tiny Kay wouldn't stand a chance against two grams, potentially more, of the super shrooms. "This was attempted murder."

The atmosphere turned oppressively grim as Oliver, the captain, and Molly all exchanged heavy glances, defined by a sharp edge of fear.

The slap of sandals sounded on the stairs. Oliver turned to find Neve glaring at him at the bottom of the steps. "Kay's awake. Well, kind of awake. In and out. She's calling for you."

Oliver didn't hesitate. He bounded up the stairs two at a time and slung himself into Kay's room. Seraphina stood by the doorway and gave him a wry glance as he breezed past.

"I'll give you some space." She left and closed the door behind her.

He hardly noticed. He sat on the edge of the bed and twisted toward Kay, gathering her hands in his. "Hey," he said, low and gentle. "Anybody home in there?"

Her eyelids fluttered but didn't open. "Oliver." Her voice was quiet, barely audible.

"I'm here." He pitched his voice louder. If she'd just open her eyes. "Kay, I'm right here."

A smile ghosted over her face. "You promised. Can't leave."

"Okay. Then I guess I won't." He slid off his shoes, came around the other side of the bed, and crawled in behind her. He stayed on top of the blankets in case Neve and Seraphina got the wrong idea. He wrapped his body snug against hers and tucked his arm around her, pulling her close. Her body relaxed against him. She murmured his name once again. A minute later, her soft snores were the only sounded the room.

Oliver blinked away the memory of Kay's terrified face and squeezed his eyes shut. He focused on the feel of her body in his arms, on keeping his own breathing steady. Eventually, he fell into a fitful sleep.

The next morning, Oliver left Kay sleeping and clambered down the stairs in yesterday's clothes, only to have a fresh set of pressed slacks and a dress shirt ungraciously slapped against his chest by Molly the minute he entered the kitchen. "Get dressed. You're going to work."

He gripped the clothes and frowned. "Work? I need to stay—"

"With Kay? I've got it covered." Neve's brittle voice gave away her bad mood. She stepped away from the coffee maker with two mugs, pressing one into Oliver's hand. "You have to go if we're keeping cover intact. Kay called both you and Seraphina last night about the bad puttanesca. You'll collaborate one another's stories. Anyone asks, Kay instructed you to take her calls today and bring any paperwork by her place tonight."

Molly had crossed her arms and regarded Neve. "We're not hiring, doll."

Neve's slow head turn was almost a threat all by itself. Her glare was twin daggers. "I typically disembowel people who piss me off before my first cup of coffee. You get a pass on account of you being one of the good guys, but if you ever call me doll again, I'll decorate this place with your entrails."

Molly's face registered shock. Oliver realized his own mouth was hanging open.

He closed it, swallowed, and tried to pretend he hadn't heard. "You're telling me I'm supposed to sit around the office all day?"

Molly gave him a scathing look before walking away. What the hell had *he* done? They'd both read Neve's file.

Neve cast a sigh of relief at Molly's back, then smiled wanly at Oliver. "I can't stand that woman. Listen, Obadiah, no one knows you and Seraphina have any connection. If you both claim to have talked to Kay this morning—which makes sense, because who else would she call if not her assistant and the designer working on her precious spa—no one will think to question it. Seraphina left a half hour ago. You come in and echo what she's already told the crew, blah, blah, whatever. Goddamn this weak, shitty coffee. What the hell is this stuff?" She grimaced and walked away.

Oliver sighed, downed the lukewarm coffee in his hand, and shuffled to the bathroom to change. He didn't like the plan but couldn't argue it was the right one.

He did his best to look and sound normal as he strode into Free Leaf Concepts. He smiled benignly at Brit, waved, and headed for the elevator, then remembered his part. "Hey, Brit, forward Kay's calls and messages to me today, would you? She called me this morning with a warning to avoid the Italian place down the road."

"Yeah, I know," Brit replied in a bored voice. "She called Seraphina, too. I don't like Italian, anyway. Too messy."

A few minutes later, Oliver let himself into Kay's office. Seraphina had gathered the team there. Brendan walked in seconds after. "Oh, hey guys. Seen Kay?"

Oliver and Seraphina spoke at the same time, then laughed it off awkwardly, which made it seem all the more plausible. "Brit said you'd already heard from Kay?" he mentioned innocuously.

Seraphina gave them a sad smile. "Yeah. She said she had lunch at a little Italian place and ended up going home early with an upset stomach. Bad puttanesca."

Oliver nodded. "She said something about food she had sitting out, but I don't see anything on her desk. Anyone see a salad in the breakroom fridge? I left scones, but I bet someone on the cleaning crew took care of those," he added with a smirk.

"If she left food out, they'd toss it," Jasper cut in quietly. He shrugged. "Or eat it and claim to have tossed it."

It took every ounce of Oliver's willpower to avoid studying every face in the room intently, Brendan's most of all. The supposed spy.

Brendan cleared his throat. "Oh. Well, okay. If you hear from her again, tell her I said get well soon."

"Of course," Oliver replied. "She was well enough to make a few phone calls, so—"

"And to be highly annoyed by the illness," Seraphina added.

Nice touch. "She'll be back soon, right as rain."

Brendan nodded and left. Oliver exchanged a heavy glance with Seraphina, wasted several minutes shoveling useless papers around Kay's desk, then excused himself. A force was gathering in his chest. Something had to give. Brendan's position and motives were murky, and Kay might be sleeping now, but there was no telling how coherent she'd be when she finally woke up. What if she couldn't tell them who gave her the salad? Oliver had a single hunch, and if Kay being drugged was any indication, now was the time to act on it.

He passed the elevator, and entered the stairwell. He bounded up the stairs and let himself onto the fifth floor. Brendan's office door was closed. Hopefully, he was ensconced inside. Same for Merit's and Easton's. Early morning, everyone was slowly waking up to the working day. Probably hovering over third cups of coffee and yesterday's paperwork.

Oliver steeled himself and knocked on Mr. Arnell's door.

The imposing man opened the door a crack. He peered down at Oliver, his brows forming a deep V of consternation. "Oliver...Pierce, is it? Have you got the right door, young man?"

He refused to fidget. He was out of his mind, taking his biggest risk yet. He might as well do it with some aplomb. "Absolutely. We need to talk, sir."

"Is this about a promotion? Because I don't deal with human resources. You should talk to Merit—"

"Merit is exactly who I *don't* want to talk to, but thanks." Oliver lost patience and shouldered himself into the office. Mr. Arnell gave way and closed the door behind him. Oliver continued before he lost his nerve. "I overheard you two in the stairwell. She said she'd handle everything. I need to know what that conversation was about."

"I...it's, uh, complicated, um...business things, you know." Mr. Arnell's Adam's apple bobbed in a long, nervous swallow. His eyes darted around the room, bouncing from place to place in an effort to avoid Oliver.

"You're scared." It was the last reaction he could have expected. Oliver shook his head, confused. "I don't get it. Are you in on the drug ring or not? Is Merit threatening you somehow?" He dug the small mushroom figurine from his pocket and held it out, trapped between his thumb and index finger. "Why do you have this? What's it for? A signal? A badge of some kind?" Easton's rapid blinking and guppy mouth incensed him. He slammed a fist down onto the desk. "Come on! No more games. Kay is in danger. We're running out of time to get to the bottom of this. You're either involved, or you know who is."

Or so he prayed. Cappy Don was going to pull him off the case so fast, he'd get whiplash, but as long as he came away with something, Oliver didn't care. He didn't have any more time to tiptoe around the greenhouses or play hide-and-seek with Brendan. The conversation between Merit and Easton was the only untapped lead Oliver had. He was going to squeeze it until it bled information.

Easton's gaze landed on the mushroom still poised between Oliver's fingers. "Where did you get that?"

"Oliver Pierce, special investigations. I found it in your desk."

"My niece runs a pottery shop in mid-town. We supplied her with an order of rare mushrooms for a window display, and she made this for me as a thank you gift."

"And the secret room on this floor? Start talking, Mr. Arnell. If Kay dies, you're an accessory." Her condition wasn't that bad, but Easton didn't know that.

He blanched and gritted his teeth in the first show of emotion beyond fear and confusion. "Follow me. I—I don't know if it's safe."

Oliver waited while Easton came around the desk, pulled a thin volume from the bookcase, and gave the whole thing a nudge with his shoulder. A partition fell back half a foot, far enough for Easton to push it to one side.

Oliver let his mouth pop open. "The stupid hidden room was in here the whole time I was fingering for loose panels? You've got to be kidding me."

Mr. Arnell glanced back at him. His displeasure was made plain in the straight ridge of his brow and the grim set of his mouth. "Only Merit knows. Well, and Neve Harper."

"Neve? Neve *Harper?*"

Easton beckoned him through. "She designed the room."

"Wait...*Neve* designed it? How is she involved in this?"

Easton gave Oliver a wry smile over his shoulder. "She isn't. I'm afraid you've got a few things backward, Mr. Pierce. Come inside, have a seat. I'll do my best to fill you in."

Oliver's mouth dropped open as he stepped over the threshold. The room wasn't filled with file cabinets like he'd imagined. There wasn't even a desk. "It's a bedroom."

"Apartment," Mr. Arnell corrected. "Small kitchenette in the corner. Sink, mini fridge. Couch rolls out into a bed. Behind the swinging door there's a shower stall. Fairly basic equipment, but serviceable."

"You should get to the filling me in part." Oliver sighed and set his hands on his hips. Disappointment didn't quite do his emotional state justice. "Because you're right, I definitely have some stuff backward."

* * * *

Kay dodged the hammer again. Finn was oblivious, swinging wildly. He wasn't trying to hurt her—she knew it in her bones—but all the same, each swing came close to crushing her. She ducked and rolled away a second time, slamming hard into the ground. Pain lanced through her shoulder.

Neve's voice crackled to life as if she spoke from the heavens. "Kay, you're fine. No one's after you. I'm with you."

Neve's face washed into Kay's vision like a wave splashed upon the shore, there and gone again. Half of it was cast in shadow, and in that shadow, disdain hid with razor teeth—the part of Neve that had never liked Kay, never wanted her around. Kay was too bubbly, too annoying, too childish and stupid.

She gasped at the point of a needle driving through her flesh. She looked at her legs, where the pain flared brightest. Neve had folded them over, backward and all wrong, like a bent paper doll, and was sewing Kay into a new shape. Into *her* shape.

"No, please. I'm not you. I promise, I'm not you." And then Kay had the needle, stabbing and tearing herself into Neve's form.

"Oliver." If Oliver came, she'd be okay. Oliver liked her. All of her. The small, hard parts, and the fluffy, giddy parts. Slowly, she began to unfold, and the threads binding her loosened.

"Good. Good job. Stay calm, sweetie. You're okay." Neve was back.

"Please go," Kay begged. The rejection Neve kept hidden was a physical pain in Kay's heart. Sorrow engulfed her, and her breath caught as sobs clogged her throat. Why wasn't Oliver there? "Oli..."

"Hey, hey. I'm here. I'm right here." A firm hand ensconced Kay's.

She'd waited a million years for that touch, and relief made her breathing shallow. Warmth gushed from the contact, spreading up her arms and over her body like a tender, cleansing fire. She held on for dear life. A pinpoint of light stabbed into her head and somewhere in the back of her mind, she recognized the overhead light in her bedroom.

Eyes. She was opening her eyes. She blinked and squinted, trying to turn her head away. She managed to groan, lift a hand, and point. The light was quickly extinguished. Kay tried peeling open her eyes again. They burned like pissed off ants had taken up residence in her sockets. Before she could say any of the millions of things rushing through her head, darkness swirled and she fell away.

A harsh cough jerked Kay into consciousness. Flames licked the inside of her throat. Panicked, her hands reached for her neck, but only one made it. The other was twined with another hand.

Long, thick fingers braided into hers. *Oliver.* Kay squeezed, reassured beyond all reason when he squeezed back. Movement made the bed creak, and Oliver's soft voice pierced the dark. Her eyes opened, but it stayed dark. It was nighttime, and there were no lights were on. And Oliver was with her. "You awake?"

Fragments of nightmares flashed in front of her eyes, and she blinked them away. "Yeah." Her voice came out a gravelly croak. "I need water."

Her mistake became evident when Oliver tried to leave the bed. She tugged him back as hard as her strength allowed. "Never mind. Don't go."

"I'll be quick, I promise. You need water, and not just for your throat. You've been in and out for over twenty-four hours. We had you on an IV drip yesterday, but you need to drink."

"Just wait, okay?" The nightmares were gone, but the terror was still a ball inside her chest, waiting for the slightest provocation to unfurl and take over. "I'm scared."

Oliver settled back in next to her. "You don't need to be," he murmured close to her ear. "They're hallucinations, Kay. And I'm right here."

She knew what they were. Snatches of time came back to her. Dancing wallpaper, a swimming bus, a heartbroken tree—utter madness. Humiliation swamped her. She'd never felt so unarmed and vulnerable. She closed her eyes, focused on her breathing. Fat lot of good her gun did her now. She had no defense against this kind of assault. No one did.

"I know it's not real," she said. "But the feelings are." She told him about Neve in the greenhouse, eating the plants, and Seraphina in the tower, searching for her. Then Finn, swinging a hammer, unaware that each swing nearly killed her.

Oliver was silent for a while. "So, your subconscious thinks Neve is a monster who doesn't really like you, Seraphina is judgmental, and Finn has no idea your guilt over how the relationship ended is killing you. Or trying to. And me, well, I'm a superhero."

For the first time in what seemed like years, Kay smiled. The movement felt foreign on her face, like the muscles weren't sure what to do anymore. "That's stretching it."

"I accept you, protect you. I saved you," he pointed out, a few shades shy of smug.

Her smile faded. "Yeah. You did."

"You sound pretty disappointed about that."

"No, I just...I think I should see Finn. Every weapon my own mind had against me stems from that. Neve disdains me for being weak; Seraphina thinks I'm cruel."

"And here I am, thinking you're great." Oliver shifted closer and his free hand found Kay's stomach in the dark, splaying over her. His thumb came to a rest in the hollow of her belly button. "I don't think it would serve any purpose except to reopen old wounds. Even if you tell Finn the truth, do you think it will make him feel any better about how your engagement ended?"

"Maybe not," Kay admitted wearily. "But the guilt is eating me up inside."

Oliver took a breath, poised to argue again, but Kay cut him off. She had his opinion, and she'd decide what it was worth later, when she was fully herself again.

"Tell me what's been going on," she insisted. "What have I missed?"

He snorted softly. "Nothing and everything. Seraphina and I covered for you at work. We didn't want to flush out the bad guy yet. So, we made up a story about you getting food poisoning and never eating the salad or scones that were left on your desk. We decided you would've seen them, at least, but apparently the nighttime cleaning crew tossed everything out."

"Huh." Kay chewed her lip. "Clever. Did Brendan buy it?"

Oliver cursed. "Fucking Brendan. I should've guessed. He gave you the salad?"

"Well, I didn't see him leave it on my desk, but he told me all about this great place and their great salad earlier in the day. It was living up to its reputation until I got a bite of something weird. I didn't eat much more, but by the time I got on the bus..."

She didn't want to say any more. Bad enough it had even happened. She wanted to bury the whole experience as deep as it would go into her subconscious and never speak of it again.

"We found the empty café bag. The scones might've saved your life."

Her smile returned, warm and welcome. "I guess you're a superhero, after all."

He chuckled softly and snuggled closer into her side. "For you, I'm whatever I need to be. Assistant, partner in sleuth. The scone crusader."

Hearing her own breathy laugh almost made her feel normal again. It also made her realize her breath probably smelled like a family of skunks having a bad day. She promptly closed her mouth and spoke quietly through her lips, with her head turned away from Oliver's face. "I'm a little hungry, actually. Water and plain toast sound kind of great."

Oliver's weight shifted as he scooted away and rose from the bed. "I'll be right back."

When he left, Kay inched toward the edge of the bed. She was lightheaded, and a dull headache pulsed from her temples. Ignoring it, she struggled to her feet and shuffled down the hall, to her bathroom. These old houses weren't familiar with en suites, but creating one was on her to-do list for her master retreat.

She locked the bathroom door, jacked the water to the hottest setting, and slipped under the weak stream with a slight gasp before adjusting the temperature. The steamy water sluicing over her skin was as good as a cup of coffee. Her mind shook itself from the remaining fog. Her skin tingled like it was coming to life after a long hibernation. She rolled her shoulders and stretched tired, sore neck muscles. She felt like she'd been hit by a bus.

After several minutes, her hands started to shake. She hugged herself and shivered in the hot water. She'd almost died. No, worse than that. Someone had almost killed her. If she'd kept eating the salad, ate it all...

She exhaled forcefully, pushing down panic. She let tears flow unhindered, let them mingle with the water running over her face. She couldn't afford to think that way—to get caught up in what might've happened. The hard work wasn't over until the bastard was caught. Then, Kay could fall apart and give in to her shattered sense of security.

She scrubbed her whole body with a rough bar of soap, scouring the bad memories away as if they were marks on her skin. She washed her hair twice. Wrapped in a towel, she brushed her teeth three times, flossed twice, scrubbed her tongue like it had grown hair, and spat mouthful after mouthful of Listerine. She kept at it until her mouth burned enough to make her eyes water.

She blinked at her reflection in the tiny oval mirror posted above the sink. Blotchy skin and bloodshot eyes. She was a mess. But she was a scrubbed clean mess, and that did wonders to restore her. She kicked away her dirty clothes and shuffled back to her bedroom wrapped in her fluffiest robe.

Oliver met her in the hallway. He had a tall glass of ice water in one hand and a plate of cookies in another.

"What happened to toast?"

He offered her a sweet smile. "You're out of bread. But one of the lab guys brought these. Oatmeal raisin. Think you can handle them?"

She scoffed playfully. "Now that I've showered, I can handle anything." As if on a cue, a wave of dizziness pulsed over her.

Oliver's hands were tied up, so he stepped close, offering his body for support. "Yeah, okay, tough guy. Why don't you tell me where I can dig out some comfy clothes for you while you lie back down for a while?"

Kay leaned into him. She kept her eyes closed but managed a nod. It wasn't the intense rush of vertigo she'd suffered earlier, at least. These were slow rolls of dizziness, like being on a tiny boat in rough water. A steady back and forth. Enough to upset her balance but, surprisingly, not her appetite. "Deal." She snuggled into a pile of pillows, with the cookies on her lap and the water at her side, while Oliver dug through her drawers per her instructions and explained what he'd found in Easton's office.

"The most bizarre twist in this whole affair so far. Mr. Arnell apparently suffers from agoraphobia. Leaving work or his home gives him anxiety. The two hours he's gone each day are for therapy appointments, and Merit is instrumental in his support system. Hence the conversation I overheard from Brendan's office. Anyway, Easton began missing a boatload of work when the issue got severe a few years ago, so he has a small apartment hidden behind the bookcase in his office. Neve designed the damn thing."

Kay pointed at the top drawer of her armoire, and nibbled another side from the cookie. "Would you grab the pink plaid panties? I can't do a thong right now. Is it relevant he hired Neve? She's an interior designer. Doesn't get more interior than a hidden apartment."

Oliver plucked the underwear from Kay's drawer with a triumphant smile. "This isn't weird at all," he mumbled before laying them on a nearby table and moving to the next drawer. He rooted around until he came up with an old T-shirt and added it to the pile. "No, I suppose not, but it would've been useful information to have. I knew there was a hidden room on the top floor and assumed it had something to do with the drug operation. Also, it explains why Mr. Arnell hired you. Neve recommended you. And since he knew something shady was happening in his company, he knew he could trust you." Oliver glanced at her and raised his eyebrows. "Surprised me, too. Mr. Arnell is Cappy Don's inside informant. None of this does much for my investigation except answer the question of Brendan. If he's not the inside source, then he's something much worse."

She set aside the cookie to pick up the glass of water with both hands. She was still off-kilter and a little shaky from being on her feet. The cool water felt like a dream sliding down her throat. She started to drink and couldn't stop, finally tearing away with a gasp. She blinked a few times and caught her breath. The rush of cold water brought her headache back in force, but the pain faded quickly. "Well, the more questions answered, the fewer are left to ask. Did Mr. Arnell say if he suspected anyone in particular?"

Oliver had a knack for finding the most unappealing clothes hiding in her armoire. A holey pair of hideous purple house pants she wore to paint joined the T-shirt and underwear. He carried the clothing over, sidled into bed next to her, plopped them down, and stole a cookie. "Amos. He said to take a closer look at Amos. Which makes sense. What doesn't make sense is that Easton is adamant Brendan isn't our guy. The evidence says otherwise. Besides leaving you the spiked salad, Brendan intercepted the e-mail from Pattie. Why would he do that?"

"And how?" Kay set the plate of cookies on the nightstand, out of Oliver's reach, and curled onto her side. "He needed to know an undercover operation was going on before he could deduce how to insert himself into the circle."

Oliver cleared his throat. "I should probably go. Get with the team on how we want to move forward from here."

Kay frowned. She was feeling better. But being alone still made her uneasy. "Are you sure? It's getting dark out. Sounds like a job for tomorrow morning."

He gave her a sideways glance. "I know you're still recovering. And I can stay if you want. But don't judge me if things get uncomfortable in here."

She squinted at him. "And they'd get uncomfortable because...?"

He squirmed and cleared his throat again. "Because you're curled up next to me scrubbed pink, hair still wet from the shower, and completely naked under your robe. My thoughts might be scattered, but that small fact has not escaped my notice."

A giggle burbled up from her chest. It was like an inhale of fresh, sweet air. After being terrorized by her own mind, a genuine laugh felt incredible. "I'm hardly a temptress. I probably look awful. And I feel stupid and weak." Her smile fled. She didn't trust herself to say more than that.

Oliver rolled on his side so they were facing each other. His gaze roamed over her face, his eyes green as ever, drinking her in. She marveled at his expression. He traced a line down her cheek, and his eyes steadfastly refused to meet hers. So unlike when they first met, and they couldn't seem to stop staring at one another. "You don't look awful," he murmured softly. "You look like my new favorite thing."

The same sense of safety and acceptance that had surrounded her in her dreams enveloped Kay. Of all her friends and past loves, it was this guy she hardly knew who made her feel most like herself. She acted on the impulse before she could second-guess it. Oliver's eyes opened wide, finally locking their gazes together, at her tentative kiss. Hers fell closed soon, as a new kind of heat swept through her, starting in her chest and moving through her limbs like a brush fire. By the time it hit her toes, her heart was pounding and she had Oliver's shirt caught in a firm grip.

He seemed frozen against her. She almost broke away, prepared to apologize and blame her weakened state, but it was as if a dam broke, and Oliver came to life, meeting her flame for flame. His hand slid expertly into the folds of her robe, finding her hip, guiding their bodies closer together. His lips moved against hers, teasing and exploring, gently encouraging her mouth to open to his. An explosion of want burst from her chest when his tongue slid against hers. She moaned, found his hand on her hip, and held it.

It was a bold move, but her body had a mind of its own. She was merely along for the ride. She basked in the connection she felt in the simple gesture as he squeezed her hand almost imperceptibly. Then she took hold of it firmly and moved it toward the warm, demanding center of her body. His finger glided easily inside her.

Oliver sucked in a ragged inhale, and hers hitched in her throat, and their eyes were open again, their gazes caught. His eyes were glassy with want. "You're sure?"

Kay wanted him to know how sure. She'd wanted this since they first met, and something about the way he looked at her convinced her he had, too. She pushed her robe back, exposing the curve of her hip, and rolled slowly onto her back. She opened her body up for him, and then started a leisurely swing of her hips, making love to his hand in the dimly lit room. "More than sure. Desperate."

Chapter 13

Kay cleared her raw throat delicately. "You're sure about this, Sera? I can work via videoconference. Or you can put the team onto something else. I only need a few more days and I'll be back, better than ever."

Seraphina's voice left no doubts. "Kay, the work from here is pretty standard. I'll have Guillermo get with Amos on the rest of our plants, and Jasper and I will perfect the measurements. The place will fit together like a glove."

"Jasper?" Kay frowned. "Mr. Arnell sidelined him last week. Are you sure you want to work with him?"

"Absolutely." Seraphina sounded pleased with herself. "We had a talk. I explained that even perceived racism will earn him a reputation. A reputation that his father's good friend, Mr. Arnell, will surely suffer if it were to become local gossip. Little Rock is a small town at its heart, after all."

Kay's mouth opened and closed. "You actually accused him of being racist?"

"He denied it, if that makes you feel better. Which is why I articulated *perceived* racism. Apparently, Guillermo is unaware that his current fiancée once dated Jasper, and Jasper is a little miffed by the timing of their relationship. There may have been a little overlap. But again, Guillermo remains in the dark, as I think is best. Jasper was pretty horrified to learn you think he's racist. Doesn't solve the problem, but clears the air somewhat."

"Jesus, Seraphina, what did you do, open a confessional booth?"

"People want to be understood, Kay. Sometimes it's as simple as asking and listening."

Chastised and annoyed, Kay huffed and burrowed down into her mound of blankets like a sullen child. "Maybe we can keep you on retainer for therapeutic services."

"If it helps."

Wise-ass. Kay rolled her eyes, then smiled despite herself. "I know I sound irritated, but in truth I'm immensely grateful. It's strange how exhausting just laying here can be. And you wouldn't believe the nightmares I've been having. Finn keeps showing up. And you and Neve, Oliver and—"

"You're dreaming about Finn?"

"No. I'm nightmaring about Finn."

"Hm. Not sure there's much of a difference." Seraphina's voice was laced with concern. "Are you sure you shouldn't go see him? Not for his sake, but for your own. Clear the air. Get whatever is weighing you down off your chest before you suffocate."

Kay bit her lip. "I guess having nightmares about the guy is a pretty good sign I've got some baggage."

"Well, you have some time to think about it. Maybe talk with Oliver. I hear he's taken to personally overseeing your well-being?"

She couldn't very well admit Oliver was the only person she could stand to be around. Seraphina was as much a part of her bad dreams as Finn. Unresolved issues abounded, apparently. But maybe Seraphina was right about this. "We'll see. Thanks, Sera. And good luck with Jasper. I hope you get more out of him than I have so far."

* * * *

Images of Kay's porcelain skin sheened with sweat assaulted Oliver. He shook his head and tried to focus on Cappy Don's spiel, but his brain didn't seem to want to cooperate. Instead, he shifted uncomfortably in his chair, struggling with memories of Kay's mouth open in sighs of pleasure, her arms clinging to his body as if he alone in all the universe could save her, and her eyes soft and silently begging for his touch.

Hazel. Her eyes were hazel. A dark ring of deep brown circled her pupil, surrounded by a wider circle of blue. So many mysteries unlocked last night. Leaving to go to work this morning had been torture, disengaging his body from hers when all he'd wanted to do was burrow in deeper and never leave her side.

Cappy Don clearing his throat was like a jet engine roaring to life in Oliver's ear. "You with us, Pierce?"

"Yeah, sorry. Lot going on. So, you're sure this is the right call?" If they blew the whistle now, they were limiting themselves, drawing a hard line in the sand. "We're after more than the players inside Free Leaf Concepts."

The captain looked tired as he leveled a glare at Oliver. "We have a handful of bad options. Wait for our research team to dig up Amos's life story, wait for the lab to come back with the names of some plants, wait for someone in a cape and tights with an awkwardly large bulge to swoop in and serve up the bad guys on a platter. Or we can break cover and let Free Leaf know we're circling. Shake the tree, see what falls out. We're close. Perfect position to have something to offer a whistleblower."

Oliver nodded but he didn't like the plan. An entire year, he'd patiently waited for the perfect evidence and timing to make their move. "What if we get nothing out of making our move now?"

Molly shifted in Oliver's recliner, uncrossing her legs to cross them again. "It's a possibility." She offered Oliver no more than a one-shoulder shrug. She was all business today. "But at the end of the day, a major artery begins and ends at Free Leaf Concepts. It's an important cog in the machine, and busting it up leaves them vulnerable. Really, Oli, our best hope has always been finding an inside guy and hoping he'll talk. If we crack down now, they'll have to assume we've collected enough evidence to justify our confidence. Obviously, we'll keep our street team in play."

The street team had been trying to weasel into the ranks from the ground up to no avail. Oliver didn't put much stock in their efforts.

The captain waved his hand impatiently. "I can read your face, Pierce. But that angle hasn't been a total loss. Those guys are in the best position to report which movers and shakers start scrambling once we crack open Free Leaf." He leaned forward and slapped Oliver awkwardly on the back. "You did good in there, kid. You took some risks I didn't exactly approve of, but I can't argue with your results. Never could."

"Even if we don't pin these guys now, Oli, I doubt the Jonesboro PD will hesitate to reinstate you. You can go home, put your life back together."

Oliver cocked his head and studied Molly. "My life is more together now than it has been in years. And no, I can't mosey on home while these super shrooms are still out on the streets, killing people. Almost killing people," he added, with some heat. "Kay nearly died. Or have we forgotten already?"

"No one has forgotten what happened to Kay. It was yesterday, for crying out loud." The low growl in Cappy Don's voice swiftly put Oliver in his place. It had been a shitty thing to say.

He sat back with a huff, still impatient and unsure, but accepting the call wasn't his to make. "You want to go in head-on, I'm game. I'll conduct the interviews, do whatever you need me to do, but I'm not going anywhere until this thing is wrapped up, from top to bottom. Just tell me what comes next."

Molly sat forward, leaning her elbows on her knees. "Wait until Kay is better. We think the interrogations will be more effective if the employees know you were acting with a partner, as well as in conjunction with Mr. Arnell. The more eyes they think have been watching them, the more evidence they'll have to assume we've got. I've already instructed one of my guys to forgo the interview with Brendan's mom—" Her phone, balanced on the chair's armrest, pinged. She picked it up immediately. Her brow creased. "Well, shit. We've already got a connection."

Cappy Don scratched his cheek. "Love when it rains. What is it?"

She laughed softly. "The kind of report I love. Now, Amos has a degree in Microbiology from UA. We already knew that." She wiggled her phone and raised her eyebrows at the two of them. "The funny thing is this report is from the contact I sent out to interview Brendan Berkley's college roommate. Amos may have finished his education at University of Arkansas, but he started at Georgia Tech, where Brendan was educated. He doesn't list it on job applications, or we'd have found this in his personnel files at Free Leaf. Curious thing to leave off your résumé, right? Anyway, care to guess who Brendan's old dorm mate says was his lab partner? One Amos Winston. It gets better. Before Amos jumped ship, they were studying the effects of increasing global temperatures on certain types of fungal growth."

Oliver grinned. "Mycology. Now, we're getting somewhere." He glanced at the captain. "Did Mr. Arnell ever mention their connection? Did he even know?"

Cappy Don shook his head. A thunderous expression clouded his face. "It would've been a hell of a lead if he had. We'd have looked a lot harder at this Amos fellow."

"We did look hard at him," Molly returned defensively. "He practically runs the lab at Free Leaf Concepts singlehandedly. But a few classes at Georgia Tech that aren't on his official transcripts would be next to impossible to track down. It's like he transferred to University of Arkansas with an empty record. Doesn't make sense. The only red flag was the timing, but not everyone goes straight to college. Nothing all that strange about a late start. I figured he took a few years off, went backpacking through Europe."

"I would've made the same assumption," Cappy Don admitted wearily. "Curious thing. Maybe something happened at Georgia Tech?"

Oliver relaxed for the first time since the captain and Molly had showed up on his doorstep. "Right about now, a point-blank interview is looking pretty damn good, actually." He was about to ask when they planned on ousting themselves when his cell rang in his pocket. He fished it out. Something about Neve Harper's number popping up on the screen sent a coil of unease snaking through his gut.

He left his chair with an apologetic wave to his team and stepped away to take the call. "Neve. How was our patient today?"

"She was alternately hungry, nauseous, hot, cold, tired, restless, sleepy, and anxious. Her doctor gave her the clear this morning but suggested she stay in bed one more day to catch up on solid sleep."

"Sleep is a good idea. She's probably exhausted. I'm headed there soon. Just about done wrapping up a meeting with my team. Has Seraphina checked in? She was still working with Jasper and Guillermo when I left the office."

"Still there according to Seraphina's last text. They're in overdrive without Kay." Neve paused and sighed heavily. "Shit. You were the last place I could think to check. I should've known something was up when Kay said she thought sleeping all day was a great idea. What a crock."

Oliver froze. "Say what now?"

Another heavy sigh. "Well, she's not at the office, which I thought was a pretty promising guess. That's where I'd have gone. She's not at her parents', whom I wished now I wouldn't have called, because they're ready to file a missing person report, and she isn't with you. Where else would Kay go?"

Oliver began pacing, wracking his brain. He should've texted her more today. He should've gone by at lunch instead of spying on Brendan. He turned at a tap on his shoulder.

Cappy Don held his old cell phone aloft, with the mouthpiece covered, and bobbed his head toward the front door. Oliver nodded his understanding. Must be someone important if he had to step out to take the call.

Oliver chewed his lip. "We have eyes on Brendan, and we'll hear if he's seen with her. Neve, I know this is going to sound stupid, but Kay isn't someone who goes off half-cocked. Know what I mean? Maybe she just needed to get out of the house for a few hours."

"Yeah, maybe." Neve didn't sound convinced, but she perked up. "You're right, you know. Kay's the equivalent of a well-spoken toddler sometimes, but her head is screwed on pretty damn straight."

"She hasn't left the house since she was drugged," Oliver stressed, as much to put himself at ease as Neve.

Neve was silent for a beat. "Okay, Owen. I'm with you. Here's the rub, though. Duke called. There's some kind of emergency with Hannah—that's his dog—and he needs me. He sounded bad on the phone. I can't leave him hanging, especially if something has happened to Hannah. That leaves you and Seraphina to keep an eye on Kay. I guess we can give her the day. Doc said she's fine. But if no one has heard from her by morning, your captain better step up."

Oliver relaxed. If Neve had pressed, he wouldn't have felt comfortable letting it go at that. He hoped they were both right. "Cappy Don won't wait forty-eight hours to look into Kay's dropping off the map, I assure you. He couldn't stop me from looking for her if he tried. There were still a few lab techs in the house when I left. I'm assuming someone would've mentioned if she'd been forced out the door, right?"

"Two lab guys. One swabbing the floorboards, another fiddling with some equipment in the kitchen. They both said she was freshly showered and in a chipper mood when she waved on her way out this afternoon. Said she'd be back soon. They've since cleared out, so there's no one to tell us when, or if, Kay returns."

Oliver rubbed his chin. "I'll stay there tonight, then. In case." He'd also send officers to canvas the neighborhood and try to track Kay's movements. Someone should've seen her get in a cab or a bus.

"Again?" Neve murmured, a smile evident in her voice. "I knew she liked you. We should've bet on it. I love winning."

His pulse kicked up a notch. If Kay was already discussing him with her friends, well, that had to mean things were pretty serious, right?

Even in the midst of an identity crisis, she had a way of lighting up every moment she inhabited. He wanted to live in those moments with her indefinitely. Last night, an insecure part of himself wouldn't let go of the possibility that the sex had been a means to an end for Kay—a healing act, a distraction. But maybe not.

The thought filled him with a completely foreign mix of anticipation, giddy excitement, and bone-deep dread. That way lies rejection. A caveman living inside him wanted to go the clubbing route, drag her back to his cave. The sane, modern part of him demanded a meeting of minds; if she didn't feel the same about him, he wouldn't force the issue.

No, that was a lie. He'd force it, at least a little. "I better go, Neve. I'm in a meeting..." He gave Molly a dubious look. "Kind of. Afterward, I'll head to Kay's. I'll be there when she gets back."

"Peachy. And I'll call Seraphina, let her know the two of you are sharing babysitting duty the next few days. The timing is crap, but Duke loves his dog more than he loves me, so that should give you some idea of how important this is. And you're right about Kay. She's smart, and I trust her, but have a care, because an attack like the one she suffered has a way of leaving a mark. When she does come back, do me a favor and don't mention Hannah. In case it's nothing, I don't want her to worry. She's got enough on her plate."

Oliver ended the call and turned around at the same time Cappy Don reentered his apartment.

The old man's eyes were alert and his shoulders rigid. Things were in motion. He hitched his chin at Oliver. "Plainclothes are taking Amos Winston for questioning now. Discreetly. He'll be held in Mr. Arnell's office until we get to Free Leaf Concepts. Lab sent a text over while I was on the line. Some plants you two had tested?" His gaze swung between Molly and Oliver. "They're still mapping the DNA sequence of the super shrooms, but they tested your samples first, hoping to fast track the process, and can confirm that neither are a match."

Oliver groaned. "Kay's mystery flower. Has to be. Kay questioned Amos once already. Maybe he'll be a little more forthcoming with a detective."

"Let's hope," Molly said, rising. "Because if we're breaking the skin on our undercover operation, we're about to tip off the whole organization that we're onto them. We better have the right guy, or it's for nothing."

"Speaking of right guys, why don't we take Brendan now, too?"

Cappy Don held the door open and motioned for them to get moving. "Because we've got more to connect Amos. The idea is he gives us enough to make an arrest when we move on Brendan. I want to question that guy behind a mirrored wall."

It was just another day at Free Leaf Concepts, as far as anyone working there knew—besides Amos, of course—so Oliver and his team, plus two uniformed officers, took the stairs up to Mr. Arnell's office. Oliver noted Cappy Don's labored breathing by the time they reached the fourth landing. The price of promotion.

Amos and Mr. Arnell were waiting in strained silence when they arrived. Easton appeared distinctly uncomfortable and lingered near the plainclothes officer standing on guard by the door, while Amos perched on a stool near the drafting table.

Oliver nodded to Cappy Don. "Give me five minutes with him."

The captain nodded. A single uniformed officer remained after everyone else cleared out. Oliver rolled his shoulders, relaxed his frame as if he were meeting a colleague for a chat over tea, and joined Amos at the table. All of Easton's work had been stored away. Oliver wondered if he were concerned with proprietary issues or simply shy of his work.

Amos had his lips pressed together, his eyebrows raised high in a perpetual expression of surprise. Oliver scanned his features, searching for nervous tics and other signs of distress. There were none. Whatever

Amos may be, scared wasn't one of them, although he seemed slightly uneasy. He'd probably never been escorted from his labs by a member of the LRPD before.

Oliver smiled benignly. "Interesting work you do, Mr. Winston."

"That right, Mr. Pierce? We misters now, that's strange. Best you tell me what this is all about. I plan on having a picture-perfect salon design waiting for Kay when she gets back. That's a lot of work."

"It is," Oliver agreed, nodding sincerely. "For now, we just need to ask you some questions about your old lab partner from Georgia Tech."

Amos sat back in his chair easily. He was either genuinely unconcerned or a mastermind of body language. "Brendan Berkley? He works here, you know. Ask him anything you want yourself." His black eyes trailed a curious path over Oliver. "Always knew there was something about you. You a little too smart for that dumb job you got. Should've figured."

"I'm flattered. But all the same, your answers would mean a lot to me, Amos. We know you scrubbed your Georgia Tech classes from your transcripts and résumé. Can you tell me a little more about that?"

"Yeah. I suppose I could." Amos nodded and relaxed even further. He gazed around the room, squinting and nodding as he recalled the details and spoke them without hesitation. "See, I had trouble with a girl. The kind that a man can't properly defend himself against. She wanted me, I didn't want her. She made up some bad stuff. Couldn't be proved, lab tests were inconclusive, so I think she had a friend inside, because rightly done, those tests should've cleared me. A man might assume they weren't rightly done, feel me? I laid my assumptions out for the dean, and we came to an understanding. I left the school, got a fresh start with University of Arkansas." He stopped and folded his hands neatly. "There you go."

Oliver didn't pause. "Brendan's roommate tipped us off to your connection. Old lab partners. What did you study?"

"Mycology, mostly."

It surprised Oliver how quickly Amos dropped the term. He scratched his chin. "Kay sent you to Capital Acres not long ago. She had questions about some plants. Three of them, one she couldn't identify."

He scoffed. "None she could identify, you mean." He wagged his finger at Oliver. "Now, that makes a man nervous, but sometimes you got to educate your boss. Kay's a good boss; she took it on the chin. But she ought to have known the plants she was asking about were toxic. I went looking for the other plant she described, but Pattie told me she didn't have nothing like that, and certainly not growing with other toxic stuff. I figured Kay must've got confused. I know she ain't what her résumé said she is."

"Can you tell me how she described the plant? Could you identify it if you were given open access to all the greenhouses at Capital Acres?"

Now that they were working out loud, so to speak, Oliver didn't doubt Cappy Don's next move would be to get Mr. Arnell's blessing to do a full search of the greenhouses. No more tripping over themselves trying to find probable cause. It was frustrating to know they'd had the director of the company in their pocket all along. He could've given them access to Capital Acres anytime. But then, Oliver was forced to admit, he couldn't have done so without tipping his hand.

Amos finally grew restless, sitting up suddenly and giving Oliver a pointed stare. "Look, man, what is all this? You a cop, I got that, so this must be some deep shit I'm wading through. You want my life history, or you want some real answers? I got nothing to hide." He lifted his hands in surrender and waited like an impatient teacher for Oliver to make his next move.

Oliver blew out a sigh. He tapped the drafting table and glared at Amos. "Someone working at Free Leaf Concepts is using the company's facilities and resources to create genetically modified psychedelics, drugs still being tweaked and perfected. Drugs that have killed people and landed many, many more in hospital emergency rooms. You can see why you and Brendan having a secret connection related to your study into fungus, of all things, might make law enforcement a tad curious."

Amos sat up slowly, shaking his head, palms still out as if to hold back a tide. His body language was genuine.

Oliver felt a thin tendril of panic lace through him. Amos didn't exhibit the signs of a man with something to hide. He appeared concerned, and slightly more nervous now he realized he was obviously a person of interest, but no more so than was understandable.

"This ain't me, man. I don't make drugs. I studied fungus for a short while, but Brendan and I, we moved on pretty quick. There's more interesting plants to pick apart. Besides, I mentioned that I'd studied mycology to Kay ages ago. I wouldn't throw that out off the cuff if I wanted to hide it. It just ain't relevant, that's all. Nobody looking for some high-end landscaping job wants fungus in their flowerbeds. I mean, there was one time Mr. Arnell's niece wanted some weird stuff for a window display, but—"

"Brendan," Oliver reminded him sharply. "You and Brendan. What else did you two study?"

"Man, that's it! I swear. I was studying orchidology by the time I transferred. I didn't know till years later that Brendan moved out here. As for us knowing each other, hell, wasn't no secret. Brit was there, too, sometimes. She mostly took notes, and later I heard she dropped out of her degree program. Three of us caught up after Free Leaf took her on, but seeing as we didn't hang on the regular, there wasn't much to say. It didn't cross my mind to put out a memo that we all knew each other in college. It's a small world for people in certain circles. Ain't like the city is swarming with people who studied plant biology. Makes sense to me she ended up working here, same as Brendan and myself. That's it. That's the whole truth, nothing but the truth, so help me God."

"Why didn't Brit or Brendan complete their degree programs?"

"Brit, I don't know. Honest, I didn't know her that well. Still don't. But Brendan earned a degree, just not one Free Leaf Concepts is interested in. He got himself a bachelor's in pharmaceutical science."

A quiet calm descended over Oliver as information slid into place.

Brit Lars, the front desk receptionist. The only employee besides Brendan Berkley, with his strategically placed office, who would know every time Mr. Arnell left the building via the stairs. She also had access to e-mails, memos, and messages between employees. Of course she did. It was her job to ensure their delivery. She was a failsafe messenger.

Oliver stood so swiftly, the stool nearly fell over beneath him. "Thanks, Amos. I have to run. You're clear, by the way."

In the hallway outside Mr. Arnell's office, tension was thick in the air around the group waiting on Oliver's findings. He grasped Cappy Don's shoulder. "Amos Winston is clean. I know who we want. I can't prove it yet, though. Someone find me Brendan Berkley. I need to speak to him immediately."

* * * *

Kay hated the white canvas tennis shoes. Hated them like she'd hated nothing else for a very long time.

Funny, the things a person could forget. Like how when it rained up in the mountains, the mud could get ankle-deep. Unlike in the city, there was not a network of concrete pathways and drains, making it possible to keep one's feet relatively dry in a downpour.

Easy to forget, also, that a pair of white—of all colors in the world—canvas tennis shoes were as good as no shoes at all when muddy water seeped through the fabric. Kay's feet were wet and cold, her heart colder still. Cold and bruised.

At his core, Finn wasn't the kind of man who let things go. But when he finally released something, he did so thoroughly. Kay was irrevocably one of those things. Finn hadn't just let go. He'd flung her to the other side of the moon.

She'd arrived in Red Hill yesterday, got herself a room at the quaint inn on the main drag, and shored up her courage with the mini bar and bad television through the night.

This morning, she'd dressed and explored the town, asking questions until she knew exactly when and where to find Finn Welk. He'd been at the bar just after three, as promised by the barber. Molly had been right about him.

Kay knew from the palpable unease inside the establishment the moment she walked inside that every single patron knew exactly who she was, and what had happened between her and Finn. He'd drunkenly told the tale a hundred times to the same crowd. Their hostility had forced her to ask Finn to leave with her. Probably the biggest mistake she'd made, outside of leaving Little Rock without telling anyone where she was going yesterday. Since he'd still been sober, Finn offered to drive while she talked. A ride would keep his head clear, he'd claimed. So they'd ridden down rutted dirt roads and old country lanes while Kay did her best to explain why, exactly, she'd allowed their relationship to end as it had.

When she was done talking, Finn had stopped the truck, asked Kay to step out, and then peeled away, leaving her stranded on a muddy backroad in the middle of nowhere and a storm cloud bearing down, with only a vague sense of which way was which.

For the first hour of walking, she'd cried.

She was done crying now. She was all cried out. An empty tank. A shell, really. She felt hollow and exhausted. Still, she trudged on, one step in front of the other, hoping a sign would pop up and give her an idea of how far she was from town. Or from somewhere. Anywhere. A farmhouse, a ranch, a cabin.

At least Finn had exacted some degree of revenge. Being left stranded in a storm on a dirt mountain road assuaged her guilt somewhat. And helped put it in perspective. Perhaps some things were best left secrets.

Her anger fascinated her. Maybe in the grand scheme of things, Finn deserved a little payback. Maybe the truth had caused him more pain than the lie. But every time Kay imagined Oliver in Finn's shoes, she knew without a doubt he'd never have taken his revenge this way. Or at all.

She cried out when a half bar sprung to life on her cell phone. She quickly dialed Neve. Neve would get in touch with Cherish Rancourt. Cherish was a member of the Red Hill Historical Society. She had lived in Red Hill all her life. If anyone could find Kay from a vague description of the turns Finn had taken, it was Cherish. Or her son, Krandall. Neve's phone went straight to voicemail. So did Duke's. Kay bit her lip. With Seraphina filling in for her at Free Leaf, she only had one person left to call.

Oliver answered out of breath. "Kay! Your parents are ready to call the police and report you missing. Neve and I agreed we'd give you twenty-four hours, but I've been worried as hell. Where are you?"

Kay scanned the trees overhead. Steely gray clouds were crowding together and threatening more rain. "I'd sure love to know. Listen, you need to make a call for me. High Mountain Ranch in Red Hill. I'm in the middle of nowhere, running on a half bar. I have no way to look up the number or I'd call myself. Ask for Cherish, but Krandall or Miles will do. I need them to look for me."

"Wait..." The line crackled. "...know...where you are?"

"You're breaking up. Just listen. I passed an ancient road marker maybe a half mile back. White square with an undiscernible number. I think I'm headed west. The road is predominantly straight, mostly rutted, but shored up recently where creeks run underneath. I can't be more than twenty minutes out from Red Hill. Remember, you want Cherish, Krandall, or—"

The phone beeped in her ear as the call was dropped. Shit. If Oliver caught at least half of her description, she might be found before dark. And since she'd given a location, she now had to remain in the same spot. She searched for a tree stump near the road and settled in for a tedious, tortuous wait. If no one came for her, it was going to be a long night.

An hour passed before she heard the rumble of an engine. She was dizzy with relief at the sight of Krandall Beels behind the wheel of his old pick-up.

He reached across and helped her wrench open the passenger door. He had a towel down on the seat already, and offered another once she was settled. She'd managed to fling mud all over her clothes from stomping down the lane. "Your friend, Oliver, he'll be in Red Hill by the time we get back to town. Less you wanna come stay out at the ranch?"

"I have a room downtown, but I appreciate the offer." She needed cell service, which was spotty out at the ranch. "I can't thank you enough for coming to find me, Krandall. How on earth did you get here so fast?"

He grunted, a customary response. "Finn told anyone who'd listen what he done. Big joke, he says. People 'round here know you, Miss Bing. Didn't take long for someone to hear word and give my mama a ring. She radioed your friend's details as I was headed out. Thanks to Finn's big mouth, I already had a good idea. I coulda told ya not to give the Welk boy no more of your mind."

She sighed and carefully removed her shoes. The sky was darkening with twilight, and suddenly she didn't want anything more than a soft bed and white noise. "Thanks again, Krandall."

Krandall waved away her offer of gas money, then more adamantly refused her offer to renovate any room at the ranch, free of charge. He answered her thanks with a series of grunts and left her at the inn's front entrance.

Oliver was waiting in her room. He sat on the far side of the single king-sized bed, his hands clasped together in his lap, and a perfectly blank expression on his handsome face. She didn't bother to ask how a detective got inside without her key. Probably flashed his badge at the receptionist. These small towns had some seriously lax security.

Kay threw her ruined sneakers on the floor. "You found me."

"Yeah." He smiled humorlessly. "Also solved a case and made an arrest. We still don't know who's behind the bigger scheme, but we put a serious dent in their operations."

"Oh, my God, really? That's amazing! Was it Brendan? Did he confess?"

Oliver pressed his lips together and studied Kay with an unnervingly direct gaze. "You'd know if you were there."

"Well, I wasn't." Her response was clipped.

Oliver was angry. She'd known he would be.

"I'm sorry, okay? I shouldn't have left without letting someone know I was okay. I thought if the guys in lab coats saw me leave on my own, they could tell you I was fine."

He cocked his head to the side. "You think I'm mad because you left? I trust you to know what you're about, Kay. I was worried, yeah. We all were. But we also all agreed you can handle yourself. Checking in would've been considerate of you, but that's not why I'm mad. I'm mad because you came here. Because you saw Finn. Because you kept it from me, like there was a need for secrecy. We made a pact, remember? No lies."

He zeroed in on her motives with stunning clarity. Once again, she had to remind herself that he was a detective. She should've known keeping a secret from him would be next to impossible.

"I didn't lie," she pointed out calmly. "This was personal. It didn't have anything to do with you."

"If that's true, you'd have let me know." His green eyes were piercing. "And the fact is that I want this. Desperately. But I don't want to be the next Finn. If you don't think you can talk to me, then I have to put some space between us before this goes any further. I can't keep falling unless I know you're gonna catch me."

Kay let out a breathy laugh, but her nerves kicked into high gear. Somehow, this thing with Oliver had become very real, very fast, and if he let her go now...the thought squeezed the air from her lungs. She moved around the bed, flung her purse onto the quilt, and sat down next to Oliver. "You didn't ask for full disclosure."

He offered her a grim smile. "Yeah, well, I need it, I guess. Me and you, Kay, we're all or nothing. I need to be in on the tough calls."

"You were, remember? You made your feelings about me reaching out to Finn pretty clear. I did what I felt I had to do."

He shook his head, still staring at her. "You don't get it, Kay. Forget my feelings. I don't need your protection. I just need the truth. Always. You could've told me to go screw myself. If my options were fuck off or support you, I'd have had your back today, and Finn couldn't have left you stranded in the middle of nowhere. I'd have been here, with you. Holding your hand or waiting in the car, whatever you wanted. Give me a chance before you decide I'm going to let you down."

Kay swallowed past a lump in her throat. "Why do you care so much?"

His features finally softened, and a slight smile lifted the corners of his mouth. He raised a hand and ran his thumb along her chin, below her lips. "Because I'm in love with you. Crazy about every inch of you. Even if I didn't want you giving Finn any ideas about a reunion, I can't help but admire that you come at everything—your job, your ex, a pain in the ass assistant—head on. You're fearless, and I love it. I love you."

She felt them before she understood them. Warm tears made slow tracks over the apples of her cheeks. She brushed them away, then reached for Oliver. She took his face into her hands and moved closer, practically into his lap. "I'm not fearless at all. For instance, this scares the hell out of me. Because I love you, too, and it happened so fast, I'm not sure when or how I fell."

He smiled, and Kay's whole chest grew tight in a grip of fierce happiness. His arms circled her, and he kissed her. "Must've been something in the air."

Chapter 14

The drive back to Little Rock the next morning was strange in the very best way. Oliver floated on a cloud, so new and delicate he was afraid to move lest it break apart and he fall to his doom. For now, he had one hand on the wheel, and the other gripped by Kay, who sat in the passenger seat and chewed over the final developments in the case. The captain had called and relayed events Oliver missed last night, after he'd handed the reins of the interrogations over to the captain so he could run off and rescue Kay.

"Brit Lars. I never thought twice about the secretary," she said quietly, gazing out the window.

"No one ever does," he agreed. "But it made sense. Throughout history, servants and waitstaff have made perfect spies. They could be counted on to need the money, and had free access to important people and places. If you could get one's doorman or groomsman in your pocket, you were as good as a member of the household. What irks me is how I applied the reasoning to Brendan without also giving Brit the same scrutiny."

"Yeah, but she didn't have top floor access."

"Only she did," Oliver pointed out wryly, suffering the weight of disappointment all over again. He'd made a gross assumption, because he'd never personally seen Brit anywhere past the fourth floor. "She had access to every nook and cranny of that place, including digital accounts, calendars, e-mails, and messages."

"Right." Kay clucked her tongue. "Explain to me again how Brendan isn't in on it. He intercepted that e-mail from Pattie and left the salad at my desk. Can we prove he wasn't working with Brit?"

Oliver squeezed her hand. "I know the justice system annoys you, but he doesn't have to prove his innocence. And for now, we're unable to prove his

guilt. He's got an answer for everything. He claims Brit took possession of
the salad he brought for you and offered to leave it on your desk. Could be
she's corroborating his story to keep him out of jail, if they were working
together. Or it's simply the truth. He was picked up on security feed in the
parking garage, and the timing fits as well as anyone can assume. Everyone
has been working so hard on the salon project, they've been glued to their
work stations. No one was really paying attention to who came and went
from your office.

"Brendan has access to a wealth of information, thanks to Mr. Arnell's
insistence on taking the stairs. Without realizing they were being overheard,
Merit and Easton discussed many things, including Easton's utter certainty
that his greenhouses were being used for illicit activity. Brendan claims
he wanted to break the case himself. That meant inserting himself into a
partnership with you, once he deduced you must be the inside investigator
based on the e-mail Pattie sent Merit. He assumed I was merely following
your instructions, since I'd never ventured to do anything so reckless before."

"Huh."

Oliver shrugged and shook his head. He wasn't sure how he felt about
the story himself. Brendan was cool as a cucumber, as difficult to read
as they came. Besides that, he lawyered up, wrote his statement, and was
released without sufficient evidence to hold him. Oliver couldn't do much
without being charged with harassment, and he couldn't risk that kind of
damaging mark ending up in their official file. When it came time to bring
charges on everyone involved in the drug ring, they needed a squeaky-
clean, airtight case.

"Brendan is a big, fat question mark if I ever saw one. Amos told us
about his pharmaceutical science degree, but Brendan claims he left the
credentials off his résumé because the field of study was irrelevant to his
position at Free Leaf Concepts."

Kay swung a perplexed gaze his way, which he caught from the corner
of his eye. "Are you kidding me? You tracked down my ex-fiancé, dug up
the reason our engagement went bust, but you guys didn't know Brendan
was a pharmaceutical major?"

Oliver's jaw clamped. "Believe me, we asked ourselves the same question.
Turns out, Molly knew but decided the info was irrelevant since he never
pursued work in the field, and has no employment history with any
pharmaceutical company. Brendan might be untouchable now, but if he's
got so much as a pinky toe involved in this thing, I'm going to find out.
And I'm going to bring him down."

Kay was silent for a beat. "There's something...a pattern of some kind. I know it's there, but I can't quite see it. Probably nothing." She sighed. "What will happen to Pattie? Brit rolled on her like it was nothing?"

"Gave her up instantly. It was Pattie's idea to engineer the break in they had several months ago. They stole Tallulah's plant to stage it as a robbery by a rival company. The purpose wasn't to take something from Capital Acres, however, but to bring supplies in. Pattie's plan had the added benefit of the company beefing up security afterward, which helped further protect their setup."

"What about their lab?" Kay demanded. Oliver smiled. She sounded like a real investigator. "If Amos isn't part of their little dream team, then they have their own lab somewhere."

"Amos was intended to be a patsy. Almost worked, too. He was in an ideal position to attract suspicion."

"That's another strange development. Something seems off, but I can't put my finger on what."

Oliver shrugged. They were still working through the network of connections. "They wouldn't want to consolidate their operation in one place. There's a lab somewhere. Maybe we can get Brit to give up the location."

Kay hummed thoughtfully. "So, what now?"

"Well, the latest batch of mushrooms has been taken as evidence. We severely crippled the supply line since we crashed Capital Acres immediately following Brit's arrest. Found the plants you mentioned, with Amos's help. He also identified our mystery flower, based on your vague description. African dream plant. Lab is testing it against our sample of the super shrooms now, but I'd bet my favorite socks they'll get a match. Passing off the hallucinogenic plant they were splicing to create the super shrooms as a rare oriental decorative was relatively easy, and didn't undergo any hard scrutiny from Rowan—the only person who might've identified it for what it was."

Kay groaned and threw her head back, bouncing it against the headrest. "African dream plant? Damn, I wasn't even close! I have some serious homework to do. Amos was right, you know. He saw through my wannabe Neve act pretty easily. I'm in way over my head. I'm really glad he had nothing to do with any of this. I would've been screwed. I'm going to need him if I'm going to pull off this spa we're working on." Her free hand covered her eyes. "I'm scared to go back to Free Leaf. I trust Seraphina, but what did I leave her to work with? Two designers who can't stop fighting long enough to get anything done, and a diva botanist. Do you think Easton would blame me if I asked the Sweetclover proprietors for an extension? Could *anyone* blame me, really?"

Oliver waited until she stopped for breath to interrupt. "Actually, you've got a few surprises waiting for you back at the office. We should be there within the hour."

True to his best guess, they arrived a little over forty minutes later.

The atmosphere on the fourth floor was one of somber industriousness. Heads down, hands busy, low murmurs passed between colleagues as if they were at a funeral. Oliver was dismayed by Kay's troubled frown. Hopefully, Seraphina's surprise would do something to right it.

Kay managed a smile for her team as their heads popped up from the drafting table, one by one. They met her with slow grins of their own and a few exchanged glances.

Only Amos was missing. He'd been given the day off after undergoing another round of vigorous questioning and a polygraph at the local precinct. Guillermo crossed his arms and pursed his lips, but glee was evident in his dark eyes. Even Jasper was there, a black marker in hand, hovering over their plans.

Seraphina rushed over and gripped Kay's hands excitedly. "You must be worried sick about Sweetclover. But I think you'll be pleased with what your team has wrangled together in your absence." She pulled Kay toward the drafting table.

"Wrangled together?" Jasper repeated in a dry tone. "I'd say it was a more meticulous effort than that."

Kay gave him a quizzical stare. He shrugged. Seraphina stepped between them and dropped Kay's hands to grip her shoulder. "Despite a rocky start, Jasper has been instrumental in helping me get up to speed. You've got a talented team, Kay."

She didn't seem convinced. She still watched Jasper like a bird of prey deciding if he were a meal worth the effort. "Is that right?"

It was Guillermo who spoke up. "*Sí, mi amigo y yo*, we come to an agreement." He grinned and slapped Jasper on the back. "No bridge can't be crossed over a few *cervezas*, no?"

Jasper's expression turned sheepish, and he ducked his head and said nothing.

Seraphina's smile widened. "Have a look for yourself."

With one last doubtful glance at Jasper, Kay turned her attention to the plans laid out on the table, illuminated by the affixed lamps.

From where he stood on the other side, Oliver noted brightly painted green trees, a deep indigo wall with some kind of design, some trailing vines over pillars. He rocked back on his heels and watched Kay's face unfold into a beatific blend of unabashed surprise and delight.

"It's exactly what I imagined," she breathed, leaning in closer.

"We're lightyears ahead of schedule." Seraphina beamed. "I kicked everyone into high gear. I wanted to give you something, and be sure you had plenty of time to make changes. You'll have lots of time to tweak stuff before your next meeting with the Followills."

Kay didn't seem to hear. Her gaze roamed over every corner of the carefully drawn plans, from the listed measurements to the sketched and inked panel of plants they intended to use. "Snapdragons and mango calla lilies. Oh, Sera, that's brilliant! Just one purple wall?"

Seraphina shrugged but her smile was indulgently self-satisfied. "Jasper's idea. When we did the deep purple all over, it was too dark and heavy. So, I took your notes about the mosaic tiles, and applied the same idea, but with shiny glass pebbles. It's the same color, but an altogether different vibe."

Jasper pointed to a thick line. "I thought of a feature wall, placed just so behind Tallulah's tree. It'll act as a kind of partition. Behind it is a perfect place to keep a coat and purse rack for clients. Or a wall of lockers, obviously a wood cabinet of some sort, not the tacky metal kind. We did a crosshatch design."

"And I know you were nervous about using orange for contrast," Seraphina added, "but the orange-yellow flowers reminded me of the sunset Oliver described, and I mean, just look at it. The colors just—"

"Pop," Kay finished excitedly. "Like rock candy on the tip of your tongue." Oliver didn't think she even realized she was bouncing on the balls of her feet. "String lights here and here, almost forming a trellis. It's magical. It's wonderful, inviting, and special and different." She clapped her hands, pinning each of her team members with a bright, infectious smile in turn. "You guys!" she gushed. Her smile pushed the boundaries of her cheeks. "It's perfect. You did amazing. I'm floored."

Her team, including Seraphina, brimmed with the kind of pride that could only come from pleasing the person one wished most in the world to please.

Oliver took in the scene with a slow inhale.

This. This was Kay's superpower, her strength. Neve had brass, and Seraphina had poise. But Kay lit up other people from the inside out, her giddy enthusiasm spreading out like a net and catching up anyone in her wake. It was a revelation to see how their faces reflected Kay's utter excitement right back at her.

"Kay Bing," he said softly.

She turned to face him. He didn't notice until his cheeks finally grew tired that he'd been grinning like an idiot alongside them all. Kay's hazel eyes were lit up like small fires, burning bright with her happiness.

He took her into an embrace, as casually as if they'd been doing it a lifetime. "There you are. Finally, we meet."

* * * *

Kay was awash with numerous feelings—pride, excitement, joy. Not to mention some annoyance, exasperation, and a smidge of sorrow. "But your wedding! It would've been beautiful, Neve. How could you do this? How could you rob me of being the most amazing maid of honor in the world? I had plans, you know. Fabulous plans."

Neve snorted. "Admit it, Kay. Trying to force your brain to imagine me in a wedding dress, doing all the traditional crap, makes your head hurt, doesn't it? It makes my head hurt. This was the only way I was ever going to become a married woman, and we all know this is true."

Neve had a point. Almost impossible to picture Neve as a blushing bride. "I suppose. Still, I would've liked to have been there, even as a witness at the courthouse. Do you feel different, now that you're Neve Kennicot?"

"Actually, Duke and I are still discussing that small detail. We've already eloped, I don't see why we shouldn't throw tradition out the window completely. He should take my last name. I'm not really prepared to give it up."

"You can't be serious."

"Why ever not?" Kay could tell from her tone she meant every word. "He makes a better Harper than I do a Kennicot. I'm only stating facts here."

Kay laughed. "Well, I wish you luck convincing Duke of your so-called facts. Listen, I better go. I just heard Oliver come in. He had to take an important call, and I'm asphyxiating on curiosity."

She greeted him in the kitchen, swung her arms around his neck. "What call was so important you had to take it outside?"

"An update on the case." Oliver wore a strange expression. He stood with his hands on his hips, biting his lower lip and staring at an unremarkable spot on the floor. "Molly said Brendan Berkley resigned from Free Leaf Concepts today."

Molly said...

It clicked, that small thing that had been driving Kay crazy for days, ever since Brit's arrest. "Oh, my God. Oliver...."

He rushed to Kay's side. He braced her hip, the other hand gently cradling her back. "Hey, you all right? What's wrong? You look like you're about to pass out."

"Molly said." She stared at Oliver. "Molly said. Shit."

"Kay, what are you talking about?" His green eyes scoured Kay's face, worried and anxious.

"Molly," she said. "I know I sound crazy repeating myself, but I'm in shock. I knew there was a pattern. The missed connection between Mr. Arnell and Jasper. The college courses linking Amos to Brendan, and subsequently, Brendan to Brit Lars. A determination to remain connected to you, the man running point on the investigation. Oliver, you said you didn't think there was anything between you and Molly. Maybe you were right. Maybe she played that card because it gave her an excuse to stay in your circle."

Oliver's brow creased in consternation. He gripped both of Kay's shoulders as if to steady her. "Babe, you're not making any sense. Molly is jealous because you and I—"

"No." Kay wanted to shout, to make him hear. "No, not jealous. It was never about that. You told me she was upset I entered into the investigation as something like a partner, but not because she was jealous. She wanted to be the one you shared information and theories with. She needed to know how close you were to tying things together. Oliver, call Cappy Don. Have him look into the background checks Molly was responsible for. I'll bet my house she carried them out herself, and altered them. Even mine, hoping to catch you off guard, keep you distracted."

"You just said she didn't want us together. Why would she use you to distract me from the case?"

"She didn't expect me to figure you out, or for us to end up working together. She underestimated me. People do that a lot."

Oliver still looked unsure.

"Oliver, think. She's in a perfect position to control the investigation, by controlling the intelligence. She took those plant samples from you and let the lab run them because she knew they weren't connected. One report is off, fine. Mistakes happen. But it happened more than once. You said yourself, Molly knew about Brendan's degree in pharmaceuticals. It's not her job to decide which information is relevant to your case, Oliver. If she kept that to herself, she had a reason. I've got one more wager for you. If you dig deep enough, you'll find she's somehow connected to Brit Lars or Brendan Berkley."

"You think Molly is involved in the drug ring." Oliver said the words slowly.

Kay shook off his grip. "If you won't look into it, I'm sure I can convince the captain my hunch is worth a little research to see if I'm right."

Oliver shook his head and exhaled heavily. He planted his hands on his hips and studied Kay. "I'll make the call."

* * * *

Kay's hands were white with old plaster, ancient wallpaper glue, and sweat. She leaped off the stepladder at the sound of heavy footfalls coming onto the porch.

Oliver had been gone the entire day. Not a text or a call, and Kay had been too apprehensive to reach out. She'd either unearthed a deeper plot, or irrevocably damaged Oliver's relationship with one of his coworkers.

"Well?" she prompted, the moment he stepped through the doorway and closed the door gently. If they were going to argue, they might as well get it over with.

For an uncomfortably long while, Oliver stood by the door. When he finally looked at her, his eyes were bright with exhaustion. His mouth was pinched close. "I owe you an apology. I underestimated you, too."

Kay grabbed a nearby hand towel and distracted herself from the heavy atmosphere by trying to rub the grime from her skin. Oliver leaned against the door as if standing were suddenly a chore. She used her foot to push the stepladder toward him. "Sit down before you fall over. What happened today?"

He dropped onto the stool and rubbed his face. "Molly was arrested. Brendan, Amos, and Brit were all questioned a second time. Brit decided to strike a deal, gave us everything on Molly. You were right. They're distant cousins. They practically grew up together. Amos and Brendan were released. For some reason, no one will talk about Brendan. We know he's involved somehow, but he's being collectively protected." Oliver peered up at her. "Unless you've got another epiphany you want to lay on me?"

She stifled a grin. She couldn't tell if he was genuinely annoyed she'd figured it out before him, or genuinely hoping she could think of some dangling thread with which they could tie down Brendan Berkley. "Sorry. I got nothing. How are you feeling? About everything."

He cocked an eyebrow, and a faint glimmer of amusement shone in his gaze. "You mean finding out I dated a drug dealer, if only briefly? Or finding out she only pretended to be hot for me so she could get first dibs on intelligence I picked up? Because I'm feeling how you'd imagine. Relieved. Thank God she was a terrible seductress. What if I'd fallen in love?"

Kay pulled a face. "Tragic."

"And I'm happy." His expression didn't mirror the statement, but he sounded pleased. "Locking these people away is a pretty good start to getting justice for Manny."

"Your friend," Kay said sadly. "I was sorry to hear about that. What does this mean for you? Are you sticking around until you bring Brendan down? Another undercover gig?"

His gaze dropped. "I'm no longer a viable option for undercover work. Photo made the paper today. Me standing next to the captain outside the precinct after Brit's arrest." Color rose in his cheeks.

"And that's got you blushing?"

A quick flash of a grin came and went. "Not exactly, no."

"I see." She saw nothing. She figured his role would change once they uncovered their guy inside Free Leaf Concepts. Would he have gone deeper undercover if his identity hadn't been shared publicly? "Then what's next for you?"

He sighed and studied the walls. The foyer was almost done, with the exception of the last few diehard strips of wallpaper that simply refused to budge. Together, they'd soaked the walls last night, and were using putty knives to force the wallpaper off.

"I toyed with the idea of going home. My old captain reached out. He's ready to welcome me back with open arms. I'm a hero." He betrayed a brief, wry smile.

Kay's heart twisted. "But..." She couldn't get out the words. The inn, their confessions. What did any of that mean if Oliver returned to Jonesboro? She couldn't follow him. She had a brand-new career and a home she'd made it her life goal to renovate. She had a wealth of love in her heart for Oliver, but she didn't know if she could give up everything else for him.

Or could she?

In her heart, she wanted to follow Oliver wherever he went. Jonesboro, Canada, the moon. This big house was important to her. It was her dream to restore it. But it couldn't love her back. It couldn't fulfill her or sustain her like love returned. Yes, she could give up her manor for Oliver.

He watched her keenly. "Or," he said quietly, "I could stay. Cappy Don gave me the update, then invited me to join him indefinitely. A team leader, in fact, on the task force assigned to the drug ring."

Did she dare believe it was hope in his stare? Kay brushed her hands together, betrayed by their slight trembling. She opened her mouth twice, only for nothing to emerge. An unnamed fear held her back.

Oliver closed the gap between them in a few easy steps. Inches from her, he stopped. He'd meet her halfway, but he wouldn't force her. The rest of the distance was hers to cover, should she choose to. "So, all the love stuff we talked about. That was real. Is real. But love and reality don't always jive. I want the whole package. I want to be with you every day, live with you in your big mansion, fumble my way through helping you realize your dream of this place. But maybe you're not ready for all that. The heavy stuff. But if you are, and if you want, I could stay."

"And if I don't?" she dared.

"Then I'll go. Because I'm not staying without you. It would defeat the purpose."

A slow smile took over her mouth against her will. At a glance, he appeared relaxed. But Kay recognized the tightness at the corners of his mouth, the way he kept pressing his lips together, and how his gaze slid from hers. "You're an idiot."

His mouth fell open.

"Didn't expect that?" she probed sweetly. "Oliver, I couldn't breathe a minute ago, because I thought you were trying to tell me good-bye. In those fifteen seconds, I sold my house and moved to Jonesboro. Not without some measure of regret, of course, but I'd do it if you asked. I'd do it to be with you." She closed the gap between them and slid her arms around his waist, laying her head on his chest. His arms encircled her. "I'm ready. If it's you, I'm ready, because this isn't anything like what happened with Finn."

"What's it like?" His soft murmur whispered against the top of her head.

"Base jumping."

Low laughter rumbled in his chest, and he squeezed her against him in a brief, fierce hug. "Not sure if that's a favorable comparison or not."

"My heart is thundering in my chest, my palms are sweating, but I'm thrilled and excited and ready to dive. I'm terrified, but I want it. So, yes. Stay. Please stay."

"As you wish."

Kay lost track of the minutes they stood locked together, but there was no need to count when they had forever.

THE END

Rumor has it, she can't resist...

MEN LIKE THIS

A Long Shot Romance

Roxanne Smith

Can she trust a man who pretends for a living?

Horror author Quinn Buzzly knows all about the dark side, but when she meets actor Jack Decker, she's moved to explore something completely different—at least on paper. With his sexy good looks, intriguing manner, and charming Irish-tinged English accent, Jack is the perfect model for her next hero. Quinn decides to spend one year in London writing a historical romance inspired by him. Until real life butts in . . .

Jack's jealous ex-fiancée sparks a media storm when she accuses him and Quinn of having an affair. But Jack knows how to play this game. At his insistence, Quinn agrees to go along with the faux romance until the chatter subsides. Then they'll stage a quiet breakup and go their separate ways. Yet Jack is a shameless—and irresistibly convincing—flirt, and Quinn has to remind herself it's an act. Or is it? If Jack means business, he'll have to find the words to convince a wordsmith that their love is the real thing . . .

Chapter 1

Quinn gaped at Richard as if he'd grown an extra appendage in front of her eyes. He might as well have. He was alien to her, despite having known him for many years. "I'm giving you about three seconds to explain."

He had the nerve to smile. It showed off the large glaringly white teeth inside his too-perfect mouth on his too-perfect face. "You don't like it?" His dark gaze wandered, his approval apparent. "I really thought you would."

They were at a nightclub called Sabini's in Hollywood—Quinn deplored Hollywood. A small treasure of a private bar hid deep in the bowels of the rowdy club: quiet, classy, and far from the maddening *wump-wump-wump* of the dance floor down the hall. Yes, she liked it.

No, she wasn't going to admit it.

She crossed her bare arms, partly from the chill but mostly to show Richard she meant business. "Our relationship demands trust. Why would you lie to me, Richard?"

He spared a quick glance at her defensive posture. "Cold?" When she didn't respond, he waved off her concern. "All I've done is taken you out. Is that so bad?"

A jolt of agitation shot through her. Had he lost his mind? Had one too many cocktails earlier? "Yes, I'd say it was! You dragged me across a nasty dance floor wearing a silk ball gown and diamond brooch worth more than your house. You said my sister planned this. I want an explanation, and I want it now."

Richard continued to scan the bar, unruffled by her outburst. "I brought you through the front because I left my key to the private entrance at home. I apologize." He sat on one of the backless cowhide bar stools and lifted a hand for the bartender. "Bottle of champagne, please. Two glasses."

The busty young woman who could've still been driving on a learner's permit smiled. Her gaze roamed freely over Richard before she dashed off to fulfill his glamorous request.

Quinn fought the urge to stick her finger down her throat. Champagne? Who was he kidding?

He turned back to her and patted the seat beside him as if beckoning her to join him like she were some wayward, spoiled child. "Your feet must hurt." His eyes were kind, and his smile knowing. "Angie has excellent fashion sense, but you shouldn't have let her talk you into those heels."

He spoke the truth.

Quinn's feet throbbed from the towering stilettos she had no business wearing. She planned to set fire to the outrageous instruments of torture the very day they lifted the burn ban in L.A. and fight harder for the ballet flats next time.

She scowled at Richard for being right but sat anyway. The blood rushing back into her feet made her woozy with relief. With some effort, she refocused on Richard. "Quit stalling and tell me what we're doing here, or I'm walking out. If I have to call a cab to get home, I swear, I'm taking my next project to someone else."

Richard's dark and impeccably shaped eyebrows shot up. His mouth fell open. Finally, a dent in his smooth surface. "You wouldn't."

He didn't sound so certain.

Quinn smiled at having the upper hand. "I damn sure would. Like I said, this is a trust thing. It was odd when you told me Emily wanted to get together in Hollywood, but I told myself you wouldn't do anything weird. Then you go and order champagne. It keeps getting weirder, and you refuse to tell me what's really going on. You don't own a white windowless van, do you? Or have duct tape in your suit pocket?"

He didn't appear amused. In fact, he managed to appear unaffected, his impenetrable feathers were back in place. Her show of humor must've left him with the incorrect impression she'd be easily managed.

"You're over thinking this. We had a successful night at the fund-raiser. You're gorgeous. I wanted to have an after-party drink with my favorite client. There's nothing *weird* about wanting to prolong a nice evening with a friend."

He couldn't have mocked her any clearer.

She couldn't have cared any less. "Except for your conniving, I'd agree. Why didn't you simply ask?"

"I wanted to surprise you." He smiled his horse-toothed smile. It ruined everything he had going for his face. "Surprise."

The champagne arrived. He handed her a dainty flute. "Drink this." The sweet condescension in his voice nearly undid the frail threads holding Quinn's temper in check, but she kept her grip on the reins—until she glanced at her glass.

It practically brimmed over with the sparkly wine. A sudden burst of insight hit her. "You're trying to get me drunk."

"Now, Quinn—"

"You used my sister to lure me here knowing I'd never come willingly. Real classy." Quinn came out of her seat, disgusted and angry. She growled at the sharp jabs of pain shooting through the soles of her feet.

Richard must've taken the growl as meant for him. "Quinn, calm down, please. Yes, I'm attracted to you. Yes, I thought this was the only way I'd ever get a date with you."

"This is not a date!" Despite her pain, she stamped her foot. The small *click* of her heel failed to make the desired impact.

Richard placed a hand on her arm. "Obviously."

Her fingernails dug into her palms as her hands formed angry little fists at her sides.

Richard didn't notice. His primary concern seemed to have shifted from her to their audience. "You're causing a scene. You asked for an explanation, now allow me to give one before you get us kicked out."

Quinn seethed but didn't interrupt this time. A lift of her brow invited him to continue.

He cleared his throat and straightened his black silk bowtie. Since they'd come from the prestigious city fund-raiser, he was in a tuxedo jacket and slacks.

They'd been a striking pair. Quinn wore a black strapless gown and styled her long blond hair into an elegant chignon that displayed the diamond drops in her lobes. They matched the cluster pinned to the front of her gown.

In this casual setting, they looked like a bad joke. Overdressed and ill behaved. "You have to understand, Quinn. We work together closely. We talk every day. It's not strange I'm attracted to you. Asking you out seemed unprofessional."

Quinn nearly choked on her unspoken reply. This *wasn't* unprofessional? Her jaw practically unhinged at Richard's startling lack of self-awareness.

"I figured if we went out casually and had a few drinks, things might take their natural course."

A shrug accompanied the statement to show how big of a deal it wasn't, but Quinn saw red. She jabbed at his shoulder with an accusing finger. "I'm not stupid, Richard. You celebrate with a glass of champagne. There are completely different motives at play when you order an entire bottle. You weren't hoping for slightly tipsy. You were going for totally sloshed. Then what? You'd take me back to your place and pretend it got out of hand?"

"No, I'd never—"

Quinn turned away. She braced her hands against the bar in an effort to stay on her bruised feet and tried to breathe. "You sure as hell would. After what Blake did, there's nothing I'd put past a man."

He had the audacity to scoff. "Blake is an idiot."

The comment acted like flame to tinder—instant ignition.

She whirled on him. He was no better. He was probably no worse, but at the least, he and Blake were exactly the same. "Oh, and you're some genius? Do you even realize what you've done? I should fire you." She shook her head to dislodge some of her anger, but it wasn't going anywhere. She trembled. "Get away from me. Leave, now."

"Leave?" He repeated the word slowly. "I'm not going anywhere. I brought you here. I'm responsible for you."

Quinn pinned him with every ounce of fire in her green eyes. They flashed when she was angry. They must be crackling like hot coals now. "Do you really expect me to get back in your car? I'll take a cab home. I don't need your protection. What I need is for someone to protect me from *you*."

He looked like he might refuse again.

She hit him with the final blow. "Our contract is riding on how fast you can get away from me. I mean it, Richard."

Their surroundings seemed to come back to them simultaneously. Everyone stared at Richard as they waited in dead silence for his reaction. Even the bartender watched their exchange with rapt attention. Richard's face flushed a dull red. He stood in a deliberate fashion as if it were his idea to leave. "This is foolish."

His clenched jaw and piercing glare labeled him furious, but Quinn had her own store of ire to draw from. She slipped into the most condescending tone she possessed. "You need to go home and think about what you've done."

He recoiled like she'd slapped him, but she'd wager his reaction was nothing more than embarrassment at getting dressed down in a room full of strangers. Maybe now he'd understand how she felt—mortified and belittled. He'd tricked her into coming here and attempted to ply her with drink for the sake of getting her in bed. She couldn't have done anything more insulting than that.

Richard stormed toward the exit. She hoped the staring eyes of the audience, hers included, burned holes in his back as he went.

Her shoulders fell the moment he disappeared from sight. Her rage fled. She wasn't built for dramatics. She frowned at the two untouched glass flutes on the bar. One sat empty while the other comically full. She'd never much cared for champagne hangovers.

Quinn wiggled her fingers in a girlish wave at the bartender still watching her with round eyes. "Can I get a beer?"

Quinn waited until she almost finished her first drink to call Angie, her best friend, the same demon responsible for her miserable, dejected feet. She plucked her cell phone from the hidden pocket inside the bodice of her gown. She wasn't totally stupid. She'd have never let Richard leave without a backup plan up her sleeve.

Or down her dress, as it were.

Angie answered on the first ring. She sounded unfazed, like she'd expected Quinn's late-night call. "How did the fund-raiser go?"

Oh, that's right. She'd done something fun tonight. "I had a great time. In fact, I wish we were still there."

"Oh, I'm sure you'll have others." Angie sounded slightly distracted. Quinn imagined her painting her toenails or watching television. "What time did you get home?"

Quinn cleared her throat. It wasn't her fault. She shouldn't feel stupid, but for whatever reason she did. Must be some kind of male superpower. "Would it be weird if Richard wanted to sleep with me?"

"Of course not. It'd be weird if he didn't." Angie didn't seem distracted anymore. "Did something happen? Oh my God, did you go home with him?" Her voice dropped to a dramatic whisper. "Did you guys do it? Are you calling in secret from the bathroom? Was he good?"

Richard had inspired an intense lack of charitable feelings, but leave it to Angie to smooth Quinn's angry wrinkles mere seconds into the conversation. "No, nothing like that, but he did bring me to a Hollywood nightclub. Shows a little spark, doesn't it?"

"Hollywood? Does he know you?" The disdain in her best friend's voice was welcome commiseration. "Where are you?"

"A place called Sabini's." Quinn appraised the room once more. Large round bulbs suspended from the ceiling hung low and cast their warm glow over the bar, thus creating quite the snug little atmosphere. "I'm pained to admit it, but the private bar is sort of nice. It's the mosh pit of sweaty, spastic idiots in the dance room next door who frighten me. I can't believe that passes for dancing these days. I thought the first guy I saw was having a seizure. He's lucky I didn't shove my brooch in his mouth to stop him from swallowing his tongue."

Angie snorted. "A creative way to divest yourself of a fortune. I've been to Sabini's before. Your Richard's a classy one. Are you two having a good time?"

"Not exactly." Quinn explained in painful detail how her night had gone so topsy-turvy.

She waited in silence for Angie's reply. She imagined her friend working through the scenario in her mind.

Finally, a response. "Well, okay. I guess my question is why you're still there."

Quinn loved easy questions. She sucked the last drop of beer from the long-neck bottle and smacked her lips for emphasis. "To get drunk. Why does anyone sit at a bar and order booze?"

"Nice. Tomorrow you'll wake up not only divorced and homeless but with a hangover cherry on top. Way to take your power back, honey."

"I'm not homeless. I'm staying at a hotel."

"Homeless isn't synonymous with cardboard box. You don't have a home. You're homeless."

Quinn waved to the bartender. Time for another drink. "Shut up and tell me what I'm supposed to do. Am I overreacting?"

Angie clucked her tongue. "Had he taken you out for kung pao chicken, I'd say yes, but this is kind of a big deal. He dragged you to some shady Hollywood club wearing a thousand-dollar ball gown and million-dollar diamonds. Not just ignorant, mind you. Potentially dangerous. This is L.A., not Friendly, Texas. Letting him leave you there was even dumber, by the way."

"Probably." Quinn tried for a deep breath. It escaped as a depressed groan. "What do I do? Fire him?"

The mere suggestion made her stomach pitch. She mustered up a weak smile for Busty the Barkeep, who promptly deposited Quinn's second beer in front of her.

"There's only one thing you can do." Angie sounded apologetic but remained firm. "You have to kill him."

Quinn pressed the phone closer to her ear. The spectacle had ceased, and people were back to their regularly scheduled partying. "Like it's ever that easy."

Angie scoffed. "You have no problem scalping a sweet, vulnerable, and ruggedly handsome pediatrician with a chainsaw, but you can't kill Richard? You even murdered the poor doctor on the very same night he finally worked up the courage to ask that cute barista out on a date. It took a lot of courage for him to step out of his comfort zone. The guy had issues."

Quinn rested one elbow on the bar and said what she always said. "You're taking it too personally, Ang. You've got to quit falling in love with my subjects."

"What in the hell is a barista doing with a chainsaw in the first place, huh? Does she moonlight as a lumberjack?"

Quinn wanted to roll her eyes at Angie's protest but couldn't. She was too pleased with herself. Her life's work revolved around inspiring heartfelt emotion in others. More's the better if the emotions were dark ones like grief and loss.

They were sort of her calling card. "Look, if I wrote Richard into a story to give him a grisly death, I'm afraid he'd notice. He *is* my agent. And you'd understand why the barista had a chainsaw if you'd bother to finish the book."

"I can't, Quinn, I just can't." Her best friend sniffed. "You kill everyone I love."

"I'm sorry. I'll write you a happy ending one day. Promise."

Angie went from sniveling to haughty in the space of a single sentence. "The only happy endings these days are in massage parlors."

Quinn was still laughing when she ended the call and returned the slim black cell phone to the hidden confines of her ball gown.

Her silk strapless Carolina Herrera ball gown.

Every bit of good humor conjured disappeared. Quinn remembered where she sat and how she got there.

Richard, Richard, Richard. He'd really screwed up tonight. Angie's solution, while amusing, wasn't pragmatic and wouldn't solve anything. Quinn nervously rolled the beer bottle between her hands.

The idea of confronting Richard in his office made her queasy. He'd downplay the entire scene and make her out to be a dramatic prude. The smoothness she counted on for publishing negotiations would come back to bite her when she found herself looking down the barrel of it rather than grinning smugly from behind it, but what were her choices?

She had to make a stand. She needed to put him in his place, be the iron fist of the feminine movement.

Then again, there wasn't much determined avoidance couldn't patch up. Key West was fabulous this time of year. Cabanas, boat drinks, palm trees, and pool boys.

When had she last gone on vacation? Disneyland three years ago. With Blake. Quinn didn't want to think about that. She wanted to daydream about pool boys. For research, of course. She was far too old for a pool boy.

She'd need a pool *man*.

"You don't match."

For an instant, the deep voice coming from behind stunned her. Since she sat virtually alone on her side of the L-shaped bar, she had no choice but to accept the man—a pool man if her luck had improved any—intended the words for her. Some drunken fool trying to succeed where Richard failed. What had she been thinking staying here? She should've picked up a bottle of tequila and moved this pity party to the privacy of her hotel room.

He had an accent, although she couldn't place the dialect. Definitely European. Rather than turn around right away to face her new visitor, she took a long, hard look at the beer bottle in her hand. Too soon to order her third? She wanted fuzzy, not pickled.

She'd put it off long enough. Quinn swung around on the tail end of an eye roll to greet Bachelor Number Two. The smart reply she had ready died on her lips.

Meet the Author

A Florida native, **Roxanne Smith** has called everywhere from Houston to Cheyenne home. Currently residing in Asheville, North Carolina, she's an avid reader of every genre, a cat lover, pit bull advocate, and semi-geek. She loves video games, Doctor Who, and her dashing husband. Her two kids are the light of her life. Visit her website at roxannesmith.net, and her blog at smithrox.blogspot.com.